THE LITTLE GIRL WAITS

by Jamie Greening

ATHANATOS
PUBLISHING GROUP

THE LITTLE GIRL WAITS

by Jamie Greening

ATHANATOS
PUBLISHING GROUP

The Little Girl Waits
by Jamie Greening

www.thelittlegirlwaits.com

Print ISBN: 978-1-936830-65-7
EBook ISBN: 978-1-936830-66-4

Published by Athanatos Publishing Group
www.athanatosministries.org

Other Butch Gregory Stories:

From Athanatos Publishing Group:
The Haunting of Pastor Butch Gregory and Other Short Stories

From Bard and Book Publishing:
The Land Begins to Heal in the collection *It's About Time*

Other Stories from Jamie Greening,
available wherever fine Ebooks are sold:

The Deep Cove series
Deep Cove
Deep Cove: The Party Crasher
The Deep Cove Lineage

Jolly Rogers: A Story About Boyhood
Speculation
The Last Message

For my daughters, Chelsea and Phoebe

Table of Contents

Part One: Innocence and Evil

Part Two: Coming Together

Part Three: Working Apart

Part Four: One To Cry, One To Die, One To See

Acknowledgements

This book would never have come to fruition without the love and support of my wife. She has read so many copies that I'm certain she feels like these characters are part of our family. What's more, her constant encouragement to, "go write" and the freedom she gave me to spend endless hours with make believe people dealing with very real problems is remarkable. Thank you Kim Greening.

Special thanks go to those who helped me proof the text: Elisha Pile, Sarah Diane Edwards, Bonnie Stancikas, and Kendall Ventura. Derek Elkins and Robert Cely read earlier versions and made many helpful suggestions and for that I am deeply in their debt. Another round of thanks to all the bards at bardandbook.com, where I get the joy of practicing the craft of writing with such a talented team of colleagues.

The wonderful people of First Baptist Church, Port Orchard, Washington have my undying gratitude. All the positives about Sydney Community Church are mere reflections of First Baptist Church, with none of the negatives. Those were 14 great years we spent together. Thanks.

The staff at Athanatos Christian Ministries, especially The Twitter Queen Maryann Spikes, The Keeper of the Codes Gerson Lacado, and The Fisherking Julius Broqueza are more than amazing: They rock! I especially would like to thank Anthony Horvath, who took a chance with me on my first Butch Gregory book four years ago and has never ceased to be a source of encouragement.

Part One:
Innocence and Evil

Chapter One

Terror Under The Bed

UGLY PEOPLE attacked the innocence of Tamara Rey's childhood on a beautiful evening.

She, of course, like most children, was unaware of the primordial evil that stalked her as she walked along the sidewalk and slowly sucked soda from a plastic cup bigger than her nine year old head. It was nearly nine on a spectacularly normal Pacific Northwest summer's evening. The glowing sun was still in the western sky, about to begin its daily dip behind the Olympic Mountains. The temperature was perfect at 73 degrees. The heat of the afternoon had disappeared along with the memory of the long winter of slate-gray darkness.

Tamara's mother was at work, but she had left two dollars in quarters for Tamara to indulge herself with a soda from the Skookum Quickie Mart four blocks down the street. She wore a light blue t-shirt, blue jean shorts and flip flops that clapped against her heel, applauding her every step for the lazy pace along the familiar path. Her school bus stop was over there on that corner and her friend lived in those apartments up that hill. Maybe she will stop and see if her friend Tiffany is home? No, she decided. I'll call her later.

A man waved at her from a blue car as it drove by. She waved back and shouted, "Hi Pastor Butch!" She doubted he heard her though.

Tamara lifted up the floor mat and used the latch key under it to let herself into the two bedroom apartment. She pulled out the peanut butter and strawberry jelly and made a sandwich to go with her giant soda. A handful of Goldfish crackers she swiped from the cupboard rounded out her evening feast. She sat down on the sofa to eat and turned on the television. There was nothing on that she wanted to watch so she clicked it off and grabbed her mobile phone and started watching YouTube videos. Her friend, the one who lived up that hill, sent her a couple of links about kittens and a popular boy band.

The sun finally set in the western horizon, the apartment darkened. Tamara did not notice the darkness because her eyes were focused on the glow of her cell phone. Her giggling at a tabby cat playing in a toilet bowl was interrupted by the jiggle of the doorknob.

Was it mama, home early from the restaurant? She hoped so. Tamara loved her mother.

A man's harsh smoker's cough crushed her hope.

It was not mama.

Slowly the dead bolt turned, then the doorknob twisted and a tall skinny white man slowly crept into the dark entryway. He wore a Seattle Mariners baseball cap on his head and had a scruffy beard.

Startled and surprised, she couldn't say anything, but the ugly man spoke up immediately.

"Hi Tam. Where is your mommy?"

Donny. She remembered his voice. He was the last boyfriend her mother had before she changed her life. Donny lived with them for three months and then unceremoniously left after taking $500 from the cookie jar. Donny was the last person to break her mother's heart. Donny was the last man who made her mother cry.

Tamara glared at him.

"What's the matter Tam? Don't you remember me?"

She shifted her weight and stepped backward.

"Of course you remember me, don't you? You remember me because you are a smart little girl. But you weren't too smart, was you? You put that key back under the mat out front. I followed you all the way back from the store, Tam. I saw you pick the key up and open the door and then I saw you put it back. That made it real easy for me. Thank you.

"I thought about snatching you when you's walking up the road. It would have been easy, but someone might have seen me. But this, this here is way easier. See, I hate to do this to you. I really do, but I've got to take you with me. You're going to help old Donny stay alive a little longer."

Tamara was smart. She realized she was in trouble. She darted into the interior of the apartment, still too startled to scream. The thug lunged after her and chased her into the kitchen. Tamara ran to her room and crawled under her bed.

The lights were off in the apartment and Donny became disoriented as he stepped out of the orange glow of the exterior security light and into the darkened apartment. He fumbled for a light switch on the wall, but only succeeded in knocking a picture onto the end table. The glass shattered. He whispered blasphemy.

"Where are you, Tam? You can't hide forever. I've got friends with me."

From under the bed Tamara heard his frightening emphysemic breathing, and it made her cringe with terror. Suddenly a ray of light shone in through the bedroom door. At first Tamara thought that was good and began to crawl out. But then she heard Donny wheeze and begin to speak again. She squinted her eyes tight so she couldn't see and she tried not to hear.

"I'm like a boy scout, little girl. I come prepared. I brung my flashlight. Come on out and play. We'll have a good time together. I'll not hurt you. We'll go get ice cream and talk. You like to talk, don't you Tamara?"

Donny walked down the short hallway and poked his head into the bathroom.

"I 'member before, when I lived here, how we used to talk all the time. You talked so much it was hard to get you to shut up. You just jabbered away all the time." He grinned, revealing a diseased smile, but Tamara couldn't see it because her eyes were still sealed shut. Donny shook his head back and forth, "You know what Tam, I miss those good ole times. I've come back to talk some more with you about whatever is on your mind. Come on out; we'll talk. Come talk to ole Donny."

Tamara's eyes peeked open and she saw the light beam was getting bigger and brighter. Donny was getting closer. Tamara clenched her whole body. She wished she had her cell phone with her, but it was on the table right beside the television in the living room. The living room was such a long way off. What to do?

A dash for the phone. She'd never make it. Screaming might draw the attention of a neighbor but would also tell Donny where she was. But if she lay here, no matter how dumb Donny was, he would eventually find her. She didn't know what to do.

The light was coming closer. He was in her room now. She saw his dirty sneakers standing in the doorway then she watched them move to the side of the bed.

Her little body shook and she suddenly became aware of the sound of her own breathing. What if he could hear her too?

She moved her hand to muffle her breathing. When she moved it toward her mouth, her arm knocked against an old toy cymbal which had been lying in that spot under her bed unmolested for two years. It had been a silent, dormant artifact from her past resting in stasis as a museum piece from her childhood collection. Like a volcano it let loose an eruption of sound when her elbow bumped it. The cymbal became a siren with a spotlight signaling to the evil man the exact hiding place of the little girl.

Donny was a wild animal pouncing onto the floor and reaching his dirty hands underneath the bed after her. He grabbed hold of her small foot as she clawed to get away. He twisted her leg hard. She squealed and wiggled with pain. She kicked him with her other foot square in the face. Had she been older and stronger, it would have surely broken his nose and given her the moment she needed to get away.

But she was not bigger. She was not stronger. She was just a thin framed little girl. The kick had only stunned him. That stun, though, bought her enough time to get out from under the bed. She ran around the bed and again he lunged for her, but this time he missed. She turned the sharp corner down the short hallway toward the front door as fast as she could.

She collided with 275 pounds of immovable nastiness.

It was a stubby, round man with a long, full, red beard. He wore a flannel shirt that hung over his protruding gut. He smelled like Spam and beer.

"I thought you said you could handle this one by yourself Donny? If I hadn't been here, this little, priceless gem would have gotten away. Idiot!"

The stinky man swung a short wooden club and struck Tamara Rey in the back of the head. She collapsed to the floor.

Chapter Two

Skookum Mart

AMBER SMITH chose the bean burrito and the Pepsi Cola. She also grabbed a Three Musketeer chocolate bar. She was trying to maximize her late night purchase of comfort food at the Skookum Quickie Mart. Although she had plenty of money in her pocket, old habits die hard. Back when she had lived on the street Amber always worked to play the angle on how much food she could get with the smallest amount of money—stolen, panhandled, or found on the sidewalk. In this game of survival, quantity was far more important than quality.

Now Amber's money was honest money, earned from honest work as a janitor at the plant. She was just coming off work and on her way to her small apartment in downtown Sydney. She liked her new life even though it had taken the murder of someone she loved to lead her to it.

The bean burritos were on sale at the Skookum, but so were the Funyuns. Amber loved Funyuns, but only with Dr. Pepper. Dr. Pepper wasn't on sale, Pepsi was. If she wanted to get the chocolate bar too, she'd have to go with the burrito and the Pepsi in order to stay under her goal of spending less than $3.50. She came in 12 cents under budget.

The thin 5'11" woman with blonde hair, creamy skin and steely blue eyes warmed her burrito in the microwave oven and made small talk with the cashier. After the timer binged she scooped up her meal, soda, and candy and stepped outside into the harsh glow of streetlamps. Most people would have recoiled at eating a midnight snack in the middle of a gas station parking lot under toxic lighting, but for Amber, these were like old times. It was as nostalgic to her as a '50s style diner for a baby boomer. As Amber ate she reminisced about her past.

She thought about her brother.

She thought about Steve.

She thought about her old way of life and her old friends.

In many ways she didn't want to remember those tragic wounds, but she couldn't seem to let them go. It was all a part of who she was now, and she was working to accept it.

When Amber finished her burrito she walked to the trash can to toss the wrapper and napkins away. She took a slurp of her drink and looked up and noticed a gray minivan pull up at middle island gas pump in front of the Skookum. A large man with an ugly red beard got out and began to pump gas. He cursed loudly as the pay-at-the-pump feature wouldn't take his cash. He briskly walked inside and then darted back out.

Another man sat in the passenger side. Both men looked nervous to Amber. She had seen that look before—the look of someone trying to get away with something evil.

She watched him pump the gas. He looked angry.

Something down inside her didn't feel right. At one point while he pumped, the ugly red bearded man glared back at her and snarled. He had seen her staring at him.

He finished pumping and jumped back into the minivan. As the van drove off, Amber tried to memorize the license plate. It was a California plate number, MTH 18 was all she could see, but there were more numbers. The rest of the numbers were blocked by a trash can between her and the minivan. Amber saw a little girl with dark hair and dark eyes look out of the window. It was a quick glance, but she thought maybe there were two little girls. The beautiful features on the child were overshadowed by a look of terror. Amber knew that look, too. The little girl was frightened.

Every instinct inside of Amber wanted to chase the vehicle. Something wasn't right. That girl was in trouble. Why would two men have two little girls in the back seat this late at night? She checked her cell phone for the time. It was 12:17 A.M.

Where were they going?

Why did the girl look scared?

How was it that Amber felt an aching pit form in her stomach?

Who was that girl?

What about her face haunted Amber?

Every instinct inside of her wanted to chase them down and run them off of the road. But that was dangerous and she'd given up dangerous ways. She decided to call the police. But what would she tell them? "Yes officer, I saw two men pumping gas at a gas station." That's hardly a crime. Besides, Amber still didn't trust police.

So Amber did what countless numbers of people do every day. She ignored an obvious sign of trouble and told herself it was none of her business and she continued on her way to her apartment, took a shower, crawled into bed, and went to sleep.

The next morning Amber woke up about 10:30. That was normal as she was really a night owl. She drank coffee while she checked her email on her mobile phone. After she answered a couple of texts from friends she clicked over to the app for the Sydney Star, the local newspaper. The lead story read, "Sydney Girl Abducted" and there was a picture. Amber bit her lip in numb shock. The little girl in the back seat was the same little girl in the picture. The story said her name was Tamara Rey.

Chapter Three

Each Passing Thud

"YOU WORTHLESS idiot!" the red bearded man said. "I told you to gas up before we started out. I trusted you to drive on the way over here, and this is how it goes? How could you not see that we needed to get gas before? Do I have to do everything? I'm pretty sure that woman at the pump saw us and saw the cargo too. If we get caught, I want you to know that before they arrest us, as the cops are closing in on us, when the sirens are blaring and they say, 'hands up,' I will use my last moment of freedom to personally put a bullet right between your empty headed beady little eyes. I swear to God I will, idiot.

"My five year old nephew who still pisses the bed is compententer than you. Aint it, like, the first rule in the bad guy's handbook to make certain the crucial-to-success getaway car is ready to go? What if we'd been chased by the police, huh? Worse yet, what if we'd run out of gas? How do you think the boss would react to that, huh? You, you, you mush-for-brains toad. We can't exactly call AAA to come give us a complimentary gallon of gas, now can we? You need to get through your dumb skull that if you make too many mistakes, the boss is going to have you terminated, and terminated means just that; kilt."

As the enraged man spoke he peppered his speech with the ugliest and vilest words in the English language. The angrier he got, the more profanity he employed. He spoke in a crude, uneducated way but did so with a type of flare that indicated he thought himself sophisticated and quite smart, a pretense betrayed by his rather unsophisticated and crude vocabulary. Although a cruel and heartless man, he spoke like the bully in the corner of the playground, alternating misplaced profanity with childlike insults.

"My last partner made an unbelievably stupid headed mistake once. His name was Rico. Nice guy but he fouled up and let a girl get away in the park. She went crying and ran to her auntie who was with her. Well, auntie got a good look at Rico and described him to the police. Do you know what happened to Rico?"

Red beard didn't wait for an answer.

"Bam! The boss himself put a little lead bullet right between his eyes in front of everyone else right on the sofa up at the hideout. He made a lesson out of Rico. Then he took him out to the middle of Puget Sound on his boat, the deep part, tied a cinder block to his leg and threw him over. You can bet Rico is still down there somewheres feeding all the little fishes.

"That's how you get terminated. If you keep making these little mistakes, eventually you're going to end up dead, and then I'll have my time wasted so as to train a new partner, you see? I don't like training partners. So, if you don't do it for yourself, think of me, heh? You self-centered imbecile."

"I'm sorry Mark. I really am." Donny paused before he continued because he knew more insults and rhetorical questions were on the way. "I thought a quarter of a tank was enough to get us to Tacoma. I didn't know that we would need more."

"That's because," Mark interrupted, "you are such an unbelievable idiot. You're thinker is broken so what you thought was wrong. You've got mush for brains. You didn't think about the fact we would have to sit with the car idling so long while we waited to snatch the girl up in Port Angeles. Then you didn't think about the distance down the road from there to here. Did yas? I didn't think so."

Mark let fly a long train of unrelated and quite impossible curses and then continued with his lesson on fuel usage.

"You can't travel 150 miles on a quarter of a tank in this gas guzzling van! I am never letting you drive again. Ever. And I'll never forgive myself for letting you drive this time. Never again. Fool me once shame on me fool me twice and shame on you or is it shame me once and twice I'll fool you." He stumbled over his own failed turn of the phrase and then he finished with an expletive, which he used like periods or, rather, extremely angry exclamation points to finish his utterances. The two men did not speak again during the trip. The minivan was dark and silent as it motored down Highway 16 toward Tacoma.

Tamara was wide awake in the backseat. Her hands and feet were duct taped, but not her mouth. Nevertheless, she didn't dare speak. The back of her head pounded from the whack she had taken from Mark.

Beside her lay another young girl. She had blonde hair and blue eyes and was a little older than Tamara. Her hands and feet were likewise taped, but so was her mouth. The girl's eyes were terrified and her cheeks were stained with tears. Tamara could tell that the girl had cried for a long time.

Tamara too, was frightened but she didn't think Donny would actually hurt her. She could remember playing video games with him when he was with her mom. The other man, the one Donny kept calling Mark, she was unsure about. He sounded mean and cruel.

Tamara whispered a prayer as her mouth moved but no sound came out.

> Dear Jesus, help me and this other girl.
> She is very afraid and something bad is
> happening. Show mommy where I am.
> Help me. Help us. Amen.

When she said her silent "Amen," Tamara Rey wiggled over next to the blonde girl with frightened blue eyes and nudged as close as she could to her. Tamara spoke into her ear, "I said a prayer. God will help us." She couldn't hug her or console her in any other way, so Tamara just got as close to her as possible. The two girls lay there side by side listening to the tires roll over the segments of freeway—thud, thud, thud, thud. With each passing thud they got farther away from home. With each thud their odds of being found alive diminished exponentially.

A half hour later the van progressed down an alley that led to a blue metal building. Mark broke the silence and ordered Donny, "Hey idiot, get your sorry rear end out and go tell the boss we're here."

Like a trained animal Donny climbed out of the van and walked to a windowless door and knocked on it. About a minute later, the door opened.

"Why didn't you just text me? You guys never learn," an irritated voice said from behind the door. Fifteen seconds later a hum, then a crack and the large garage bay door opened. Mark drove the van inside. When the minivan cleared the portal the bay door again clicked alive and reversed direction until it came to a stop against the pavement. The two little girls were sealed inside the monster's lair.

Chapter Four

A Typical Day

EIGHTEEN HOURS before Tamara Rey was kidnapped, Pastor Butch Gregory stood in the hallway of West Puget Sound Hospital, filled with two cups of Seattle's not so best coffee, and pondered life and death. Across from him sat two women, both of whom were knitting something. Or was it crochet?

"Good morning," he had said to them when he first walked by. They both bowed their heads and smiled, but didn't speak. "Waiting here long?" He followed up. They both just smiled back. "I was told to wait here to see my friend. How about you?" Again, they both just smiled and bowed their heads a bit.

They didn't speak English.

They kept smiling at him and soon they began to talk to each other.

Sounds like Japanese.

A sinful xenophobic thought flooded his mind as he arrogantly assumed they were talking about him. He pushed that thought away. There was nothing interesting enough about him for anyone to take notice or talk about; not even in a boring hospital waiting room with nothing else to talk about.

He waited to see Lester Wooley. Lester's daughter called Pastor Butch earlier in the morning at about 5:30, after Lester stabilized. She said he had a spell in the kitchen sometime after midnight. They hoped he would get better today and go home tomorrow.

But he would not get better, though, for cancer was taking its vindictive toll. Butch figured Lester would linger a while longer and that this should probably be his last trip to the hospital, but he knew better. They would keep bringing him in again and again. Pastor Butch accepted that at some point the human body reaches fatigue and deterioration, a point where hospitals and doctors are no real help. They only create more trouble and discomfort while simultaneously generating money for the health care industry. To the hospital, Lester was just product to be milked for as long as possible and for as much as possible. To Pastor Butch Gregory though, Lester was a soul ready to make the inevitable transition from corruptible to the incorruptible, from the natural to the supernatural, from the here to the hereafter.

Lester was alone. His wife Jane had been dead for four years. All of Lester's friends were dead. Most of his family either lived far away or rarely came around, except the one good daughter. There will be a lot of sobbing and remorse at Lester's funeral. It was always the ones who had ignored their parents the most who shed bitter tears over flag draped caskets. Children who invest time in their parents' older years cried too, but they wept without shame or regret. Crying over grief and pain is one thing, but crying because of guilt and wasted opportunity looks entirely different. In many ways, it was part of his job to know the difference.

Pastor Butch looked up from his contemplation and gazed at those two Japanese women. They probably had someone they loved and cared about on this floor somewhere. Was it a brother? A sister? Most likely it was a husband? The two women looked like sisters, maybe one of their husbands was here. Perhaps it was an adult child having a procedure. He wanted somehow to communicate with them, wishing he knew enough about their needs to pray for them.

Lack of knowledge was hard to overcome, but he prayed for them anyway, silently and alone. The urge to pray over nearly everything was strong in Butch.

A nurse walked out of the large double doors.

"May I go in now?"

"Sure," the nurse said. "He's asleep."

Pastor Butch walked into the intensive care wing and was surrounded by about fifteen stalls with a bed in each stall. As he walked by he noticed all the stalls had patients. Each stall was private, with a see-through glass wall on three sides. Thin blue curtains hid most of the occupants from view. He walked to the middle area of the unit to the care station where doctors, nurses, and support staff shuffled charts and answered phones.

"Which bed is Lester Wooley in?" he asked, but he already knew the answer. He could see Lester across the unit as well as his name written in blue dry erase marker on the white board at the nurse's station but this was not his turf. It was the hospital's, and he needed to play by their rules.

"Bed 11," said a young man as he pointed at Lester.

He took a moment to switch off his iPhone and then he crept into the depressing room. He stood at the foot of the bed and looked at Lester's face. His cheeks and forehead sagged in a drug induced relaxed sleep. Butch studied Lester's large nose and ears, the lines under his green eyes, bald head, and the toothless mouth gaping wide open. Clear bags hung from the metal tree near the bed. A large beach style purse sat on the floor in the corner with a hardback book sticking out of it. It had to be Lester's daughter. Where was she? Maybe she'd stepped out for a cup of coffee or to get a bite to eat? Perhaps she is calling her husband?

He walked up to Lester's side, placed his hand on his head and prayed his standard near-death prayer.

> Lord, this good man's life is coming to a close. Receive him now, a sheep of your fold, into your arms. Prepare his soul to meet you and make his transition into eternity a gentle one. Take away his pain, take away his doubts, and minister in the deep hidden recesses of his being, that place where only you can reach. I would love for you to heal him and make him better; but I would not take away his joy of being with you soon. So we submit to your will, as in all things. And we pray as you taught us to: Our Father, who art in heaven. Hallowed be thy name. Thy kingdom come, thy will be done, on earth as it is in heaven. Give us this day our daily bread, and forgive us our debts as we forgive our debtors.

As Butch neared the finish line of the traditional Lord's Prayer in the traditional language, he unexpectedly heard another voice in the room with him. He opened his eyes and saw that it was Lester's voice. Lester was whispering the words, even in his deep sleep, right along with his pastor. Together they finished the prayer.

> Lead us not into temptation, but deliver us from evil. For thine is the kingdom, and the power, and the glory forever. Amen.

Lester never woke up, never moved, but the old saint had prayed.

The middle-aged pastor slipped out of the room, walked out of the intensive care unit, smiled at the two Japanese women still sitting and knitting in the hallway, and walked toward the elevator. The hospital was a labyrinth with towers and cross bridges strategically mingled with dead ends. He would have to take one elevator down, walk across the ground floor, and then take another elevator up to the parking garage. Or was it down to the parking garage? He had to think about that for a second.

Soon he was in his cobalt blue Honda Civic motoring against the flow of the morning commute. Most of the traffic drove northwest into the city for work. He drove southeast out of the city to the nearby town of Sydney, Washington where his church was located. Butch

Gregory moved to Sydney 15 years ago to serve as the lead pastor for his small parish church.

That is how long he had known Lester Wooley.

That is how long he'd been making trips to West Puget Sound Hospital.

After the 20 minute drive he pulled into the empty parking lot at Sydney Community Church. No one else was there yet, but the summer sun was already very high in the sky, even though it was not yet 8 in the morning. Butch parked alongside the old administrative building where his study and all the offices were located. As he opened the door the alarm barked its warning signal informing him he had 30 seconds to input the code. He punched it in and walked down the hallway.

A pile of mail and a heap of administrative work greeted Butch. It was the same pile and heap he pushed off to the side of his desk yesterday, which in turn was the same pile he pushed off to the side the day before that. He couldn't remember how long he'd been pushing that pile off to the side. It was on the side of the desk which had the trash can underneath it. He seriously considered just pushing it a few inches further and banishing it forever to clerical Gehenna.

That would feel good but it would not be good.

Instead of engaging in his rebellion, he quickly checked his tablet to confirm what day it was and to see what was on his calendar. Wednesday. He had an appointment this morning with the women's ministry leader about baby shower protocol. Butch would have to act like he cared.

After that he would have to sign promotional certificates as soon as possible because the children and youth ministries would be promoting to the next grade. Following that a late lunch was planned at one o'clock with a Baptist pastor named Fred. This particular pastor nearly destroyed his church and Butch was trying to help him put it back together. In the evening he had a baptismal orientation scheduled. Butch closed the case on his tablet and began his morning devotions.

After his morning devotionals he put some time into his Sunday sermon. He was preaching on the Beatitudes. "Blessed are those who mourn, for they shall be comforted," is what Jesus said. While he worked on the sermon he couldn't help but think about Lester. He couldn't help but think about himself.

His meeting with the women's ministry leader was tedious but painless. She asked him, "What is your theology of baby showers?" His only reply was, "I have none." He discerned from her scowl that was not the right answer. "What I mean is," he tried to cover his sarcastic error, "that it is such an important issue, that I think you know best. I defer to your wise and skilled theological understanding of all things post-natal."

When he returned from the baby shower meeting Mildred handed him the stack of certificates for signature. There were 12 of them. He quickly added his John Hancock to each, but the last one lingered. Finally he signed his name promoting Tamara Rey to the next level. He sensed something urgent. He took a moment to pray for Tamara and Nikki and then he wrote a note on a yellow sticky note: *Check on N.J. and T.R. next week.*

Butch rushed out of the office to meet Fred the Baptist for lunch. It was typical.

Pastor Fred described to Butch how stubborn, prideful, and arrogant his people were over spicy burritos and grilled chimichangas. He told Butch how he had laid down the law of how things were going to be and the people rebelled. He explained how he was God's anointed and appointed leader and that he just read a new book all about how to make every church a megachurch, but his people didn't have the faith to follow through with his vision.

Butch listened as he munched on the delicious cilantro infused salsa and fresh tortilla chips. When Fred paused long enough to take a swig of iced tea, Butch took advantage of the silence to get in a word of his own. He asked Fred if he'd talked to God about all of this.

Pastor Fred seemed to not hear his question, for as soon as he sat his perspiring glass down he launched into another diatribe about how unspiritual everyone else was.

Again, Butch listened. Then he told the pastor that maybe he should slow down and allow the congregation to catch up. He suggested he ask the Lord to show him if he had any pride or arrogance issues which might be causing friction with the people. Butch was speaking from experience because he had learned that most of the problems between him and his church stemmed from his own stubbornness or prideful arrogance. Between bites of carne asada he relayed to Pastor Fred about his horrible failure six years ago when he tried to change the Wednesday night meal program at the church based solely upon a book he read. The book detailed a church in Philadelphia that had revitalized itself through a successful mid-week prayer meeting. Butch openly confessed how hurtful it was because he had in his mind how things ought to be, how Sydney Community Church should do the same things in the same way the Philadelphia church had done, and he explained to Pastor Fred how he hadn't listen to his lay leadership and what they were telling him. Butch grimaced in his heart as he told the story because he remembered the four families that left the church over it. When he finished his example, he suggested to Pastor Fred that perhaps a little compromise was in order with his church.

Butch took note that Fred looked confused, as if he didn't understand what he was hearing. Butch realized Pastor Fred was so organizationally locked-in and viewed ministry from an aloof CEO perspective he couldn't comprehend the spiritual dynamics of what Butch was saying. Butch knew it. He had read the same book Fred kept citing. It is true, Butch thought, the book contained many insightful ideas and important strategies, but Fred forgot, or perhaps never knew, that 90% of ministry is mastering the context and knowing the people. Not just knowing; loving people.

Fred was filled with knowledge yet lacking in love.

When the bill came Fred looked uncomfortable. He told Butch, "Because so many people have left our church, we've had to cut back on our expenses. Do you mind picking up this today? I'll get it next time."

"No problem," said Butch. He hoped there would not be a next time, but feared it was doomed to happen.

In the parking lot Fred continued to froth in anger at the people at his church. Butch asked Fred if he could pray with him.

> Lord God, you are the real pastor of the church Fred serves. Help him to know how to speak gently to the people so that they will trust his leadership and his guidance in the future. I believe you want this congregation to grow and to be healthy. I also believe that Fred is a good man who earnestly intends to do your will. Where there is anger, Lord, I ask that you replace it with compassion. Where there is lack of vision, I ask that you replace it with sight. Where there is a lack of knowledge, I ask that you replace it with insight. And Father, where there is bitterness, I ask that you remove it and replace with appreciation. In Jesus' name, Amen.

When the "Amen" was said the two men went to their cars. In his car, Butch prayed the prayer he really meant.

> Jesus, don't let Fred mess his church up too much. When it does completely blow up, help me to be nowhere near the explosion. Find something else for Fred to do, because he's not much of a pastor, maybe open up a denominational job for him. And if possible, keep him away from any more church growth books. In Jesus' name. Amen.

Then Butch pulled out his little notebook and scribbled his thoughts of the meeting.

> I predict in less than 5 months Fred will either be terminated from his pastorate, resign in frustration, or the church will decline so rapidly it will close. The only thing that can keep this from happening is for his hard heart to soften.
> Note to self, send him a book, maybe a book on prayer or preaching. He needs new reading material.

With that he was off. It was now 2:30 and he swung by to pick up his daughter Sarah from a friend's house. At home he spent some time talking with his wife, Lucy. Since Butch had left the house so early in the morning to go to the hospital, he hadn't seen her for any real length of time since yesterday.

Lucy Gregory stood at exactly 5 feet tall with short curly brunette hair atop her petite frame. Her eyes flared green and her face was round. She met Butch Gregory when he was the education minister at the church she attended during college. Early in their marriage her acumen as a business woman had provided nicely while Butch served at smaller churches that didn't pay much. Sydney Community paid enough, however, that she could devote herself to being a full-time mom and plunge fully into the church ministry.

Butch and Lucy caught up on Paul and Sarah's new school year schedule and the end of summer church activities—a picnic for the Senior Adults, a trip to the water amusement park with the youth, and an outing to the sandy beaches on the coast with the singles small group. Over the years the church had grown to such a degree their weekly calendar was filled with church activities. But that was okay. They liked church. The church seemed to like them.

Soon it was 4:45 and time for Butch to head out for the baptismal orientation. He met with the six candidates in the sanctuary and showed them the baptistery, the robes, the dressing areas and explained some of the theological underpinnings of the baptismal moment. He talked about life, death, dying to self, washing of sins, and of rebirth. There was no way he could explain all of the meaning of baptism, so he hit the high points and then gave them a follow-up brochure of reading material. All of this had been covered in the class they'd all attended, but he wanted to review. Baptism was important.

Then he went through the details of the procedure—where to put hands, how to bend the knees, and what to do when coming out of the water.

A young man, about 25 years old, raised his hand to ask a question. "How cold will the water be?"

Pastor Butch Gregory laughed, "Not cold at all. We have electric heaters that will make the water very warm—almost hot tub warm. I don't do cold baptisms."

He finished up the orientation with an overview of the three questions he would ask them in the baptistery. "When we get up there, I am going to ask each of you, individually, 3 questions. The first question is, 'Do you publicly profess Jesus Christ as your Lord and Savior?' and the second question is 'Do you renounce the devil and all works of evil?' and the third question is 'Do you promise to serve the Kingdom of God through a local church for the rest of your life?' Now, the answer to those questions needs to be yes—and you need to say yes out loud. If the answer is not yes, then we can talk about that some now. Don't wait until we're in the middle of church to do it. Are there any questions?"

"What does that big word, re-now nd-tsted mean?" came a hand from a little 11 year old girl.

"That is a good question Rhiannon. It is just a fancy word that means you don't want to have anything to do with the devil. So the question just means you don't want to have anything to do with the devil and all the evil stuff he does. Does that explain it?"

"Thanks Pastor Butch."

There were no other questions, so Butch prayed over the group and then they left. He went back into the room to turn the lights off and put the robes away and as he hung them by the heater pump underneath the stairs leading up to the baptistery he thought back to the idea about baptizing in cold water. He shuddered and rubbed his arms for warmth at the thought.

The older men in his church always razzed him about the heated baptismal pool and they often compared him with worn and much rehearsed stories of "pastor so and so" who used to baptize in the Puget Sound in the month of December. In the old men's eyes this type of endurance was the only meaningful indicator of true, genuine spirituality. Butch always doubted the veracity of these stories. Puget Sound was constantly 55 degrees Fahrenheit, summer and winter. It was dangerous to be out there in that water for any length of time, especially in the winter. Butch knew that hypothermia was a physiological issue, not just a comfort issue. He was certain there was more than a little exaggeration in the old timers.

About three years earlier, out of pure curiosity, Butch tried it to see what it would feel like. It was the week before Christmas. The first snow had not come yet, but it was very, very cold and very, very wet. In short, it was typical Pacific Northwest weather in the month of December. Butch drove down to the beachfront looking out toward Seattle's skyline and he sat on the bench. He sat there a while, in his jeans and sweat shirt, and tried to work up the nerve to walk out into the water.

Butch didn't like water. He didn't really like being wet. He loved baptizing, but not being wet. The only time he liked water was for beverages, his hot tub, and hygiene.

Standing in the frigid Puget Sound water in December, or anytime for that matter, just didn't seem like fun. He had brought a hot water bottle and a bevy of towels and blankets. When he was a child he fell through the ice of a frozen pond behind a friend's house. It was not life threatening, but very uncomfortable and the needlelike sensation had never left his memories. He did not want to revisit it again.

Curiosity was a demanding task master and it compelled him to act.

He sat on the beach thinking about the Irish monks who used to stand in the smashing cold surf as a penance. He thought about airplane crashes in frigid river waters. He thought about Leonardo DiCaprio in *Titanic.*

The longer he sat there, the less bold he got.

So he stood up, took off his shoes and stepped toward the water. He grimaced as his first step hit the cold surf. The second one caused him to gasp, but he kept going. In all of his contemplation he had not thought about how far out to go. The tiny waves were beating him already. As the water reached his upper thigh and then his groin area, the coldness overwhelmed his nervous system and shot a convulsive shiver through his body.

He shouted in agony. That was far enough.

A woman walking her dog on the beach shouted back. “Are you okay? Do you need help? Should I call 911?”

Butch tried to answer her. He intended to say, “I’m okay. I am conducting an experiment. I’m not trying to harm myself.” That is not what came out of his mouth. What came out of his mouth was, “I’m kkkkkkkkkkkdddtttttttng a peer mint.”

He counted to 20, mentally said the liturgy he always said at baptisms, went through the three questions and then walked out. Now the problem was the wet clothes stuck to his body. It was horrible. His underwear was wet. His jeans were stiff. He was turning blue. He sat in his car with the heat blasting.

It was then that it hit him that he hadn’t told Lucy what he was doing. He didn’t know how he was going to explain this. But that wasn’t the worst. There was a lingering effect from his experiment. He caught and maintained a nasty cold which ruined his Christmas and New Year.

The pastor’s thoughts lingered on that old memory as he turned out the lights and locked up the building and went home. As he drove down the avenue that led away from the church he recognized Tamara Rey walking along the sidewalk. She was drinking a very large soda.

She must be walking home. Her apartment is not far from here.

He waved at her, but he didn’t think she saw him.

Chapter Five

Merchandise

AFTER THE minivan entered the garage, Mark dragged Tamara and the blonde little girl by the hair out of it and shoved them inside kennels made for large dogs. In the place most garages have cars, this one had cages. Each girl was put in a separate cage. The cages were bolted to the ground. Donny took the tape off of them and Mark pointed his chubby finger. "If you kids screams or yells, I will kill you." He moved his hand across his throat to emphasize the violence of his words. Then he swore. "Keep your mouth shut and you will live. Nobody gets hurt." Then he lit a cigarette and smoked it while Donny locked the cages. They turned the lights off and walked out, leaving the girls alone in the dark.

"What is your name?" asked the blonde girl after a few moments of fearful, dark silence.

"Tamara. What is your name?"

"Britney."

"I heard the two men talking about Port Angeles. Is that where you are from?"

"No. I'm from Sequim. I was visiting my grandma for a couple of weeks in Port Angeles before school started again. Tamara, are you from Sydney?"

"Yeah. What happened to you?"

"I was at the park playing," Britney began. "My grandma was taking a nap, and she lets me walk over to the park so the house will be quiet. The park is nice. It has swings, a big slide, and large shady trees. So I was playing all alone on the swings when that man—the fat one, called out to me. He said he needed some help, that he was trying to find where the ferry to Victoria was. I knew right where that was because last month my mom and dad took me to Victoria and I remember directions real good so I walked over and began pointing the way to go. He asked me to show him on a map so he had me walk over to that," she pointed to the gray minivan.

Britney began to weep as she continued to tell her story.

"Then the door opened quickly and that other man, I think his name is Donny, grabbed me and yanked me inside. He put something over my nose that made me go to sleep. When I woke up, I was taped like you saw me. I was in that car the whole time with the fat one while the other one was stealing you. There was nothing I could do. I'm sorry."

"It is not your fault," Tamara consoled her in a hushed whisper. "These are bad people. Don't worry, my mommy will find me. When she does, we'll get out of here together."

"I hope so. I am so afraid."

Tamara curled up in a little ball, and with her fingernail she flicked at the hard concrete floor.

Mark, Donny and another man who was tall and skinny with blonde features and acne scars entered the room. Now there were five evil men who surrounded the six children. Tamara expected the new children to be shoved into cages too, but instead Tamara and Britney were brought out. They were lined up against the wall, each one separately, and their picture was taken. They photographed them individually from the front, from the side, and from behind. Then, they made them take off their clothes and they took pictures of them naked.

All of the children were crying. One of the new girls screamed and cried so loud that Mark promised to slit her throat if she didn't stop it. She did stop screaming; the tears never ended. Tamara Rey tried to pretend she was at the doctor's office. She remembered that her mommy told her that it was okay for a doctor to see you like that, because a doctor checked to make sure everything was okay with your body. That helped Tamara get through it but the hard part was that the men were not looking at Tamara in the same way the doctor did.

When it was over the girls were told to put their clothes back on and they were put back into the cages. The boy, though, was taken to a back room with one of the men who brought him in. The boy came back about 20 minutes later, shaking.

The tall acne scarred man took the digital camera into his office, which was in an adjacent room and systematically downloaded all of the photographs onto his computer. Then he compiled them into six different folders, one for each child. He didn't know what all their names were and he didn't care. Each victim was assigned a number. Tamara's number was 913-8-15. Britney's number was 412-8-14. Each number meant something different. The first number was a categorization of ethnicity or features. The number 9 meant Latina and the number 4 meant Caucasian, blond. A number 3 would mean Caucasian, dark while a number 2 would be Caucasian with red features. Lot 2 always drew more sales than either 3 or 4. The number 1 meant Asian. One of the girls which had just come in was Asian. Asian girls were always in high demand and therefore came with a higher price tag.

That meant it was already a good day for the man clicking the mouse and organizing his inventory. A hateful smile curled upon his thin lips.

The second number in the sequence was for gender identification. One was a girl, and a two was a boy.

The third number identified approximate age. He learned to stop asking the children their age, because they either lied or it just made them cry more so it was easier to just guess it and assigned an appropriate number. The smaller the number is, the younger the child. Younger Asian girls tended to sell better. So, a top priced product would be one that started with a 114. The highest number he'd ever entered for age identification was 7, which, to him meant a 17 year old. There was once a girl who he was pretty sure was 18, but no one would buy an 18 year old. The middle number set, separated by dashes, was the month the girl was obtained. This particular batch of product was harvested during the month of August.

August is always a good month. No school, so kids are cut loose on the streets, the weather is warm and the days long, the perfect environment for harvesting. At other times of the year their greatest profit margins came from shopping malls and high school football games. He hated the football games. So many people and so many things can go wrong. But school bus stops in January, now that was another big profit margin month. The pickings were so easy at bus stops. Unguarded and isolated children left all alone in the precious moments before the bus arrives. Easy money.

The last number in the identity code was the numerical order for that month. Tamara was the 15th girl harvested on that day and Britney, taken just before her, was number 14.

The ugly man sat at the computer and catalogued the images and placed them in the proper file sequence with the matter-of-fact business sense of a professional. One might expect similar efficiency from an accountant or a real estate agent. His cool capitalist mindset would have been the same if he were taking inventory of stock located in a warehouse somewhere. It was all just merchandise, waiting for eager buyers.

And there were plenty of buyers.

That these were human beings was irrelevant to him, but oh so important to his buyers. For most of them, the power of owning and controlling another human with total dominance was part of the thrill.

He didn't care about that. It is just business.

After the inventory was catalogued, he uploaded the images to a protected website. The website was pass code secured and heavily encrypted. Only buyers could access it. They could look through the files and the photographs from the comfort of their own home, place the order, and literally have the girl delivered. Most of the buyers were from the Pacific Rim, Central and South America, and Eastern Europe. Sometimes orders came in from the States, but that was still rare. He took a certain pride in his work in that aspect. Unlike the petty pimps and the lowly thugs found in every city everywhere else, he was a global businessman with a model for international trade.

He was the Jeff Bezos of the child sex trade.

Around midmorning Donny fed the girls breakfast. The breakfast consisted of crackers, canned meat, and room temperature water from the tap. The little children gobbled it down, though, fearful and without complaint.

"I brung you some chocolate bars too. I thought you kids might like that." He handed out the candy to the kids as if it would atone for the evil he introduced into their lives. He knew what he was doing was worse than wrong but his cowardice always dictated his decisions.

Tamara took the chocolate, but her mind was on the half eaten sandwich sitting on the sofa. What would her mother think when she came home? Would she ever see her mother again?

"Donny, why are you doing this to me?" Tamara asked.

"I had no choice Tam. It was you or me." He paced in front of the cage, feeling more a prisoner than the she was. "Sorry, but that's the way it goes. Look, they would have killed me, but they ain't gonna kill you. You're just going to have to grow up a little faster, that's all. You are a prized possession." He stopped pacing and stared at her. "Really, I guess, you're like a beauty queen treasured by men all around the world. They won't kill you Tam, you are too valuable. People want you. Me, on the other hand, well, I'm just the hired help I guess. Nobody wants me."

"Please let me go home Donny. I don't want to be a beauty queen. I want to go home. Take us all home. Please." She began to cry.

"Shhhhhh Tam. You'd better be quiet. I'm nice to you, but the rest of these guys, they ain't so nice. I'm not the one who knocked you on the head, remember? Do what you're told and you'll make it through this. If you don't obey, then, well, things can get real nasty real quick and I don't want that to happen. Just don't make no trouble. I'll tell ya what, I'll see if I can't get a soda or find another piece of chocolate or something. I'll be right back."

Donny left, but he didn't come back, and she was glad he didn't. She didn't want soda or chocolate. She wanted him to disappear forever. Tamara felt hate. She hated Donny. It was the first time she ever felt that particular emotion. She didn't like it.

About one o'clock in the afternoon an important email arrived at the garage. The blonde headed leader with the acne scars was working in the front of the building taking care of the cover operation when the message came through on his mobile phone. He stopped what he was doing and walked around to the back and woke up Mark.

"At sunset you leave for the waiting room, got it."

"Okay, I'll wake up Donny."

"No, Donny stays here. After his screw up with the gas that you told me about, I can't trust him. Take the other two guys from Snohomish with you. Donny stays, you got it."

"Sure thing, boss."

The boss growled one more directive. "Make sure and change out the license plates on both vehicles. Use the Nevada plates."

Chapter Six

The Scene of the Crime

SANDY FIELDS was one of the first responders to Nikki Jones' apartment. She called Pastor Butch and told him that Tamara had been abducted. Sandy was a deacon at Sydney Community Church. She had assisted Pastor Butch at their baptisms. She told Pastor Butch what she knew: Nikki was okay, but Tamara was missing.

Sandy took a risk by informing Butch because the new fire chief was not receptive to the faith community and had already warned Sandy a few months earlier when she called Pastor Butch about a DOA who was from Sydney Community.

Before he left for the apartment he checked one of the Seattle television station's websites. It indicated a child abduction had occurred in Sydney but gave no specifics. The news vans hadn't arrived yet, but Butch knew they would be here soon.

As is so often the case Butch Gregory was flying blind. When he arrived, he didn't quite know where to stick his head. He was confused; this was not his element. There were no seminary lectures on how to interface with a crime scene neither were there any lessons on what to say to a parent whose child has just been stolen away from her home in the middle of the night. Butch's situation was made more precarious in that he really didn't know what had happened. He stepped under the upside down police tape marked POLICE LINE DO NOT CROSS. He crossed the line, and no one even noticed. The apartment door was wide open, the lights were on.

Nikki Jones' living room looked and felt far different from the last time Butch Gregory sat in it. Memories of that first visit invaded his mind. On that evening he had come to this same apartment on a hunch from a Sunday School teacher. Tamara Rey came to church by herself and she was asking her teacher questions about faith, heaven, and Jesus every week. Pastor Butch came by the apartment that evening not knowing what to expect. What he found was Nikki Jones, a single mother coming out of a broken, dysfunctional relationship with a horrible man, trying to make ends meet. He also found a sweet little girl who was smart and attentive.

That night Pastor Butch talked to Nikki and Tamara about faith, love, and commitment to Christ. Before his visit was over they both were one step further in their walk with Christ. Back then, on that first visit, the apartment was filled with hope. Now it was filled with fear and the dread of death. Uniformed Sydney police officers filled the small two bedroom apartment. Many of them were not, apparently, doing anything, other than standing there. A couple of detectives were taking fingerprints. One officer was taking notes on a green steno pad.

The room also had three brown uniformed Blackjack County Sheriff's deputies and a man and a woman in dark suits. Butch assumed the two street clothed people were FBI, but didn't know that for sure. It could just be from watching too much television. It didn't seem possible to him that the FBI would even know a town like Sydney existed.

As he stepped deeper into the apartment Butch spotted the most important person in it, the one he'd been looking for. Nikki sat on the sofa, in the exact same spot where she had prayed to become a Christian. Her hair was tussled. She looked bleary eyed and numb.

Butch said in a low voice, "Nikki."

When he said her name Nikki Jones came out of her daze and her eyes met his. With one motion she leapt off the couch and ran to him, tears coming down her eyes and said, "Pastor! They took my baby. They took my baby. Why? Why did they take my baby?" It was not an accusation, but a plea for insight and understanding. Butch opened his arms and embraced her with the loving, caring steady pastoral embrace he'd given to widows, to orphans, and to the dying. A hug is usually the best consolation for the inconsolable, and it is always the safest bet.

"I know," he said, "but I don't know why. We will try and put the pieces together. God will help us. He always does."

One of the police officers rolled his eyes and mumbled. Butch ignored it, and hoped Nikki hadn't seen it. He knew this would be a crisis of faith for her as a new, growing Christ-follower as well as one of the most traumatic things a parent can go through. In fact, he pondered as he held Nikki tightly, it would be a crisis of faith for anyone. He pushed back the fear that it could happen to one of his children. He pushed that though aside. The last thing she needed was the police to be spreading doubt or for him to be anxious in this dreadful moment.

Butch sat down on the couch beside Nikki and held her hand. He noticed a woman on the other side of Nikki in a chair. "Hi," said the woman. "My name is Dr. Candace Coles and I am the traumatic response psychologist for Blackjack County. Most of the officers call me Dr. CeeCee. Can I talk to you for a second?" As she said this, Dr. CeeCee stood up and motioned with her head for him to follow her. Butch did and she pulled him aside in the corner of the room.

"I've been talking with Nikki for the last half hour about mentally choosing to not succumb to her worst fears and that she should trust the police and hope in them to find Tamara."

"We do not hope in the police, Doctor. Our hope is in someone else." He had little use for psychologists.

"Well, I thought perhaps, since you are her priest and I see how she livened up to you, that you might help me."

"I'm her pastor, and I intend to help Nikki," replied Butch. In one motion he turned his back on Dr. CeeCee and walked back toward the heartsick mother. He again sat beside her, took her two hands into his, bowed his head, and began to pray.

> Dear Father, we don't know what is going on. We only know that this is bad. I ask on behalf of this mother and her little girl that you let this not be nearly as bad as we fear, and that Tamara is okay, somewhere. Keep her safe and let her be found without harm. Holy Spirit, bring some kind of comfort to my friend Nikki, comfort I can't give or that no human wisdom can give. Hold her close to you right now. I ask this in the name of Jesus Christ. Amen.

Nikki exhaled a barely audible, "Amen."

Butch then looked right into Nikki's eyes and asked, "What happened."

"We've already got the details, Reverend," interrupted Dr. CeeCee. "I am sure the officer will let you read the report."

"I know," replied Butch. "But, I want to hear Nikki's voice. I don't know what happened at all, and she can best tell me in her own words."

That was only partly true. He did want to hear Nikki's voice. But he also knew from years of ministry that when people hurt, telling their pain and rehearsing their story helps the healing process. He didn't know why this was so, but it was so. He wanted to give Nikki one more opportunity to process exactly what happened to her and to Tamara. Besides, he really didn't know what had happened. He was still as in the dark on details as he was when he arrived. Pastor Butch knew that police reports are always interesting, but usually they fail to convey the whole story.

Nikki slowly opened her mouth and began to speak. "I don't know, Pastor. I got off work at 5 this morning and I came straight home. The door was shut, but not locked. That was odd. I came inside the apartment and went to Tam's bedroom to check on her. Her bed was still made. She wasn't here. I tried not to panic and just assumed she spent the night with a friend without telling me. It wouldn't have been the first time. So, feeling bad that it was so early, I waited until about 6 to call her closest friends. She wasn't there, Pastor. She wasn't there. It was then that I noticed one of the pictures was knocked down and that a half eaten sandwich was on the coffee table."

Nikki began to cry uncontrollably. Butch held her hand and waited.

"Pastor, that was when I saw the small blood stain by the front door."

The Pastor's eyes widened and then sank. His heart collapsed inside of him.

Butch sat in stunned silence. He held her hand. He didn't say anything. What is there to say?

Nikki wailed for her daughter. It was a haunting lament Butch had never heard in his entire life. He pulled her close to his chest and prayed silently. He asked God to undo this and make it right somehow. He also asked God to help him, and help him right now. He didn't know what else to do.

As he glanced across the sofa he could see that Dr. CeeCee didn't know what to do either.

Butch walked outside of the apartment and saw three different news vans from the Seattle television stations. He took his iPhone out of his pocket and called Michael Hill.

"Hey Mike, have you seen the news this morning? No, no you haven't. Well, you know Nikki and Tamara from church, right? Yeah, of course you do. Well, Tamara was abducted last night, right out of her apartment. Nikki is pretty torn up about it—"

"Yeah, look, I don't have much time here. I feel like I need to get her somewhere safe and calming." He walked down the driveway to the sidewalk running along the street. "Mike, I was wondering if Nikki could stay at your house. It is going to be a zoo around here, and she needs someplace where she can be alone and process all of this. I know this is short notice, and all, but I need your help.

"Good, are you sure? Good. I will bring her over, then, as soon as I can get her away from here. I don't know what the police might have for her to do or say or sign. Thank you. I'll see in you a little while."

Butch walked back through the police line, into the apartment and spoke to the command officer. He gave the officer his name and business card. He also told him that he'd seen Tamara walking up the sidewalk towards her apartment last night. Then he said that he wanted to get Nikki out of here. The officer was surprisingly compliant and said sure. He just wanted a couple of phone numbers to know where to contact her. Then Pastor Butch Gregory walked back into the apartment, towards the couch. He took the shocked woman by the hand and said, "Come with me," and he led her to his Honda.

He drove her to the Hill's house. She knew Michael and Florence from church and they welcomed her with big hugs. Butch sat with them for a while and explained to Michael what happened while Florence scrambled some fresh eggs, toasted some sourdough bread, and fried up some sausage for Nikki to eat, which she didn't. Nikki just sat at the yellow and white kitchen table and stared off into nothing.

Pastor Butch prayed again for Nikki and Tamara and went on to the office. He knew that the Hill's would minister to her and give her the space she needed to hide from the media.

Chapter Seven

Visitation

THE CLOCK said 2 A.M. Butch woke up in a sweat. He never did that. He studied Lucy on the other side of the bed and envied her deep slumber. Her irenic sleep was in stark contrast to his feelings of anxiety. He felt antsy, nervous, and agitated. He knew the day's stress and the unsettling nature of Tamara and Nikki's situation had gotten to him.

Was he having a heart attack? He checked his arms and there was no numbness. He didn't feel unusual pressure on his chest. He was just uncomfortable. It had been 24 hours since Tamara had been abducted and no news, no leads, no development at all. The only thing the police would say was, "We're working on it." He felt frustrated and he only wondered how Nikki must feel.

Butch got out of bed and slid his feet into his house shoes. He walked down the hallway, past his children's rooms and into his study. He turned on the small reading light and sat there. The feeling he had wasn't only anxiety about the day's events. It was something else. He'd had it twice before in his life. The first time was when he received his calling from God to go into the ministry. The second time was when he was told by the Lord to accept the pastorate of Sydney Community Church.

Something was up.

His old hardback Bible that he used for his daily devotions sat on top of the August copy of *Christianity Today.* He shoved aside Erickson's massive *Systematic Theology* that he'd brought home a couple of days earlier and opened his Bible and began reading in the Gospel of Luke. He'd been reading through Luke in preparation for a sermon series in the fall. He had come through the biggest teachings in the book and was winding his way toward the passion narrative. He picked up in Luke 19 with the story of Zacchaeus. Butch enjoyed the story about the repentant tax collector, but he stumbled when he came to verse 10. Jesus says,

> For the Son of Man came to seek and to
> save the lost.

When he read it, he heard a voice inside of him echo, *to seek and to save those who are taken.*

Butch knew from his biblical formations that Jesus' statement here is linked to the great teaching in Luke 15 about God's passion for those who had lost their way in the world. He flipped backward the three pages in his Bible to Luke 15. Luke 15 was still fresh on his mind and he knew the stories well, but he reviewed the three stories in that chapter again anyway.

A lost coin.

A lost sheep.

The coin probably symbolized a wedding dowry. The shepherd in the story had to leave the rest of the sheep and take his shepherd's crook to fend off the wolves and the evil of the world to save the lost sheep. Finally, the father waited expectantly for the child to come home from a far country where he had squandered his life.

Different backgrounds, different genders, different socio-economic classes, and different expectations about the world, all united by the human need to find, to recover, and to save what or who was lost.

He fiddled with the worn pages of the Bible and heard the voice again inside his mind remind him she does have a pastor, she does have a shepherd to go find the lost sheep.

His face turned pale as Jesus began speaking directly into his heart. It wasn't an audible voice. It was, though, epiphany.

Jesus said, "You must go find Tamara. I am sending you. She is alive. I am with you."

That was it.

The Lord gave no special instructions. He didn't tell him where to look. He just told him to go.

"Lord, I can't do that. I am a pastor, not a detective. I have no crime fighting skills." The Lord said nothing.

This isn't funny. I've got a ton of work with the church. There is the building campaign, the new staff member to train, and not to mention my responsibility to my family.

The Lord said nothing.

Why me, Lord?

The Lord said nothing.

All Butch heard was the disturbed silence the Divine often gives to those who ask too many questions. Pastor Butch sat and listened for an excuse not to act all the while his heart burned within him and his mind turned toward Nikki Jones. She was alone, crying, and hurting. He also thought of Tamara. Perhaps she was in distress. He imagined her locked up in a hotel room somewhere. He was afraid of what horrible atrocity might have been done to her. He thought of every book he'd ever read about abduction, child serial killers, and the international child slave trade.

His mind shifted uncontrollably to his kids who were asleep down the hall. If he weren't around wouldn't he want someone to go find them? Would he not be grateful to anyone who would help his wife find his daughter or son? Yes, he would.

But would he want an unqualified bumbling fool to do it? No, he would not. He must be misunderstanding God. Butch looked up toward the heavens, opened up his palms and prayed one of his shortest prayers. "I can't do it Lord," and then he went back to bed.

He still couldn't sleep. Images of Tamara Rey being dragged from her apartment with blood oozing from her body gnawed at him. In his mind he could hear her scream and see the fear etched on her precious face. He tossed and turned hoping comfort would come; but it didn't. He dozed off once but something akin to panic startled him awake. Then he remembered the police officer he talked to at Nikki's apartment who told him there was probably no way Tamara would ever be found. "These things never turn out well," he told Butch that awful morning.

At 4:30 in the morning the exhausted pastor again got out of bed as sleep continued to elude him. Butch quietly walked through the dark hallway, beyond the living room and moved onto the kitchen floor. Butch kicked off his house shoes and felt the cold, smooth tile under his feet. It felt good. Then he turned on the small light above the stovetop, grabbed a clear crystal glass from the cupboard and filled it with water from the tap. He thought about making coffee, but knew the smell would wake his wife and oldest child.

Passing through the doors he sat down at the dining table and stared straight ahead. He didn't turn the chandelier on but the glow from the stove's overhead light in the kitchen was enough. He didn't really want much light anyway. He didn't really know what he wanted, other than to have this anxiety leave him.

In the dimly lit dining room Butch took a drink of water and gazed down into the crystal glass and watched the particles float around inside the glass. Just enough shafts of light came from the kitchen's stove light to illuminate the glass so that he could observe their random movements. He felt like one of those particles—adrift on the current—helpless to do anything about the direction he was traveling. He took another sip of water and looked across the table to the other end. He blinked. His mouth gaped open. He took another drink, and then blinked again. Sitting across the table from him was his kid brother.

His brother who had been dead for over thirty years.

"Shark?" Butch whispered his name loudly in disbelief.

"You have to find her," replied Shark.

"Find who?"

"The little girl, Butchy. She's in trouble and you are the only one who can find her. You have to do it."

"I don't understand Shark. How are you here? You're dead. I was there. This doesn't make sense. We buried you. How can this be?"

"Butchy, don't try to think too hard and don't live in the past. Right now Tamara needs your help. She is scared and she is praying. God wants you to find her. He sent me to tell you. Now, go find her. It is your mission to do this, but you will not be alone."

"But, how? The police said—"

"The police," Shark cut off his big brother's sentence, "though well meaning, are not able. You can do what the police can't do. You see the world differently than they see it. There are barriers for them that will hinder the work. You can move quicker than them."

"Shark, what you are asking is impossible. I don't even know where to start. I mean, I'm a pastor not a detective. Where would I look, what would I do? I have a theological library, not a forensics lab. I think you've made a mistake." Butch shook his head repeatedly at the end of each sentence.

"No, Butchy, no mistake. You have to do this. But not alone. There is a woman who knows some things, and these are things that can help you. She will contact you this morning at your office. She has a role to play and her own calling. She will help you, but you have to hurry. You only have ten days. After that, it will be too late. Oh, and stop telling God what you're not. That is twice today you've said you're a pastor not a detective. Stop it. You are what he has called you to be, and quite frankly, he doesn't like it when you question his decisions."

"What woman?"

"You'll know tomorrow."

"What about Tamara, where is she?"

"I can't tell you that."

"What? Why? Why bother showing up and give me orders and then not giving me the most important information I could possibly have? That makes no sense Shark. None."

"Well, there are rules. I just can't tell you everything."

"Whose rules?"

"Whose rules? Really? You know whose rules."

"God?"

"Yeah, God: The One True God: The Lord. He rules and these are his rules."

"What kind of rules are those? There is nothing in the Bible about anything like this."

"So cerebral. I thought by now you would have figured out that the Bible doesn't give all the answers or all the rules; it certainly doesn't give the rules for those of us who are dead."

"Are you a . . . are you an angel?"

"You know better than that. I'm no angel. I'm your brother."

"But how are you here and why now?"

"No more questions; besides, you know why. I can, though, give you a hint.

Not in the forest, but near the sea
the little girl waits in uncertainty.
You must travel through woods and sky,
and in the desert eyes should pry.
On your search there will be three;
one to die, one to cry, one to see."

"That, that doesn't make a lot of sense Shark."

"It will. When you are near the completion, it will give you confidence to know that you are on the right track. It will make sense later. Oh, and there will be another who will help you as well. He is as one who is unwilling to take medicine but whom, nevertheless, knows the medicine is good for him. I must go now. Remember Butchy; pray."

Then he was gone. As dramatically as he had appeared, Shark was gone. He didn't gently fade or pixelate away. It was instantaneous. Butch was again sitting all alone at his large, oak dining table. There were so many questions that came to his mind he couldn't properly process them all. He sat dumbfounded until he heard his alarm clock going off in the bedroom. It was 6:00 A.M. and he'd barely been aware of the passage of time.

Chapter Eight

This is Really Happening

"PASTOR BUTCH, there is a young woman here to see you. Says her name is Amber. I don't see her on the appointment book." Mildred's voice was cold on the phone intercom. That was because she was grumpy. It made her unendingly grumpy when people popped in to see one of the staff, especially Pastor Butch, without the prerequisite appointment. Mildred had been Butch's administrative assistant for ten years, and over that decade she had added a watchdog function to her position description. She saw herself as Butch's guardian, protecting him from the hordes of barbarians who sought to invade the tranquility of the pastor's prayer and study. Whether Butch wanted this shielding or not was a question Mildred never asked. It did irk her that Butch had never sent a drop in away. Mildred always wanted him to.

"Hum," Butch grunted as he tried to remember the name, then he added, "Send her on back, Mildred. Thank you."

Butch quickly rifled through his mind like an old filing cabinet; "Amber, where do I know that name from? Amber?" When she walked through the door and he saw her face, the memories flooded him. Three years ago he had buried Amber's brother, Pastor Adam Smith. It was a tragedy of Greek proportions and a media nightmare.

Adam was cut off too soon. Shot dead by a lunatic in the middle of a worship service.

Didn't Amber know her brother's killer? It was such a mess, impossible to figure out. Now here she is in my office? I'd better be on guard.

What more could happen this week?

Pastor Butch smiled and extended his hand, "Hi Amber. It is good to see you again."

"Not really, Butch. Not really." There was an awkward pause, and then she continued. "Part of me hoped I would never see you again. Ever."

"I think I understand that," Butch said in the pastoral tone he'd been working on since his first year of seminary. "You went through a lot, and I am probably a painful reminder of all you went through. I must say I am surprised to see you. I touch base with your sister-in-law Elaine from time to time. The last time we talked she told me that you are building a very good life for yourself. She tells me you are even attending Adam's church now. Is that right?"

"Yes, I do. But I want to cut the crap Preach. I'm not here to talk about my brother. That is over and done and there is nothing I can do about it. Besides, we don't have time for memory lane right now." Butch sat up straight in his high back office chair and then leaned forward in an "I'm all ears" posture. Amber noticed this. "For some reason, Preach, it is in my mind that you're the one to help me. Two nights ago, not last night but night before last, I saw a little girl I am sure was in trouble. Yesterday I called the police—do you know how hard that was, for me to call the police—and they took my report but I know it is just a piece of paper in someone's outbox waiting to be catalogued, numbered, and then filed in someone else's drawer. Meanwhile, I can't get her image out of my mind. I am pretty sure that the little girl I saw is the little girl who was abducted two days ago. Her name is Tamara Rey. I am also sure she goes to Sydney Community Church."

Butch gulped hard. "How do you know she goes here?"

"Because God told me last night." Amber Smith paused to gauge Butch's reaction to her claim that God spoke to her. When he didn't flinch, she began again with her rehearsed story. "I guess I can trust you with things like that since you are a pastor and all. But last night I had a dream. In my dream the little girl was in this church singing and laughing. The next minute in my dream you and I were chasing after her. She was just out of reach and we couldn't get to her. We kept running faster and faster but we never could get to where she was. There were ugly, evil men who kept pushing us out of the way and in the dream we had to get rid of the evil men to get to Tamara. I knew when I woke up that it wasn't a dream. It was something God was talking to me about. That is why I came to you."

Butch sat with his hands on his knees. He had been working hard all morning to tell himself that what had happened with his brother at the dining room table was all some sort of psychosis. But here, here in his study he saw Amber and knew this was the woman Shark told him about. This is the woman who would help him find Tamara Rey.

Amber continued, "We've got to help her. We've got to find her and I don't think we have much time."

"I know," Butch paused. He again swallowed hard, took a sip of coffee and followed, "God told me too."

"I guess he's doing a lot of that lately. How did he tell you?" Amber asked the question out of pure curiosity. She wondered if her experience was the same as his.

"I'll fill you in later." Butch pivoted to his left in his roller chair and tossed his hands up, "What are we going to do," he mumbled, to himself not so much as to Amber. He surveyed the terrain of his large desk. Since he had arrived at work he'd tried to stay busy to keep his mind off of Shark. So there was a Hebrew lexicon, three commentaries, two ripped out magazine articles, and six different Bibles all opened on his desk. He was studying Genesis 22. However the herald of news had changed his priorities dramatically.

"Amber, we've got to work through this, but right now I need to tidy up some things around here so I can focus my attention on this—this odyssey. Can you stop by my house this afternoon around 3? I'd like to introduce you to my wife and plot our next move."

"Sure," Amber said, "but this is quick. I thought I'd have to talk you into doing something. That was as far as my plan went."

"Someone else beat you to it, I was already talked into it. But now we need new plans," answered Butch, "and we haven't much time."

After a few moments of conversation followed with directions to his home, Amber left. Butch walked over to the tall metal cabinet and rummaged through thick files of old sermons. He would need to preach something old this upcoming Sunday if he was going to spend all week chasing ghosts and missing persons.

No, no, no, no. His thumb hit one old sermon after another. No, no, no, no. Finally, something caught his eye labeled "Get Over Yourself: The Art of Praying for Other People." He checked the date on the file—he preached that sermon 6 years ago.

Had it been that long? He remembered preaching it, but as he read through the manuscript none of the text was familiar to him. He only remembered the title but couldn't remember any of the substance. If he didn't remember it, the congregation most certainly wouldn't. Such was the blessing of a file cabinet full of old sermons.

They forget six year old sermons, but they also forget six day old ones as well as sixty minute old sermons. They even forget six-minute old sermons. Sermonizing was a double-edged sword in more than one way.

He walked up the hallway into the main reception area and had Mildred cancel all of his appointments for the rest of the week—his premarital couple tomorrow night, the men's prayer this afternoon, and even the big pastor's lunch he was to be at tomorrow. Butch didn't know exactly what the rest of his week would be, but he knew he needed to clear his calendar. His actions clearly made Mildred grumpier because she did not engage him in small talk. Whenever Mildred did not approve of Pastor Butch's decision she took a cold, professional tone which is what she did as he ticked off everything that needed to be canceled.

On his way back down the hallway a nudge in his gut erupted into full blown inspiration. Butch stopped by his associate pastor's office. Pastor Philip Coleman had only been on staff for 6 months. Fresh out of seminary and green around the ears, Philip was often frightened by church people. Butch hated to do this to him, but he had no choice, and it felt right. "Philip, you are preaching this Sunday. I'm going to be out the rest of the week, for the most part. If anything comes up, just handle it."

"What? Handle what?"

"Anything. If anything pops up, just handle it."

"Are you expecting anything to pop up? I mean, what might pop up?" His eyes were platters and his cheeks flushed rose red.

"Philip," Butch looked directly at him, "ministry is not something that can always be predicted. It usually just happens. People get sick, they experience tragedy, get angry, make decisions you don't like, gossip, slander, get pregnant, elope, get divorced, go to jail, move away, move in, move out and a host of other things which are completely unpredictable and unscheduled. What I am telling you is that if anything does happen, I trust you as you listen to the Lord to make the right decisions for the church and for the individuals involved. I also trust you to do the right things. When I come back, I will support whatever decisions you make and we will work through any problems that are still around. I am counting on you to shepherd this church in my absence. You are a highly trained minister with an outstanding skill set given by the Lord. Ministry is 90% intuition and I trust your intuition. You will be fine. Okay?"

"Sure, sure," Philip said weakly. "Thank you for your confidence. I will not let you down."

Butch patted the young unmarried man on the back and momentarily reminisced upon his own early ministerial career. Once upon a time the same essential pep talk had been given to him when he needed it. Now Philip needed it. Philip was a good man and a good minister. He just needed some confidence and experience. As he thought about it in Philip's doorway, that speech might have been for him too for he was right in the midst of the most unpredictable situation he'd ever been in.

"Now Philip," he started, "the first thing I need you to do is call an emergency board meeting for tonight. Work with Mildred to contact all of them and tell them I need to meet at 7:00 PM with all of them. Tell them it is important and they need to be here." Butch walked away, but he remembered one more thing. He stuck his head back inside Philip's office and said, "Oh, and you need to prepare to do the baptisms this Sunday."

"Baptisms? I don't know how to do that? I've never done that before. They didn't teach us that at school."

"Well, it's easy. Just be careful—you don't want to lose anyone." Butch let that sentence hang in the air and then he reassuringly grinned at Philip and said, "I'll walk you through it this afternoon. It is not hard. The water does all the work."

Butch entered into his office. He took that old sermon about prayer and put it back.

If Philip preaches on Sunday, then I can store this away for yet another rainy day. Then he packed his satchel with his laptop, tablet, Bible and a couple of books and pulled the file labeled "Jones, Nikki and Tamara Rey." Butch had files on everyone and everything. He had made this one just after that first visit to their apartment last winter.

He sat back down at his desk and looked through it. He was very surprised at how much information was inside it. There was the enrollment form which Tamara filled out at Vacation Bible School. It was her first contact with the church two summers ago. Butch noticed that under the line "Are you a member of a church?" Tamara had written "Probably not." Then there was the original contact report from the children's minister stating that Tamara was open to spiritual discussions. That same note indicated that contact with the mother was, "very difficult due to work schedules." Following that was the yellow legal paper Butch had scribbled on after his visit and then a copy of a baptism certificate for both Tamara and her mother Nikki.

Behind it was a copy of the covenant they signed at the new member's class. There was an achievement award from Sunday School for Tamara when she memorized ten Bible verses. There was a certificate for Nikki completing the Dave Ramsey financial course.

Butch found a photograph of the two of them together with a deacon and the music minister at the Easter banquet in April.

Butch recognized all of these papers, but at the very back of the file was a final slip of paper he'd never seen before. It was brown in color and facing the other way in the file so Butch couldn't see what was written on it. He plucked it up and noticed it was not simply brown paper, but actually old parchment paper. There was a note on it written in perfect calligraphy.

What?

Not in the forest, but near the sea
the little girl waits in uncertainty.
You must travel through woods and sky,
and in the desert eyes should pry.
On your search there will be three;
one to die, one to cry, one to see.

He looked up and said, "Thank you, Shark. You knew I'd never remember all that."

This is real. This is all really happening.

Part Two:
Coming Together

Chapter Nine
Lucy, Meet Amber

BUTCH ARRIVED home from the office at a quarter after 2 in the afternoon. He was very hungry because he worked through noon to get everything cleared away then he drowned Philip with the dos and don'ts of baptizing. Lucy had a big bowl of hot spaghetti noodles with plenty of freshly grated parmesan cheese and warm garlic bread waiting. Through the years lunch had developed into their special time. Evenings were often crowded with meetings, phone calls, and study but lunch was a repose they could share most days.

"I don't know what to do, honey. I don't know if I am going crazy or the stress is getting to me. It seems, well, unbelievable."

"Well, you're not going crazy, you are crazy," she laughed as she said it and grabbed his hand.

"Thanks a lot."

"No, really. If I've learned anything from being in ministry together with you it is that you have to be a little bit off-balance to do this right. Only crazy people go into ministry. Sane people don't, they stay away from it. Sane people work at companies that pay insurance and give sick days and accrued vacation time. Sane people enjoy professions that don't cause minor addictions to antacid. Sane people find places to work that involve steady pay increases, retirement accounts, and union protection. But we are not sane. Face it; we are crazy, but we knew it would be this way. This is what we signed up for."

"Yeah," he wrinkled his nose as he formulated a response, "but that is a different kind of crazy than this. I mean, right there in that chair," he pointed, "my dead brother talked to me this morning and then later he left me this ridiculously enigmatic riddle in my file." Butch waved the parchment like a flag of surrender.

"Lucy, I know enough of psychological practice to diagnose myself and that is the bad part. Could it be that the abduction of Tamara is triggering old guilt about Shark and causing a kind of schizophrenia? Maybe I never healed from that old wound and it is manifesting itself in this present crisis. Did I hallucinate the whole conversation with him this morning then write that note to myself and plant it in the file? That, frankly, seems more plausible than to accept the completely unhinged idea that Shark talked to me, and the equally preposterous thought of Jesus turning me into a detective."

"But what about Amber? You didn't hallucinate that young woman who came to see you this morning?"

"Yeah, I know. That is where it gets extremely bizarre. When she walked into my study this morning an odd sensation flooded over me. It was almost precognition. Then when she unloaded on me; well, I just knew."

Lucy held his hands in hers and said, "Butch, do you really think it is crazy to believe God is working in this world to help a little girl and that he wants to use you to do it?"

"No, God wants to help Tamara, I believe that. What I don't believe necessarily is that I am the one to do it. There are people who could do it better than me. I don't even like to watch crime dramas on television. I'm a coward and I'm old and I don't have a clue as to what I am doing. The world is filled with millions of people infinitely more qualified to do this kind of thing than me."

"Ok, I get that," Lucy agreed as she nodded. "Now which Old Testament prophet would you prefer I reference, because you sound like Moses and Jeremiah and perhaps a little bit of Elijah. Hum? Maybe I'll call you Eli-miah-oses for all three who are rolled into one giant Butch Gregory?"

"I hate it when you do that." Butch exhaled as he complained. "That's my job to bring up the Bible and stuff. You're supposed to just tell me it is going to be alright and that I don't have to do anything I don't want to."

"Oh really? What is good for the goose is good for the gander. You know I'm right. Besides," she pulled his hands close to her chest and looked into his eyes with a seriousness that Butch knew she only exhibited when she'd given something deep thought, "since you told me this morning about Shark being here, and really since I learned of Tamara's abduction, I knew that something special was cooking. I feel it inside of me, too. You have to do this. I don't know how, and I don't know how long, but you have to do this. There is a frightened little girl out there somewhere and for reasons beyond the comprehension of either one of us, you are the one whom God has chosen to go help her—to go find her."

He nodded, "But I'm so afraid. If I mess up, she could end up dead. I," he stammered, "I—I—she is so sweet and innocent; I don't want to make a mistake that would get her hurt. This isn't like fouling up a ministry start or making a mistake with an Easter event. If I mess this up, then people could get hurt. I could get hurt. Tamara could die."

Or he could die.

The doorbell rang, and Lucy Gregory bent over and kissed her husband on the cheek and said, "That's right, but if you do nothing, not only will she definitely die, but you will also be disobedient to the one who called you; the one who called us. I would be most angry with you if you disobey God. Got that preacher boy?"

"Come on in," said Butch as he gestured his arm toward the inside, welcoming Amber to his home. He then introduced his wife. "Amber, this is Lucy, Lucy; Amber." The two women shook hands cordially. The three of them sat at the dining room table and confronted the reality that they were about to embark on something completely out of their realm of experience.

"Amber, I don't know exactly what your belief system is; and I don't want to assume anything, but I believe the Lord has called me to find Tamara Rey. In order to do that, I need you to tell me everything you saw and everything you know, even if you've already told the police. You should know that I am not working with the police.

"Me neither. They've still got a pretty thick file on me from before."

"Well," Butch said, "I just wanted you to know that I'm on my own here. What I need is for you to help me by telling me everything that happened."

"You don't have any business going after that little girl by yourself. This is not going to be about me telling you what I know and then you going off and doing it all alone. I'm not helping you. Instead, we," she pointed back and forth between the two of them as she emphasized the word we, "are looking for Tamara."

That was the moment when Lucy Gregory decided she liked Amber.

"Are we clear on that Preach? Because if we are not clear then we've got problems."

"Sure," Butch answered in a resigned tone. He didn't like it, but it felt right to him.

"Good," Amber said, "now, to answer your questions. I didn't see that much at the Skookum Mart, but I think what I saw was important. When I walked outside I saw this mean looking man pumping gas. He seemed, or felt, very dangerous. Inside the van, looking out of the side window was a little girl who appeared to be very scared and frightened. Her eyes were screaming, 'Help me!' I think there were actually two girls, because I thought I saw a wave or two of blonde hair in the backseat with her. The next day I heard about Tamara, saw her picture and I made the connection."

"What did the man look like?" Butch was trying to make a mental picture of who they might be looking for.

"There were actually two of them. The one who pumped the gas was large, maybe 260 pounds or so. He had a round face and a full red beard. The other guy, who was in the front seat, was thin and weak. He had that typical meth addict look to him. He wore a Seattle Mariners baseball cap and he had a beard too, but it was scraggly. They both looked like goons."

"Did you see anything else?"

"I saw the license plate on the car. I didn't get the whole number, but it was a California plate. The first five digits were MTH18. I didn't see the rest."

Lucy asked, "What kind of car was it?"

"It was a minivan. I think it was a Toyota."

"You'd think the police would have found this vehicle by now," Lucy said. "That is a lot of detail you've got here Amber."

"I know, but there were several hours between when I saw them and when the police actually got on the case. They could have been half-way through Oregon by then—or Montana maybe or even into Idaho."

"Or Canada. Or by plane or boat to anywhere," Butch chimed in.

Or dead.

He buried his face in his hands. A morose despondency settled over him. He knew well the vastness of the limitless terrain. On the western side of the state the thick forests and rugged mountains made finding anyone difficult. The vast and mostly depopulated eastern side of the state hid a lot of nefarious activity. Idaho, Montana and Oregon were even worse.

They could hide forever in Montana.

Heaven forbid they should cross the border into Canada. Butch knew if that happened, then Tamara would never be located. Finally he lifted his head from his hands and said, "I don't even know where to look."

"Well, together, I think maybe we can find her. But we might need help." Amber said this to Pastor Butch, but then she turned her attention to Lucy Gregory. "Lucy, you're husband and me are supposed to work together on this. We have to help each other."

Suddenly and without any forewarning, Ambers eyes filled with tears and her voice cracked. "It doesn't come easy for me. I'm a 'live and let live' kind of person who doesn't usually get involved in other people's lives. But it seems to me that it is what my brother would have wanted me to do."

Now Lucy was crying too. The pastor's wife had a strictly enforced "no one cries alone in my presence" policy. It was a good policy for her calling in Christian ministry. The mere sight of someone else in tears brought them freely and unabatedly to her eyes, but there was more as she cried with Amber. Her heart was broken and her soul was stirred. She knew that Amber was right. The Lord was clearly leading in this moment and in these deliberations.

No more words were spoken about their resolution. Lucy simply asked the two of them, "What now, where will you start?"

"Well, it seems like we should start by looking for a Toyota minivan."

"Not necessarily. I've been thinking about that," said Amber as she wiped her eyes with her shirt. "When I was living on the streets people would often talk about children being taken like this. I had this friend who told me once that there was an abandoned old building in SoDo where a lot of these children were 'processed.' From there they would be sent to Portland, Vegas, LA, the Midwest and even sometimes to the East Coast."

"SoDo?" asked Lucy.

"South Downtown—SoDo, is the old industrial part of Seattle." Butch gestured with his hands pointing in the general direction of Seattle, "lots of seedy places and a lot of old, run-down buildings. There is always an effort to revitalize it, but there are still many difficult places there. You've been through it many times on the way to the stadiums."

"Oh, that place. Yeah, not very pretty, except the baseball diamond, and oh, isn't Starbucks' headquarters down there?"

Butch continued, "Yeah, Starbucks is just about it. For the most part it is where the homeless people mingle when they are not panhandling on the waterfront or at Pike's Place or protesting in Pioneer Square." As he said these words, he felt guilty that Amber might take offense to his broad caricature of the homeless.

"I'm sorry. I didn't mean to imply anything. That's just how I've always understood SoDo."

"That's okay, and what you said is true, Preach. SoDo is not the postcard part of Seattle, but there are other places we might want to try as well. Aurora Avenue is home to a variety of both legal and illegal sex businesses. I think that is our target, not homeless people."

Lucy asked, "What makes you think they are in Seattle, anyway. They might be here in Blackjack County somewhere. There are plenty of places to hide in the woods. It might be easier to start looking here. Seattle is such a big place it seems all you'd be able to do is walk the streets and yell Tamara's name and that doesn't seem very effective."

Amber agreed, "Yeah, I think you're right. It is important to know where to start. We could lose a lot of time if we don't get it right out of the gate, so I think, maybe to figure that out, we are going to need even more help."

"Help?" Butch ached at the thought of help, but then he remembered Shark telling him there would be two people helping him.

"Yeah, help," Amber said. "We need to go to Wyoming."

"Wyoming?" Butch must have looked as confused as he felt.

"Yep. We just need to hop in that nice Honda of yours and drive. I'll tell you where to go Preach."

"Okay, I guess. Honey," Butch looked at Lucy, "I don't know what time I'll be back." He glanced at his watch. It was nearly 3:30. He looked at Amber, as if to ask what time she thought they would get back, but Amber just sat there. She offered nothing.

"Okay," said Butch again as he exhaled. "Will I need a change of clothes? I do need to be back at the church by 7 for the big board meeting. Will I be back by then?"

"Wyoming is not that far away."

Chapter Ten

Wyoming Wallace

BUTCH DROVE while Amber told him about Wyoming. Wyoming was not a location but a person, an enigmatic man she had known for several years. Wyoming Wallace grew up in Texas, but his parents named him for the place of his conception. That place is believed to be the cab of an eighteen wheeler in Sheridan, Wyoming during a particularly amorous blizzard.

Wyoming's parents were truck drivers based out of Amarillo. They delivered pipe and machinery all over the American West. Wyoming had brothers named Denver, Dallas, and Omaha. His sister was Redding, but she went by Red. Denver preferred to be known by the initials DV and Dallas had come to be known as Big D. Omaha earned the nickname Chief when they were children, partly because he was bossy but also because of the familiar Native American icon on Mutual of Omaha insurance's logo.

Amber explained that somehow Wyoming ended up in the United States Army, and was among the first boots on the ground in Afghanistan following 9-11. Before it was all over Wyoming served in both Iraq and Afghanistan. His time in Iraq was during the most difficult moments of the war—after President Bush famously declared "Mission Accomplished" on the flight deck of the U.S.S. Abraham Lincoln but before the actual elections that led to the formation of a civilian government.

Amber told Butch she didn't really know anything else about his past. He lived alone in a single wide trailer on a clearing behind his folk's house and kept to himself a lot. As she talked, Butch nodded. He knew the symptoms of war weary soldiers. Several of the soldiers from Sydney Community Church came home from Iraq with extreme post-traumatic stress disorder. In some of the cases, the PTSD was so severe they couldn't attend church because of their fear of large crowds.

"How did you come to know Wyoming?" asked Butch bluntly.

"Well, when he came back from war, Wyoming had a hard time adjusting. Many of the homeless men you see on the streets are soldiers. When they come home, society doesn't have a spot for them. Wyoming never got messed up in meth like a lot of 'em did, but his friends, like me, were mostly on the streets." She looked outside the window toward the large trees.

"We saw Wy a lot down there and everyone kind of knew he was the one you wanted in your corner if things went bad. On more than one occasion he came to my rescue—and I mean that literally—he really rescued me two different times when I know that I would have been beaten up or raped. That is why I thought of him when I began to wonder about how we could find Tamara. We need someone strong, a man who knows how to deal with mean people, and who can be mean if we need him to be. That is a perfect description of Wyoming Wallace so I thought we'd pay him a visit." She felt a twinge of guilt crawl slowly upon her. Lying was not something she was comfortable with.

"Amber, how'd you end up on the streets anyway? I knew your brother and met your parents. You come from a stable home and had opportunity. Is it true you even spent some time in college? How did you end up living on the street? It doesn't make sense. I mean, I don't mean to pry but none of it makes any sense to me," he took his right hand off the steering wheel and held it out toward her, pleading for understanding.

"You traded in a home and a family for a frightening life of poverty and homelessness. Help me understand who you are; because if we are going to be partners I need to know who I'm working with. "

"Well," Amber started, "I was an English major for the two years I spent at UDub. I got—"

"Wait, you were at the University of Washington?"

"Yes. Does that surprise you?"

"A little. You were an English major?"

"Yes. But as I said, I became involved in a couple of groups on campus that were dedicated to helping the homeless and I ended up spending a few nights out on the street from time to time and then I developed some real relationships with homeless people."

"Aren't most homeless people mentally ill?" Butch asked it as an honest question seeking clarification but realized as it slipped past his lips that it sounded like a passive-aggressive accusation.

"Some are," Amber admitted without taking offense to the question, "but not all. Some of them just get tired of the pressure from school, work, bills, mortgages, children, spouses and such so they leave it all and go underground and live on the street. That is pretty much what I did. I was a good student and all, but I felt this overwhelming pressure to succeed. I guess I could blame my parents or even my brother, but it was really more from inside me. Finally, in my sophomore year during Spring break the pressure of midterms and projects overwhelmed me so much that I just, well, I just left."

"You just left, huh? Where did you go?"

"At first I stayed mostly in Seattle but there are so many street people in the city that all the best places were taken. So I migrated back over to West Sound and found it much easier going. I guess in my mind it was just a great adventure I was on. Some people backpack through Europe or take an internship at a big business. I took the road less traveled by and that has made all the difference."

"Amber, I don't think Robert Frost was writing about leaving college and living on the streets."

"No, he wasn't. Yet for me, that was my road. I learned a lot on the streets about who I am, what I care about and I also formed great relationships. Like Wy. If I hadn't been living on the streets I would have never met him."

"Why do you say we need Wyoming's help? Don't you think we can do this alone?" Butch thought about Shark.

"Wyoming Wallace knows things—things that might come in handy. He's also tough." Amber giggled, it was the first time Butch had ever seen her laugh. When she giggled Butch thought Amber reminded him of an older version of his own daughter. She continued, "No offense, Preach, but you don't exactly exude tough. You're the kind of gentle man who reads children bedtime stories. We need a tough man who can fight off the monsters. If we are going to rescue that little girl, we need a double-shot of tough."

Pastor Butch did not like the characterization she had made of him. It hurt his pride and his ego. Amber Smith turned him into an unhelpful Mr. Rogers at best or a bumbling idiot at worst.

She guided Butch through the back woods of the deep forest like an expert pathfinder until finally the dark blue sedan pulled up to a single-wide trailer house. A DIRECTV satellite dish was mounted on the side of the trailer. A rusted barrel was smoldering with what appeared to be yesterday's garbage. The stench of burnt plastic filled the air. A black jeep sat parked under a tree towards the rear of the trailer. There was no yard to speak of, as the trailer was set in the middle of a clearing that had been hewn out from the tall pines. Rusted-out Buicks, Chevys, a Honda and a Kia along with the bed of an old Ford Ranger formed a kind of post-apocalyptic hedgerow separating the trailer's clearing from the forest.

The wary pastor spied a very large dog.

Big dogs panicked him beyond measure. Dogs unlock a primordial urge for him to run. That urge was a nearly uncontrollable part of his psyche. He knew the fear was illogical and he'd worked hard to get over it. Over the years he kept intending to ask his mother if he'd been attacked by a dog as a small child, but he'd never gotten around to it. Classic denial.

The dog barked thunder.

Cold sweat formed on his brow and his muscles clenched.

Oh Lord, why did there have to be a big dog?

He looked at Amber for a reprieve or at least support, but she was already unbuckled and was opening the door.

Trembling, he followed her lead and they both got out of the car. The dog barked twice. Each bark resonated deeply. No doubt people heard the monster's roar all the way to British Columbia. "Well, your Mr. Wyoming knows we are here," said Butch nervously.

"Yep. Here he comes." A man emerged from the door and onto the front steps.

"By the way," Amber whispered, "Wyoming is his first name. Wallace is his last name."

He wore blue jeans with an un-tucked checkered green and blue short-sleeve shirt. Brown work boots were on his feet and swirling sandy colored curly hair rebelliously popped from underneath a baseball cap emblazoned with the Boeing insignia on his head. A fat, stumpy, black maduro cigar rested between his lips, which were covered by a bold van dyke beard. He stared at Butch and spat. Then he glanced at Amber.

"Hi Amber," said Wyoming Wallace.

"Hey Wy," said Amber waving her hand.

Swallowing hard and trying not to think about the dog, the pastor held out his hand and said, "My name is Butch Gregory."

Their hands met and the tough man replied, "I'm Wyoming."

"Wyoming, Butch is a preacher. We need to talk to you about something important."

"I should've figured," Wyoming Wallace shook his head and put his hands into his pants pockets. "Amber, I don't need Jesus and I don't want to talk to any reverend about my eternal soul." The cigar was clasped between his teeth the whole time he spoke, which gave an edge of anger to his tone. Finally he brought his left hand up and pulled the cigar out and finished his dismissal. "Thanks for the thought though, but I'm not really interested. If I need prayers or anything, I'll contact one of the chaplains on the base." He took the cigar out of his mouth and held it in between his thumb and index finger and pointed toward the driveway through the trees and gestured outward with it. "Nice to meet you Reverend, but I've had my fill of god-talk and I'm real busy right now."

Butch began, "We're not here to talk about your soul, Wyoming. We need your help. Actually, there's a little girl who needs your help."

Butch had mentally prepared a much more eloquent plea, but when he opened his mouth, that is what came out.

"A little girl?"

"Yeah, a little girl who lives in Sydney. She was taken two nights ago; snatched right out of her own apartment."

"I think I heard about that. Was that on the news?" he puffed, then continued, "Well, that's too bad, but what can I do?" Wyoming's voice was low and he spoke slowly, such that each word hung independently on the air. This speech pattern along with his overall rugged composure gave every syllable out of his mouth weighted seriousness. Butch was a little jealous of this natural affectation. Wyoming Wallace would be very effective in preaching and counseling. Of course, he would need to get rid of the cigar and work on his people skills a bit.

Amber glanced at Butch and stared at Wyoming and said, "We're going to look for her. The police will never find her, I know that, you know that, and the statistics tell us that. Most abducted children are never found. Someone has to do something. I thought maybe you might help. I know we'd have a better chance of finding her if you were with us."

"Hum," Wyoming grunted.

There was a long pause as the three of them, and the dog, stood in the afternoon warmth of the Northwestern sun. Long shadows fell across the ground and longer still was Butch's face. He could tell this wasn't going well. He didn't know what to say to convince this man to help them. Nevertheless, the longer he stood there, the more convinced he became that Wyoming Wallace was supposed to help them. He thought about Shark.

Suddenly, Amber's voice cracked with emotion, "She's a little girl, Wy," Amber extended her arms in exasperation. "She's in trouble. If we don't help her, no one will."

Wyoming Wallace shook his head. "She's not my problem. I've done my bit for king and country. Good luck to you two, but I'm not interested in helping anybody anymore. It's hard enough looking out for myself. Now I suggest the two of you get back in your car and leave the way you came."

He took another long draw into his mouth, turned his back and returned to the inside of his trailer. The door shut solidly behind him and then the air-compressed arm on the screen door slammed shut behind that. The loud bang of the cheap aluminum was a death knell to their hopes of recruiting Wyoming Wallace in the rescue attempt.

Butch Gregory surveyed the scene: Amber, the dog, the trailer, the trees, the rusted out cars and the satellite dish. With a quick nod toward heaven he screwed his courage to the proverbial sticking place then turned instantly and marched right up the steps to the aluminum screen door and began to bang on the aluminum door like an obnoxious salesman. The behemoth dog barked, causing a shiver of fear to shoot down Pastor Butch's spine. The dog came right up to the pastor and barked louder and louder. Butch buried his fear and kept knocking. The dog's mouth was salivating and his teeth were bared.

"In the name of Jesus, I rebuke you, you hellish hound."

"His name is Olalla," Wyoming yelled from inside the door. Then he opened it and pointed to the dog. "That is where I picked him off the side of the road, out near the firehouse in Olalla, so that is what I named him." He patted the dog on the head. "I'd be careful. He doesn't like strangers and he is very protective of his house. Now I told you to go. Are you deaf?"

"No, I hear just fine and you need to hear more. This conversation is not over until you've heard one more thing. There is a price to pay, Mr. Wyoming Wallace, for disobeying the Lord. I know in my heart that God has a plan for you to come with Amber and me in our search for Tamara. I don't know why, really. Indeed, I don't even know why I'm doing this but I just know it is the right thing to do. If you shut this door on us again, you are shutting the door on God's work in your life. I don't believe, Mr. Wallace that this is just about a little girl in Sydney. Something about this is for you—you need this. Again, I don't particularly know why but I know it is true."

"Are you finished Reverend?" asked Wyoming.

Butch paused, stared toward the ground and said "I guess; that's the heart of it, anyway."

"Good. I've got nothing against you, and I like Amber just fine. But I don't care about your god. I certainly don't care about anything he might be doing in my life. I'd prefer if he just left me alone. I've had enough people mess with my life. Now, I will say it one more time, Reverend. Get back in your car, and leave."

Wyoming punctuated the statement by blowing a big puff of cigar smoke into Butch's face. Butch turned and descended the porch steps. On his way down Olalla growled at him; Butch growled back. He and Amber got into the car and left.

"Well, Amber, it looks like we're on our own," Butch said as he drove around the bend that was in the driveway and beyond the rambler Wyoming Wallace's parents lived in.

"Yeah," she sighed, "but I really wish we weren't. We need him."

"Look Amber, I'm not a street smart person and I've no idea what kind of life you or this Wallace man has led. But I've learned there is really only one thing you absolutely need."

"What's that, a bag of Skittles and a six pack?"

"No." Butch didn't even smile at her awkward joke. "The Lord. If the Lord is for us, who or what can be against us? The Lord is all anyone really, truly needs. Somehow, someway he always knows what he is doing. We just have to trust him. Right now I trust that he is calling us to find Tamara, and we have to get started tomorrow. I believe he is calling your friend Mr. Wallace too, but he has to make his own choices. He can say no to God if he wants, but he'll have to live with the consequences. It is between him and Jesus now and I'll put my money on Jesus. Always.

"Now, when we get back into town, I have a meeting with my board. While I'm doing that, you need to wrap up any loose ends you might have and tomorrow morning we start in earnest. I've got a friend in law enforcement. We can pick his brain and see what advice he might have. His name is Henry. Maybe he can point us in the right direction."

"I guess so," said Amber with a dose of regret and doubt. The doubt came from what she knew that Butch Gregory did not, that which she had held back from him when he asked why they were going to Wyoming's house. Wyoming Wallace was in her dream too.

Chapter Eleven

What is this all about, Preacher?

AT 7:00 PM Pastor Butch Gregory called the board meeting to order. The governing board of Sydney Community Church consisted of the big three. The deacons were the first of the big three and by far the most powerful group in the church. Behind them the next group of powerful people were the program leaders. These consist of the lay leaders for finances, children, property and worship. The last of the big three were the staff.

Remarkably almost everyone had made it to the meeting even though it was called on such short notice. The one exception was a deacon who was back east working with the Navy.

Butch opened the meeting in prayer.

> Dear Lord, thank you for bringing all of these great leaders here tonight. My prayer is that you would allow our meeting to be peaceful, smooth, and more importantly filled with your presence and wisdom. So often Lord we do not know what we should do. Show us your path and your will that we may travel in the right direction. We also ask that you help us to accomplish the work which you have called us to do; both in our church and around the world. In Jesus' name. Amen.

Amens resounded around the fellowship hall. When the whole board was together, the group was too large to meet anywhere but the sanctuary or the fellowship hall. One time they had tried to meet in the children's wing because of a Boy Scout Program going on in the fellowship hall. It was disastrous. The hefty deacons were too much for the small chairs, which kept collapsing under their potluck enriched girth.

"What is this all about preacher?" asked Mike Bowman. Mike Bowman was Pastor Butch Gregory's eternal nemesis. It didn't matter what Butch Gregory was for, Mike Bowman would be against it. Butch knew that the first salvo would come from his direction. He had prepared himself so he would not be caught off guard.

"Well, I'm glad you asked," he said smiling. "Most of you probably know about Tamara Rey's abduction. It has been on T.V. and in the papers."

"Yes, we know all about that. Very tragic indeed, but Butch why call a meeting?"

"I'm getting to that, Mike. For reasons beyond explanation I feel called by God to go find her. The Lord has led a young woman named Amber to help me and we are starting out tomorrow. I need a leave of absence, perhaps indefinitely, starting right now. What's more, while I'm on this leave of absence, I need to continue to use my office and the resources of the church which are normally at my disposal. In other words, I will not be doing church work, but I will need the church to help me get the work done which I believe God has called me to do."

Butch had practiced saying those words in his mind. He felt a wave of relief wash over him after having actually said them. It wasn't as hard as he'd thought it would be. Wyoming Wallace's front door was much more difficult than the board meeting.

Butch's relief was temporary.

"What?" The interrogative came from the mouth of a deacon named Cindi. "You want a leave of absence, indefinitely? To go on a wild goose chase? That is the most irresponsible thing I've ever heard in my life. You're a pastor not a detective, and if you make as poor a detective as you make a preacher then you will only get in the way and muck everything up for the real pros. There is no way you could ever find that poor little girl. You couldn't find a hot dog at a baseball game."

"I agree Cindi. I even tried that same line about being a pastor and not detective on God too. He wasn't buying it."

"Hold on a minute Cindi," said Morgan Dempsey. "I'm sure our pastor feels this is something he must do. Let's just think about this for a minute before we start making ugly comments."

"What?" This interrogative came from Johnny, an elderly deacon emeritus. His lack of hearing was famous around the church. He hadn't missed a worship service in ten years, but thanks to the loud noises in the Shipyard where he worked, he hadn't heard a sermon in fifteen years. Johnny's wife, who was on the finance team, leaned over and yelled in his ear, "The Pastor wants to leave."

"Leave? What did we do wrong? We love Pastor Butch. Why would he want to leave? Where is he going? California? Oregon? Over to Seattle? I knew it. Some big church is stealing him away from us. If we give him more money will he stay? I say we double, no triple his annuity."

"No, no honey," she yelled into his ear. "He's not leaving to go to another church. He wants a leave of absence to find a girl."

"Girl? But he has a wife? What kind of mid-life crisis is he going through?" With that Johnny squared around from his wife to face Pastor Butch. He wagged his finger and said, "Listen here, we will not tolerate any funny business out of our pastor. That might work for T.V. preachers, but not here. If that is the way you're going to be, then pack up and leave right now. Shame on you. I thought you were different."

It amused Butch how Johnny had gone from offering him more money to demanding he leave in mere seconds.

"No, not a girl like that, the little girl who is missing. Remember, the one we saw on television, the one from church?" his wife shouted. "Why don't you put your hearing aid in hun?"

"I don't need a hearing aid. I hear just fine."

At that, she shot him a glare of death. Deacon Johnny then realized everyone was staring at him. Meekly he mumbled, "Yes dear" and slipped his hearing aid into his ears.

"Butch," Doreen said from across the room, "this is crazy."

"I know," Butch again agreed. "But I have to. As crazy as it sounds, Jesus has told me to do it."

"You need to have your head examined," barked a man named Lawrence. "Jesus is smarter than to ask you to do something like that. There are other people in this community, why, there are other people in this church who are more able to do this than you are. This is crazy and stupid."

It was at that point that Miss Betsy gently raised her hand to speak. Miss Betsy was the saintly matriarch of the congregation. She had been a member since 1952. Everyone knew that her family had donated a great amount of the money for the sanctuary when it was built and her husband had left a large stock portfolio to the church mission team when he died. That, plus her overall Christian character gave Miss Betsy a loud voice in every room even though she spoke rarely and softly when she did. Her authority and power went well beyond respect or gravitas. Miss Betsy carried apostolic-like clout at Sydney Community Church.

"I don't know what, exactly, Pastor Butch has in mind but I've seen a lot of pastors in my life and never have I trusted anyone more than Butch Gregory. If he says God wants him to do this, then we'd better support him in whatever way we can. I mean, it's not like we are helpless. Besides," her voice turned very serious and contemplative, "who would want a pastor that didn't listen to God, and who didn't have a desire to help innocent people? Does anybody here really want a pastor who is so removed from people's suffering that all he does is sit behind his desk and keep his hands clean? I don't, and I wouldn't. We have a great man and I think we should let him do what he needs to do. We will still be here when he gets finished."

"Betsy," said Mike Bowman, "I wish I could see things the way you do, but it is not that simple and, if you all will forgive me, a bit naïve. Church is like a business," he raised his arms out and patted downward with his hands like he was pushing something into place, "and a business needs stable, steady people leading it. There is nothing stable or steady about what Butch is asking us to do for him. It is the direct opposite. What Butch is asking is whimsical and half-baked. We need a pastor who always makes sense and is more CEO like. We accept that Butch is kind and gentle and that he is caring but he is not a visionary. Right now, Pastor Butch is being very unprofessional, and, quite frankly, could be accused of neglecting the sheep." He took a deep breath and said, "We will be the laughing stock of Sydney if we sanction his proposal."

Miss Betsy replied sharply, "But the good shepherd leaves the ninety-nine and goes after the one."

Had Betsy been watching him in his study last night?

Lisa and Samuel Rickover both raised their hands. They ran the children's ministry. Samuel started, "Tamara is in our Sunday School class. I've gotten to know her ever since she started coming here. She is a very beautiful big hearted little girl."

Lisa nodded and said, "This morning in our prayer time, both Sam and I felt the incredible, overwhelming feeling that Tamara Rey was alive. We also felt from the Lord that Pastor Butch was somehow involved in how she was going to be found. We can't explain it, but when Pastor Philip called this morning and told us about the meeting; we knew what it was about and what Pastor Butch was supposed to do. If we stand in his way, we'll be standing against the will of God."

Another deacon named Stanley said, "I had the exact same feeling tonight. It was right after dinner and I was reading. Somehow I had this impression that tonight I was supposed to say yes to whatever Butch wanted."

Two or three other people nodded their heads in agreement. The spiritual dynamic of the discussion surprised Butch. Apparently Jesus had been working on others as well, not just Amber and him. It encouraged and frightened him. His thoughts were then interrupted by a loud question.

"But who is going to take care of us while you are chasing windmills?" It was Mike Bowman again.

"Pastor Philip will be here," Butch pointed right at Philip. Philip stared at the ground.

"I talked with him about this and I have complete confidence. He is ready for a little more responsibility anyway. I trust him and he'll do fine."

It wasn't Philip's performance that Butch was concerned about, it was a few of the hard-nosed people in the church being mean and hurting Philip while he was away that worried him. It was wrong to say or think that the whole church was difficult. The overwhelming majority of the people who attended Sydney Community Church were kind and striving to be Christ-like. It was the evil tithe of about 10%, most of which were on leadership of some sort, who were mean and vindictive that might cause problems. It was those people who made ministry sometimes miserable.

But he didn't say any of that. He just looked at Pastor Philip with a duplicitous grin because he wasn't going to tell Philip that he needed to stop by the store and pick up some Rolaids. The less Philip knew, the better. Some things you just have to learn on your own.

The deacon chairperson brought the issue to a vote and it passed. There were only four dissenting votes. The board agreed to give Butch his leave of absence. There were lengthy discussions as to whether or not Butch should be paid while on leave. A couple of the finance people suggested that since he'd be gone, the church should not pay him. That motion was soundly defeated after Miss Betsy offered to pay Butch's salary out of her own pocket.

God bless you Mrs. Betsy, Butch thought. And God bless the wonderful people of Sydney Community Church.

Ministry is sometimes hard, but he felt how great this congregation's love was for him and for the Lord. Although he was slightly afraid of what the coming days might bring, it brought him deep warmth to know he had the support of his church, and that they had squashed all the opposing voices with evidence of the Holy Spirit's activity in their lives. It also felt good to know that Jesus had been talking to others as well as to him, Lucy, and Amber.

Chapter Twelve

The Not So Still Small Voice

WYOMING WALLACE was sound asleep next to Jennifer's naked body. In the deep recesses of his mind he dreamed of Butch Gregory knocking on his door.

In his dream he sees Butch outside the glass pane on the cheap aluminum screen door of his trailer knocking over and over again. The reverend keeps saying something but Wyoming can't quite hear it over the loud knocking.

Wyoming moves closer to the door and puts his ear to it and hears that Pastor Butch is saying a name. Butch Gregory keeps repeating the name with each knock at the door.

What is the name?

It is a name he's never heard before, but somehow Wyoming knows exactly who it is. The annoying reverend keeps repeating and he will not stop pounding out each rattling knock. Finally Wyoming can hear the name. Butch keeps saying, "Leyla."

Pound the door.

"Leyla."

Pound the door.

"Leyla."

Pound the door.

"Leyla."

Pound the door.

Wyoming now wears his battle fatigues and stands on a street in Fallujah. He is in the early stages of the invasion of Iraq and he is sweeping through the streets with his unit looking for Iraqi insurgents. They lost three soldiers earlier that morning in this same neighborhood and now they are looking for those who'd done it. Officially, it is a reconnaissance mission but to the men carrying the weapons it is retaliation.

The sun is setting, and they want to finish this block before dark. Automatic weapons erupt and fill the street with death. The soldier to Wyoming's right, taking the position closest to the street, falls. He is bleeding from a gunshot wound. At the same time there is a great explosion. Wyoming knows that it is some kind of an I.E.D. on the street in a car they had just patrolled by. Confusion erupts and the unit returns fire in every direction. Someone shouts, "Inside the house, across the street. Move."

Was that the sergeant giving orders?

Wyoming's training takes over his actions, as it does with everyone else in his unit. Fear is there, but duty, instinct, and courage take control of his legs, arms and mind. All the soldiers run across the street while laying down weapons fire in quick succession. When they arrive at the house, two (or is it three?) soldiers lob explosives into the windows and they wait for the detonation. A second round of fire opens up on them from the opposite side of the street, the side they just came from. Wyoming sees the enemy, three boys laying prone on the rooftops. Wyoming curses under his breath—they can't be more than 15 or 16 years old. Wyoming and the others return fire and kill the three teenagers with deadly efficiency.

Now the door of the home is burst open and Wyoming is the first one in. As he enters he sees from his peripheral vision motion in the doorway of the adjoining room. Reflexively he turns his weapon toward the motion and realizes it is a little girl. She is frightened. Her big dark eyes peek out from her dark hair and her whole body trembles. She is holding her hands over her ears. There are several dead bodies on the floor all around her.

It is a miracle she is still alive.

Wyoming lowers his weapon and walks across the room to where she is.

Now he hears another sound. Someone else is here. He raises his weapon and walks beyond the little girl into the adjoining room and a man with a machine gun is in the room and looking out of the window and shooting at his friends who are still on the street. Wyoming raises his weapon and kills him from behind.

Now the other soldiers enter the room. Wyoming sees them in this dream, but now he sees them from the little girl's eyes. He feels her fear, and he knows her innocence. He knows what she is thinking. She just wants the noise to stop. It is so loud. She doesn't know why all this is going on. She is five years old and her mother is far away and her father is the man he just shot in the window.

Why are these men here?

Where is my mommy?

The soldiers enter the room just like Wyoming did, except when they spot the little girl fear pulls the trigger. Wyoming feels the pain of the shell that explodes inside his skull—her skull.

Now he is himself again, a soldier in fatigues holding his weapon. He is still stuck in this nightmare. Wyoming is standing over her body. Her body is riddled with bullets. The simple brown garment she wears is torn to shreds.

She is dead.

He is crying.

The little girl stands up; but her body is still lying on the floor.

The little girl takes Wyoming by the hand and says, "Leyla."

Pound the door.

"Leyla."

Pound the door.

"Leyla."

Pound the door.

"Leyla."

Now Wyoming is in his trailer again looking at Butch Gregory knocking on his door. Except now the pastor is covered in blood and Amber is standing behind him. Someone tugs at his hand. It is Leyla. She speaks to him and says, "Help them find the little girl." When Leyla speaks, it is not the voice of a child. It is Amber's voice.

Wyoming Wallace woke up. He laid in his bed for several minutes as his breathing slowed down then he got out of bed, pulled on his pants and quietly shut the door behind him so as not to wake up Jennifer. He walked into the kitchen and poured himself a glass of whiskey over ice and drank it. Then he poured another.

He sat there in the dark and thought about that day in Fallujah for a long time. He had dreamed about it before, but never like tonight. Never had he felt like he was reliving it all over again. Tonight the dream seemed more immediate and more pressing. Even though he was awake, he felt as though he could still hear the ring in his ear of the Reverend Gregory's thundering knock and the echo of the name, Leyla.

Where did that come from? That's new.

He'd never seen or heard that name before, yet it must be the dead girl's name. Leyla. Until that moment she had been just an anonymous Iraqi to him. A casualty of war. Now he knew her name; although he didn't know how he knew it.

Wyoming heard a gust of wind blow strongly outside. He stood up and walked over to the window to peer outside. Last winter he had almost lost his home when a very tall pine was blown down during a windstorm. He peeked outside, if for nothing else to get his mind off of the little girl that was in his dream, to get his mind off his past. But the trees were not rustling.

They were not moving at all, not even a little.

Nevertheless, Wyoming heard the sound of rushing, howling, blowing wind. The table he'd just been sitting at began to shake; just a little at first and then it wobbled and moved, sliding from side to side on top of the floor. The whiskey glass flew off the tabletop and shattered onto the floor.

Wyoming could feel wind blowing hard against his face. A cyclone formed there in the small dining room of the kitchen trailer. The vortex grew in power until it lifted the table up off the linoleum and hurled it across the room and into the kitchen where it smashed into the white refrigerator. The four wooden chairs were spun and took flight in various directions—one shattered as it hit the ceiling, one crashed into a wall and its four legs stuck into it like it was a knife thrown against a target, the other two collided with each other and splintered into kindling and the floor with splinters. The splinters then took to the air and became deadly projectiles whizzing past Wyoming's head.

Wyoming wanted to run but he was paralyzed with disbelief. Suction was created as the whirlwind grew in intensity and pulled him away from the window and toward the center of the room. Wyoming couldn't resist the pull as the wind lifted him up off the floor the same way it did to the table and chairs. The pressure of the air ripped his wristwatch off of his left arm and he saw it fly off and burst into a thousand shards of gears and mechanical guts. The wind continued to shove Wyoming Wallace into submission, forcing his body to obey the currents that flailed him up and down, all around the small trailer's main room. The wind had an intelligence of its own and as Wyoming's resistance abated and his strength ebbed, it spun him into a horizontal position and raised him to the ceiling.

The pressure from the wind would either push him into the ceiling or snap his spinal column.

He was about to die.

He'd had that sensation three times before in his life; but none of those had been like this. Wyoming shut his eyes and, for the first time since he was a teenage boy, prayed.

Lord help me.

Inside Wyoming's mind he heard the immediate reply, "Help my servant save the girl this time."

"I can't."

His refusal fueled the whirlwind. It began to spin him violently counterclockwise while at the same time shaking him up and down.

"I want to, but I can't. Pick someone else."

The violence and ruthless speed of the vortex increased and the wind spun him around and around as it pushed him up close to the ceiling and then released him to fall just inches above the ground. Wyoming spun and fell and rose like a shaft being driven by a great invisible piston.

"Okay! Okay!" he finally shouted. "I will help him."

The next instant he was laying back in bed beside Jennifer's beautifully serene body, as if none of it had ever happened. He looked at her and she still slept soundly. Trembling and sweating, he arose from the bed again. His heart raced. He didn't bother with pants but walked into the dining room and turned on the light. The table was right where it should be and the room, which had just moments before been in tatters, was back to normal.

Was it a dream? A dream within a dream?

It must have been a cruel and self-punishing nightmare; the whole thing: Fallujah, the reverend at the door, and the vortex must have all been a dream. He was about to walk back to bed when he noticed the whiskey bottle and the glass were sitting on the kitchen bar. He walked over and picked up the glass. It still had ice cubes in it, and the strong smell of alcohol.

His wristwatch was sitting right beside the glass, ticking away in perfect time.

Chapter Thirteen

I Don't Want To Get Involved

TWO YOUNG women sat on a park bench in Sydney's downtown waterfront area and drank Red Bull as they talked about work.

"Any luck tonight?"

"No, I haven't turned a trick in three days, but then again, I haven't exactly tried real hard."

"Me neither. I'd rather just stay at home and watch TV, you know what I mean, but I'm getting kind of desperate for some money, so I need some work tonight."

"Yeah, I guess I do too, but my heart really ain't in it."

"I hear ya. I can't wait until I can get out of here—find me a good man, settle down, and start all over."

"That all sounds good, except for the man part. I've had my fill of men. All they ever do is hurt you, use you, or manipulate you. I've had enough. I was talking to an old friend about that today, ya know—that very thing."

"Really, who?"

"Do you remember Amber—the girl who used to live downtown in her cardboard box castle?"

The other woman nodded recognition. Everyone down here knew Amber.

"Yeah, well, we was talking today about the old times. She had lots of questions. You know, she never really walked the streets much and now she has a real job."

"Yeah, seems like someone was telling me about that awhile back. What kind of questions did she have?"

"She wanted to know if I knew where they might keep a girl who was snatched, wanted to know if I knew where they might take a little girl, says she is looking for a girl named Tamara. Says God told her to."

"Ain't that the little girl on the news? The one grabbed out of the apartments on the other side of town?"

"Yeah, that's her. Anyway, Amber says her and some preacher are looking for that little girl. I said, 'good luck' and all but I ain't getting into nobody's business. That's how you end up dead." The woman said "dead" with an elongated pronunciation, exaggerated wide opened eyeballs, and accompanied it with a hand across the throat movement that emphasized the finality and importance of the point.

"Yeah, it is dangerous to stick your neck out for someone."

"Not me—I'm looking out for myself. That is how I've made it this far."

"Yeah, me too, and that means I better get to work. I won't make no money sitting here chatting with you all night."

"Got that right. See ya tomorrow night," she said and then got up and walked west down the waterfront toward the Holiday Inn Express. The second woman stood and walked east toward the Quality Inn. But before she got to the Quality Inn, she stopped underneath the large totem pole near the ferry terminal and looked out across the water.

She thought about the little girl. She'd seen her picture on the television news and it made her sad. Ten years ago she was the one who went missing. She ran away from home, found her way to a state park, and was soon in a van heading up the freeway with men who smelled like they lived in a trash can. It was those men who passed her off onto two or three others until she ended up here, working the street for a pimp she couldn't stand, in a town she'd learned to hate, living a life that was meaningless.

She pushed back tears and looked up toward the bejeweled sky and the creamy moon. For a shimmering shooting star moment she felt like her life was connected to something important.

She had a pretty good idea of where that little girl might be kept—or at least where the people who took her might be.

She also knew that Amber lived just a few blocks from downtown in one of the old cruddy upstairs loft apartments.

The woman reached inside her tiny purse. Her purse contained a tiny sparkly wallet, a can of mace, keys, a package of condoms and other tools of her trade, a pen and small heart-shaped pad of sticky notes that she used to write down the address of a john if she had to get a taxi to a high end client. The congressman always wanted her to come in a taxi.

On the pad of paper she scribbled out a note to Amber, folded it over once and purposefully walked through the darkness of the cruel street, crossed the indifferent intersection, and walked down the other side of the hidden ally until she came to the dilapidated building Amber lived in.

The lower floor was an antique book store, but the upper floor had been carved up into four efficiency apartments. She walked down the narrow passage between the buildings and climbed the metal fire escape which passed for stairs. Finally, she reached the metal grating platform that served as a porch for the upper level. She counted the numbers of the apartments as she walked by: One, two, three. Amber was the third one. She quietly slid the note under the door and prayed,

"Lord, I sure better not get trouble for this."

She crossed herself as if she were at mass, and then she tip-toed away toward the pavement below.

Amber heard the sound, but didn't recognize it. She was asleep on her small bed which was on the wall right beside the front door. She arose and turned on her lamp. She spied the piece of paper, folded in half, which had been slid into her home. She quickly snatched it and hurriedly unfolded it.

i heard you were looking for someone and
thought this might be handy. start here.

3639 lakewood ave, tacoma

do not come looking for me,
i don't want to get involved.
please burn this after you read it.
j

The J was circled, and was lower case, and the dot above the lower case j was written as a heart.

This was from Janet, an old friend from her homeless days. She had seen Janet just last month at the Goodwill store in town.

How the heck did Janet know? Where did she get this? How—

Amber opened the door and loudly called out, "Janet," not thinking or caring that it was 3:30 in the morning. Then she slid on her shoes by the door and ran out onto the stairwell. Running down the treacherous steps she called out again, "Janet," but there was no reply. When she got to the bottom she darted through the narrow lane between buildings and emerged on the sidewalk. Janet was walking away from her headed east toward the Quality Inn.

Amber ran and quickly caught up to the young woman.

"Sista, I told you not to bother . . ."

"I don't care," Amber cut in, breathing hard. "This is life and death Janet. A little girl's life and future is on the line. How do you know about this place?"

"I just know."

"Have you seen Tamara?"

"No, nothing like that. I just know that, well, I just know how things work and that most of the little girls end up here at one time or another. I can't promise nothing, but if I was looking for a little girl that had been snatched, this is where I would start."

"What else do you know?"

"Nothing, nothing at all. I shouldn't have told you that."

"Yes, yes you should have and you should tell me more. Look, I know you've got troubles, we all do, but I need all the help I can get."

Janet's eyes swelled with water and Amber took her by the hand.

"Listen, come on up to my apartment and let's talk." Janet didn't have much resistance because her heart was breaking. She followed Amber back to her apartment. Amber made some coffee and the two women sat and talked. Janet relayed how she had run away from home when she was 14, about the men who had abused and used her, and how she had been, in many ways, where Tamara Rey is right now.

Except, no one came looking for her.

When the sun came up over downtown Sydney, Amber told Janet to get a couple of hours sleep on the couch. After Janet dozed off, Amber grabbed her phone and punched in the address in the maps app. She knew where the Lakewood area was in Tacoma, as it ran through the city from downtown, by the freeway and out toward the military base. When it popped up, she saw that it was the gang controlled part of town where shootings, rapes, and disappearances were all too common. She grimaced at the thought of going there, but this was exactly the break Butch and her needed to get the search going.

Chapter Fourteen

There Will Be Three

AMBER WAS waiting for Butch Gregory at his office. He arrived at 8:30 and she told him about the paper and the address.

"Who gave this to you?"

"I can't tell you. It needs to be secret?"

"Why?"

"Because she wants to be left out of it?"

"Why?"

"I don't know why, Preach."

"Could you call me Butch?"

"I could call you Butch, but I won't."

"Why?"

"I like Preach better. You look more like a 'Preach' than a 'Butch' anyway."

Butch could see this was going nowhere so he ignored it and went back to thinking about the lead. He was very familiar with Tacoma and always tried to avoid the Lakewood neighborhoods. He knew a couple of police officers in the Tacoma Police Department and remembered them telling him about situations when they were shot at over there. It was a very dangerous place. He furrowed his brow.

"Well, I suppose we could go and scope it out and see what's there. It might be a vacant lot or a meth-house. It is also possible this is old information. Perhaps that is where things used to happen but not anymore. However, it would be good to know and it is at least someplace to start."

"That is what I was thinking," replied Amber. "I checked the satellite map and all I could make out were roofs, so something was there recently."

"Well, let me fill my coffee mug, and then let's drive down and go have a peak. First, though, let me contact Lucy and tell her where I will be, in case something happens."

"That's not a bad idea, Preach."

"What about your work, Amber? Have you been able to get a leave of absence or something to do this?" Butch asked it as he filled his cup.

"No. I called and quit. No big."

"It seems like a pretty big deal to me. What will you do when this is over?"

"I'll worry about that when the time comes." Amber had been jovial as she mentioned quitting her job, but then her tone took a serious turn, "For now, this is all that matters."

The two of them stood beside the coffee pot in the large open front room of Sydney Community Church's administrative building. He had just grabbed his iPhone to text Lucy when Wyoming Wallace walked through the front door. He walked over to Amber and glared, then he looked right at Butch Gregory. For a split second Butch considered dialing 9-1-1. The intensity of the moment hung for a small eternity, until Wyoming exhaled, looked at his wristwatch and said, "I'm in. What is our first move?"

Chapter Fifteen
A-OK

BUTCH'S BLUE Honda Civic eased into the toll booth for the Narrows Bridge as the trio neared the city of Tacoma. It had been a quiet trip. Butch and Amber had already developed a burgeoning rapport over the past 24 hours, but the presence of Wyoming created tension. The tension was caused primarily because of the unanswered questions. Why had he changed his mind? Why was he so aggressively angry when they first approached him? Why did he seem so reluctant to be involved?

The tension of the unanswered questions kept both Butch and Amber from asking them, and, Wyoming, true to his nature, offered no explanation. He had simply shown up that morning and agreed with the already decided plan of going to Tacoma and chasing down the lead. No explanations were volunteered, and none were asked. This lack of resolution caused Butch to wonder and doubt. Amber didn't care as long as Wyoming was with them because she knew he was meant to be with them. Butch believed that too, but he didn't like opaque or veiled motives. He couldn't determine what the mysterious man's motive was. He didn't trust Wyoming Wallace.

The ambiguity, though, was exactly how Wyoming liked it. It was something he learned playing poker; make sure you never show your cards or tip your hand. It didn't matter to him one bit whether he and the other two got along or liked each other. The odd vision he'd had in his trailer told him what he should do but it didn't tell him how he should feel about it. Besides, how would they ever understand such nonsense as whirling tornados that appear out of nowhere, almost kill a person, and then disappear with no sign of ever having existed? He was a soldier, and soldiers know how to take orders. He had been given orders and he intended to follow orders. What he didn't intend to do was talk about it, and how he felt was nobody's business.

Butch rolled down his window and paid the five dollars to the bridge toll clerk, grabbed his receipt and pulled away from the booth.

"Why don't you have an automatic pass for the toll?" asked Wyoming.

"Well, I just never got around to it. I do come to Tacoma quite a bit; I've just never thought to get one. Maybe I will someday."

"I wouldn't ever get one," replied Wyoming.

"What? Then why did you say it like that?" asked Amber.

Wyoming Wallace barked, "Yeah, well, I don't think I ever want the government having access to my bank account."

The pastor smirked at the paranoia. He'd heard that line before.

Amber sat in the backseat and admired the view from the bridge's deck plating high above the choppy waters. Beneath the Tacoma Narrows Bridge some of the strongest currents on the West Coast swirled around the large pillars which held the infamous bridge in place. Submerged on the bottom of the Narrows directly below the bridge was the highway decking of the first, short lived Narrows Bridge nicknamed Galloping Gerdie. It collapsed in 1940 and was the stuff of regional legend. To the north the blue water stretched between the Kitsap Peninsula and the City of Tacoma with multi-million dollars homes on both sides. To the south there were barges and sailboats moving in opposite directions. Some were on pleasure trips and would finish the day either at one of the many waterfront villages, like Sydney or even perhaps Seattle, Port Townsend, or Anacortes. Others were headed further south toward the state capital of Olympia. The sun was out today, and for that Amber was thankful for not only did it irradiate the blue water with added beauty, but the spectacularly clear summer day meant that Mt. Rainier was in full view. The glacier covered volcano is an ever-present feature of the Northwest panorama. Its towering peak lingers on the mind of the region's inhabitants, even if the mountain summit is covered in the haze of slate gray skies most of the year. But today Amber can see the unique double peak, the low snow level on the mountain's base, and the brightness of the ice as sun reflects off the sunrise side. She remembered when she was a child how she and her brother, Adam, would sit in the backseat and try to hold their breath as they crossed the expansion bridge, and as they held their breath their father would slow down to make traversing it that much longer.

The happy memory ended quickly as the car came off the bridge and Wyoming pointed to the first exit and said, "Take this exit. We should come in from the back way."

"I'd planned to take the freeway."

"We should come in from behind. It is good strategy."

"They don't know we're coming," Amber chimed in. "What difference does it make? Besides, this is just an investigative trip. We don't know what we're likely to find. It might just be a great big empty lot now. Who knows?"

Wyoming did not reply. Apparently Amber's argument was not even worthy of a rebuttal. Pastor Butch did as he was told and turned off the freeway onto the city street. It really made no difference to him.

The freeway was faster than jogging through the University District and running alongside the railroad tracks, but he didn't care.

Fifteen minutes later they arrived at the location which Amber had uncovered: 3639 Lakewood Avenue. It was a mechanic's garage. Specifically it was a garage named A-OK Mekaniks. Amber read the blue block letters outlined in red on the white sign aloud and sarcastically said, "They must be graduates of Sydney High."

"Block around," Wyoming ordered.

Pastor Butch turned the sedan onto the front street of the business, which sat on the right hand side. Then Butch drove to the next side street and turned right. There was a very narrow street a half a block down on the right.

"Turn here," Amber suggested.

Butch was worried that might be too close. He could feel his natural cautiousness kicking in as he thought about how people inside the business would be able to see and identify his car. The car his wife sometimes drove; the car which he used to take Sarah and Paul to school; the car he had yet to pay off. But, he knew what Amber was getting at and he agreed. If they were going to do this, then they had to take chances. So he turned right again and followed the narrow street which led right behind A-OK Mekaniks.

Two lots apparently comprised the business. One was on the right side of the small street, and the other was on the left side of the alley. The larger building was on the left. It was a metal building which had three small bay door openings and one large blue metal door. All of the bay doors were closed. On the right hand side was the back wall of the same building which faced the front street. Butch drove slowly along the alley. On the left hand side there was a vehicle. Amber looked closely and then gasped.

"That's it. That's the minivan I saw the night Tamara was taken."

Wyoming was skeptical. "Are you sure? The plates are out of state and do not have MTH 18 in them."

"Yes! I'm sure. That's the minivan I saw at the Skookum." Amber squealed as she suspected their search might end quickly and that Tamara might be inside this garage. Butch slowed down and stopped as this new revelation came out but Wyoming insisted that he keep driving.

"Turn left up here and then park on a side street. We need to think." Wyoming's directions made perfect sense to Butch. He came to the main thoroughfare, the same road they had turned off of to block around and then he turned left, drove up two blocks, turned right and then parked on the curb in front of a home that was badly in need of yard work and maintenance. All the homes in the Lakewood neighborhood looked in need of yard work, repair, and maintenance.

Butch shut the car off. Wyoming reached inside of his coat and pulled out a snub-nosed Smith & Wesson .38 revolver. Wyoming popped the cylinder, checked the shells, spun it once and then with a hard click he pushed it back into place.

Pastor Butch watched this expert handling of the pistol with both awe and disdain. Then he asked, "Do you really think that is necessary?"

"Absolutely it is necessary. It pays to be careful. Besides, I have a permit. It is perfectly legal for me to protect myself, and for what I'm about to do, I have every reason to believe I might need to protect myself."

"I do not approve of firearms. Handguns are no solution and the government should have banned them a long time ago. Jesus told us that we should turn the other cheek and take up our cross. He never said anything about owning a gun. The world would be a lot safer without them." As Butch spoke he thought specifically of the many instances of domestic violence where he'd seen handguns violently employed as well as several accidental shootings involving children.

"Fine. I respect your opinion Reverend. I, however, have spent my entire life with pistols, rifles, shotguns and all manner of weapons. This is," Wyoming's slowed down his rate of speech, "who I am. Now Reverend, if you want to help this girl, you never know what might happen, and I am not having this conversation with you. We don't have time for a theological debate right now. This," he held up the pistol, "is part of the reason you need me on this expedition of ours. I know how to use this and that is what makes me an asset to the operation." Then he smiled and slid his pistol underneath the light jacket he was wearing and into the shoulder holster under his left armpit.

Amber sat silently in the backseat. The sight of the pistol shocked her and brought back so many thoughts about her brother. But she also knew that Wyoming was right. It might get bad in there.

"What's your plan, Wy?" she said from the backseat, trying to change the subject.

"We need to find out who is in there and if Tamara, or any hostage, is being held here. To do that, we need some kind of diversion." Wyoming's speech patterns were naturally slow, but as he thought about the strategy, his speed slowed down even more. "I suggest that

… the Reverend go into the front door … of the mechanic's office on the front side and pretend to make an appointment—say you are new to the area—and pretend … pretend to make an appointment to have a transmission looked at sometime later this week. Yeah … a transmission. Then hem and haw and stall as long as possible. Don't tell them … don't tell them your real name or where you really live … no matter what, even if your cover is blown."

His eyes squinted and he looked straight ahead while he thought. He tugged at his van dyke as he finished formulating his plan. "While you do that I … well … me and Amber … we will check out that large building on the other side of the street. I bet that is where we will find something … find something if anything here is to be found. Got it."

"Sure," said Butch.

"Uh huh," agreed Amber.

"We should pray," the pastor said.

"We don't have time for this god stuff." Wyoming opened his car door.

"There is always time for prayer," Butch reached out and grabbed Wyoming's arm. "I'm willing to go along with your pistol, which, as you say, is part of you. Well, prayer is a part of me, so, we make time for prayer." Wyoming reluctantly shut the car door and sat with his gaze straight ahead said, "Get on with it." Butch Gregory bowed his head and closed his eyes and prayed:

> Dear Lord Jesus we hope our mission ends right now by finding little Tamara Rey alive and well in this mechanic shop. Protect us, and help us come out alive and let us at least find information. We need your guidance and your hand going before us. In Jesus' name. Amen.

The three walked back toward A-OK Mekaniks and then parted ways at the narrow street that led between the two buildings. Butch walked down the sidewalk and around the corner toward the front door. Before entering the shop, he prayed again silently:

> Lord, I'm about to tell a lie. Help it to be an okay kind of lie, like the one Rahab told or maybe the kind of lie that Anne Frank's family told the Germans. Protect me, but moreover protect Amber and Wyoming, and help us find Tamara alive and well. In Jesus' Name. Amen.

There was no one at the counter when Butch entered the building through the wooden framed door. Behind the counter there was a storeroom with rows and rows of parts as would be found in any auto-parts shop. The shop smelled of cars—oil, lubricant, and the various fluids which combine to give auto-repair businesses a distinctive odor. To the left was a double car bay with lifts and an underneath work area cut out of the floor. There was a white Ford Taurus in the far bay and nothing in the near one. No one was working. Butch checked his watch to see if it was lunch; it was only half-past ten.

Where are the OK Mechanics? His pun pleased him.

He searched for a bell to ring or perhaps a sign that said "Be Back At" then he heard the sound of a man clearing his throat coming from the bay. The man was in his late twenties, had dirty blonde hair, terrible acne scars on his high cheekbones and reeked of cigarette smoke. He was wearing a pair of blue coveralls with thin red stripes. The name "Knuckles" was written on the front in red stitched letters. Knuckle's visage was creepy and menacing. A consciousness of evil oozed off of Knuckles like puss from an infected sore. Butch became queasy. A lump formed in his throat and a bead of sweat materialized on his brow.

Certainly, his mother didn't name him Knuckles.

"Can I help you?" Knuckles voice was unnaturally deep. It didn't fit his appearance. Butch expected a higher pitched timbre.

Sweeping his fears aside, Pastor Butch Gregory did his duty and began his ruse. "Why yes, yes you may."

Butch then launched into the speech he had worked up while he walked from the car to the entrance. He based the whole thing on a pastor friend of his named Roger. Roger has a proclivity for driving old cars. Butch delivered the entire spiel in character as if he were Roger.

"I have this old Volkswagen Rabbit that keeps having gear shift problems, ya see. It is very old and has over 400,000 miles, but it keeps burning out the clutch. I got the Rabbit when I was a college student and it was great back then. It never really needed any work much and it always gets spectacular gas mileage. It is such a wonderful car. I once drove all the way from Tampa to San Francisco and never had any trouble at all. Boy that was a trip to remember!" For effect Butch made a howling sound as he added, "Oooh whee!" for good-ole-boy punctuation.

"My wife and I were newlyweds then and we toured two, or was it three, yeah, it was three because we saw one in Pennsylvania, one in Virginia, and one in Arkansas, so three, three civil war battlefields, ate fish from the Mississippi River, saw the oldest Native American Ruins in Colorado. Have you ever seen those ruins? They are something else. You have to drive up a long, curvy mountain type road to the cliff dwellings. A thousand years ago or so the Anasazi people lived up there. We saw their homes, their ritual dwellings and all that historic stuff. My wife, she really loved all that. Then we drove to the Grand Canyon—I mean, if you're driving across country you've got to stop at the Grand Canyon. It's mandatory, right? Right up there with baseball, apple pie, and Chevrolet, right? Right? You know what I mean? I know you know what I mean. Ya know."

Knuckles looked bored. That was the exact effect Butch wanted. If there was anything that two decades of preaching had taught Butch, it was how to bore people by talking.

"Anyhoo, then we shot out through Nevada and spent a night or two in Reno, or maybe it was three? Come to think of it, Reno is kind of a blur. I might have to ask my wife how many nights we did stay in Reno because I don't really remember. Well, we kept going from there and jogged up to Mt. Shasta and did some outdoorsy stuff before we finally arrived in San Francisco. Boy that was quite a trip.

"And that car, that little Rabbit was spectacular. The first repair I ever had to make on it was to replace the battery, and that was at 100,000 miles!

"Anyhoo, as I was saying, it started burning out the clutches about a decade ago. It seems each clutch would only last for a little while. Well, here I am again and I need to have that clutch replaced. I'm new to this part of town and I was wondering if you could maybe schedule me for sometime later this week and replace my clutch."

Knuckles looked very confused, but eventually he smiled and said, "I'm sorry; I'm the only mechanic on duty right now and I am filled for the next three weeks. Sorry."

Butch exhaled. He would go to Plan B because he knew he had to keep Mr. Knuckles here a little while longer. Of course, he just made Plan B up while he was in the middle of executing Plan A.

"Well, could you at least look and see if you have the part. I have this old friend who is coming to see me next weekend from out of town, he's from Spokane, and he is a great mechanic. If I can get the part, he says he can probably fix it for me in a couple of hours. So, do you think you could look to see if you have it?"

"We don't have it."

"Are you sure?"

"Yes."

"Could you at least look?"

"We don't keep parts like that just laying around, especially for 25 year old Volkswagen Rabbits. If I ordered the part, it would take at least ten days to get here, and your friend would have come and gone by then. I suggest you find an auto repair shop that specializes on imports. We generally only go American here."

Okay, Plan C.

"American you say. Well, that's outstanding, ya know, because I also have this Chevy Silverado, you see, which has a busted headlight. My wife got ticketed last week for driving with a busted headlight and since I've got you here and I've come in anyway, could you maybe see if you have a replacement headlight bulb back there? I know there is probably one at the NAPA, but I always end up buying the wrong thing. It would really help me out if you could pull the part and make sure I have the right thing. I'd hate to do this twice."

That last sentence was the truest thing he said. The song and dance was killing him and he didn't ever want to do this again. He was bluffing with the pick-up headlight. Butch didn't know much about cars, but he did know that Chevy was the most common kind of car, and that Silverado pickups were one of the most common pickups. Most any auto parts supply should at least pretend to have one. He was beginning to feel bad though. These lies were adding up.

Knuckles turned around and walked back toward the storeroom rows behind the counter and began to scan the shelves.

"What year is your Silverado?"

Crumb. Butch hadn't thought that far. Quick. Quick. Quick.

"2000."

"Is that a Silverado 1500?"

"Yeah," it made no difference to Butch. He only hoped that wasn't some kind of trick question and there really wasn't any such thing as a 1500.

This lying business is tough stuff. How do politicians pulled it off so well?

About three minutes went by while Knuckles looked for the part. To Butch the minutes seemed like hours. Eventually the attendant came back to the counter and said, "Okay, I've got your part. It looks like it costs $130 plus tax. You still want it."

Realizing that his bit was about up, but knowing he still needed to stall as long as possible, Butch said, "Sure." He didn't mind paying the $130, but all he had was his debit card and the last thing that Wyoming Wallace had told him was to not give them his real name. What would he do now? Suddenly he remembered something from his college days. He would pretend to have forgotten his wallet. It was a gambit he and a few buddies used a time or two to get a free meal.

But it never came to that. Just as Knuckles was ringing up the part a woman screamed. It was Amber, and she screamed, "Preach!"

When he heard the scream Butch glanced up, but Knuckles looked backward toward the sound at the rear of the building. It was a moment of inspiration. Pastor Butch somehow knew exactly what to do. There was a display of car and truck batteries on the counter where he'd been talking to Knuckles. The instant Knuckles looked back toward his customer at the counter the pastor smashed the green Interstate Battery right against Knuckle's cruel forehead. The victim of Butch's attack slumped over and fell hard against the floor.

Now he had to add attempted murder to his lies. This was not a good day.

Amber emerged from rows of shelving that were behind the counter where Knuckles had retrieved the headlight.

"Where is Wyoming?"

"I don't know."

"What happened?"

Chapter Sixteen

Fury

MINUTES EARLIER, when Butch Gregory had walked to the front of the building, Amber and Wyoming quietly walked down the small road to the place between the two buildings of A-OK Mekaniks. When they were near it they stood behind a row of overgrown rhododendrons to survey the landscape. Amber pointed out a man standing in back of the front building smoking a cigarette. He was a tall blonde man with an ugly face. He leaned against the gray minivan and lazily enjoyed his smoke break.

After about a minute of waiting, the man threw his cigarette onto the ground and walked through the backdoor into the main building. Wyoming whispered, "He just heard the Reverend come in the front door. This is our chance. Now we go."

They took advantage of the opportunity and half-jogged, half-walked in a semi-crouching position toward the metal building on the opposite side of the road. There was a large blue metal door on the front along with the large bay doors. It was locked and far too much out in the open. The two moved down the side fervently seeking a window or an unlocked door. Fortunately, there was a backdoor. It was locked as well, but enough out of the way for a little street-smart magic. Amber whipped out a pocketknife and in about fifteen seconds had worked past the doorjamb and wedged open the doorknob locking mechanism and the portal was breached. In the process, though, Amber broke her blade. She lifted her left arm to halt Wyoming and pivoted her head from left to right and up and down. Experience told her to wait for alarms to sound, in which case they would run. There were no alarms. The coast was clear.

The large warehouse was well lit from long skylights running lengthways on the roof. Both of them had expected to find cars in various stages of repair or disrepair. However, that is not what they found. Instead there were filing cabinets, cardboard moving boxes, and cages like one would find at a zoo.

Wyoming mumbled a swear, "Oh my god," and took the ball cap off his head in disgust. Then he cursed louder.

All Amber could say was "Dear God no, not this."

Wyoming walked over to one of the cages. He quickly estimated a measurement of four feet high, four feet long, and four feet wide. The cages were empty and clean, but one of the cages had a little girls shoe in it, a neon green flip flop. In another cage something was written on the ground, but it wasn't very readable. Wyoming spotted the letters and pointed. Amber stepped inside the cage and inspected it. It was not written with chalk or a pen, but looked like it had been scratched into the dirty concrete floor, like a petroglyph at an ancient archaeological site. When Amber read what it said, a wave of sorrow swept through her.

"What does it say?" asked Wyoming.

Amber stood and walked away; disgusted and sick. Frustrated at the silence, Wyoming squatted down above the etching and read the wrenching name etched onto the cold hard floor.

Mommy.

"When I find these animals," he balled up his fists, "I will kill them with my bare hands. But I will castrate them first." Wyoming growled and punched a filing cabinet.

Amber felt the same way, but she recovered her emotions and stayed on task. She knew they didn't have much time. Taking notice of the boxes she said, "I wonder what is in these? Or for that matter, what they are for?"

The boxes were stacked neatly in rows with some three and others four high. The rows were pushed against the far side of the room facing the cages. They were taped and sealed shut with nothing written on the outside except the manufactures labels. Amber had just cut open one of the boxes with her broken blade when Wyoming interrupted, "what about these filing cabinets."

"We'll get to those in a minute," she replied as she ripped open the top of the box. Inside was canned meat, crackers, dry cereal, peanut butter, and microwavable noodles.

"It's food!"

"That makes sense. Open another one."

Amber nodded and ripped the next box. Same thing, except this one had a couple of children's t-shirts and toilet paper as well.

"What do you suppose all this is for, Wy? I don't get it." asked Amber.

"I suspect it is for the trip that these kids take when they are sent to wherever they are sent. This food is to keep them alive so they can stay profitable. It makes me sick just thinking about it. Look," Wyoming said pointing to a shelf. "Look at this." Amber strained her neck and spotted it to. Sitting on the middle rack of a metal shelf was California Plate MTH 18-456. "Whaddaya know."

The door slammed.

"Who are you?" The question was a dart shot from across the garage. A thin man with ugly teeth, wearing a Seattle Mariners baseball cap, and a very scruffy beard walked toward them. It was not the same man who had been smoking earlier.

Amber recognized him as the passenger in the minivan but she tried to hide the recognition from her face.

"We were sent by the boss," Wyoming gambled. It was a safe bet. The man walking toward them didn't look like the boss of anything.

"The boss?"

"Yeah, the boss, he told us to come check up on you." As he said that, Wyoming coolly walked over to the smallest garage bay door, unlocked the metal pins and raised it so that it slid upwards on its rails. As he walked he grabbed one of the boxes of food and held it in his hands, like he was going to take it out of the door.

"What boss?" the man inquired as he continued towards the two of them.

"Run," Wyoming whispered under his breath to Amber. She glanced at him confused but then she caught on. When the man in the Mariners cap was about ten feet away Amber took off running. At the same time Wyoming threw the box of food in his hands at the man and shouted at Amber, "Run fast."

Amber ran out the bay door across the street into the other building looking for Butch. She called out to him as she ran toward the front of the shop and that is where she found Pastor Butch Gregory standing over the body she'd seen smoking the cigarette.

"Where is Wyoming?" Butch asked.

"I don't know," she replied, catching her breath.

"What happened? Are you okay?" Butch was worried.

"Is he dead?" Amber asked, pointing at Knuckles.

"No, I don't think so. But I think he is out of juice. I don't know how long he'll stay knocked out. Where is Wyoming?"

"We found where they keep the kids, in cages out back but they are all empty. We were snooping and then we ran into some trouble and Wy told me to run. I came running to you."

"Let's go find him."

"Are you sure that is a good idea?"

"No. I'm not sure of anything except that we are a team. Mr. Wallace might think he is invincible, I assure you he is not. But first, help me drag Knuckles here behind the counter."

"Knuckles?"

"That's what his nametag says."

"I bet he named himself Knuckles," Amber added as she checked his pockets. There was nothing in them except cigarettes, a lighter, and a stash of cash neatly folded in a patriotic eagle paperclip. With Houdini hands she stowed the clipped bills into her pocket when Pastor Butch wasn't looking.

After they pulled him out of sight Amber locked the front door and turned the OPEN sign around to now say CLOSED. Then the young woman and pastor walked through the back of the shelving area and into the street. Amber gasped as they came out because the bay door she had run out of was back down again.

"Follow me!" Amber said as she started to run. Butch was not very good at running, especially in black Florsheim wingtips. By contrast Amber was swift and nimble. Amber darted along the side of the building and came to the same door she had jimmied open with her pocket knife fifteen minutes earlier. She paused and waited for Butch to catch up, and in the repose she spied her broken knife blade on the ground.

Once he arrived, she began counting.

"One, two, three!" on three they both burst through the door to save Wyoming.

But Wyoming did not need saving. He had the man with ugly teeth tied up against one of the cages and he was striking him repeatedly on the face. The victims Mariners cap was on the ground beside him and his beard was matted with blood and saliva. Blood ran down the beaten man's face and onto his t-shirt. Wyoming looked up at the two as they walked toward him and then he heaped all his anger and hate onto the man's cheek with one more punch. Then he let fly the same questions he'd been asking with the same slow fury.

"Where are they? Where are the children? Where is the little girl?"

"I don't know, okay. I told you I don't know."

Butch stood back, appalled at what he saw before him. This violence and all of this action was far outside his normal experiences and it ate away at his nerves. The pastor's emotions were conflicted. He hated this man who had hurt these innocents and he wanted Wyoming to beat him more. The other part of him couldn't stand the sight of violence, even if the reprobate was guilty.

"Stop it," shouted Butch. "Stop hitting him," he wiped his eyes with his hands and shook his head. "This is not right," then he looked at the beaten and bloody man. "Just tell us where they were taken. We will not hurt you anymore."

"I already told you. All I know is they went south from here."

Wyoming lunged at him, "Ninety percent of the world is south from here." He gathered himself momentarily, and slowly added, "What you're telling us is not very helpful."

"What is your name?" asked Butch.

"Donny."

"What is the name of the man you were with the night you took Tamara?"

"Mark."

"How did you know about Tamara—where she lived and when to get her?"

"I knew Tamara through her mother. You see, I owed these guys a lot of money and they told me they'd let me off if I got them another girl. I didn't want anyone to get hurt; I just didn't know what to do?"

Rage bottled up inside of Wyoming. "You sold a little girl into hell so you could survive another day just so you could waste it on more meth and more junk? You piece of crap."

Donny spit blood and then looked at Butch and said, "They don't tell us nothing." It was hard for Donny to speak because his lips, tongue and cheeks were swelling as well as his eye sockets. "We just hold the kids here and then send them off. Then we lay low a while and go get more product. That is what they call it, product. They've never let me go with them, to wherever they go that is south. They don't trust me." He spit again. "Look, I always try and take good care of them and I never hurt them—you gotta believe me."

"We don't have to believe anything." It was the first thing Amber had said since they'd entered back into the garage. Then an idea occurred to her. "You know, the guy in the other building might be more helpful."

"What other guy?" Wyoming asked.

"We had an issue with the store clerk. We left him on ice," Amber said.

"What did you do to him Amber?" Wyoming asked.

"Nothing. Preach did it."

Wyoming looked at Butch and said slowly, "I am impressed."

"Let's go get him," said Amber.

Hastily the three of them put their bludgeoned captive into one of the cages and locked it with the padlock hanging on the door.

"Where do you think the key to the cage is?" asked Amber.

"Hopefully a thousand miles away," said Wyoming.

Then they left the building and walked to the storefront. Wyoming pulled his pistol from the holster and led the way as the three of them crouched through the shelves and snuck up toward the front counter. The body was gone. The front door was open. Apparently Knuckles woke up and left.

"Well, we'd better get out of here before he returns with friends." Wyoming said this as he began walking out the front door.

"Wait a minute," interjected Amber. "What about getting information on where Tamara is? We came here to get information."

"We've gotten all the information we're going to get. This was a processing area and now they have moved. They might already be out of the country."

"No. We have a few more days left; I know that for a fact." Butch felt weird saying this because he'd not shared the encounter with his dead brother with the other two. Nevertheless, he knew that they were not out of time yet. "The search must continue," Butch shouted as he slammed his fist upon the Formica counter. He took a breath as the other two looked at him. "She is still in the country and we still have time."

"If you say so," said Amber.

"But what we don't have is time to snoop around anymore. Since your friend got away, it is only a matter of minutes before things get hot around here." Wyoming Wallace looked very serious as he said this.

"Okay," Amber gulped, "then, should we call the police?" She didn't want to call the police, but it sounded like the right thing to say.

"Yep, we certainly should call the police," said Wyoming. "After we're across the bridge. Anonymously."

Part Three:
Working Apart

Chapter Seventeen

Government Plates

WHEN THEY arrived back in Sydney all three were bi-polar about the day. On one hand they felt elated at having been hot on the trail—hot enough to actually be where Tamara had been. On the other hand, nothing was gained and they were no closer to finding Tamara than they were before they left for Tacoma.

Butch sincerely believed their labors were complete. The way he figured it, the police would take the safely anonymous tip, find the man named Donny in the cage and then do real detective work and locate the child trafficking ring and save Tamara. He had confidence that the authorities would have resources and skills that he and his collaborators didn't have. God couldn't have expected much more from them. His conscience, however, was nagging at him. Duplicity and violence did not sit well with his soul.

Amber's soul was fine, but she was a significant contrast to Butch's rosy optimism. She nursed an abiding anxiety and doubt. Down deep she feared that the search might turn into a futile effort with useless wandering, always moving but never getting anywhere. She was frustrated that somewhere tonight Tamara Rey would still be someone else's prisoner and it made her angry. She had not wanted to call the police. She wanted to rummage through those files.

The only one who felt completely good about the day was Wyoming, though there was an ache down in his gut about the children who were being hurt. Nevertheless, he felt really great to deal punishment to the low-life who had hurt little boys and girls. It gave him an inner satisfaction. It was an inner satisfaction that he knew neither the Butch nor Amber would ever understand. He knew his role in this operation was action—and he had served his purpose. He made a mental note to sharpen his knives tonight. Something told him that there was more to come.

The three spent the afternoon in Butch's conference room writing ideas and brainstorming on the whiteboard normally used to teach Bible lessons or outline sermon series. Butch, Amber and Wyoming converted it into a briefing room.

South? What might that mean? Portland? Olympia? It might mean California. That was Wyoming's idea. He believed the children would be scurried down the coastline to where the real money was.

Amber used Butch's laptop computer and did some research on A-OK-Mekaniks but found nothing of any significance other than some poor reviews about their work. Everything they thought of was either too vague or a dead end.

Wyoming suggested checking the registered sex offender database to see if any of the images matched the man named Knuckles or the other one who said his name was Donny.

At around 5 in the afternoon they decided to regroup tomorrow. Wyoming wanted to get a good night sleep. He didn't go into details about the lack of sleep he'd had the night before. Amber said she needed to think about things too. However, what she really intended to do was talk to Janet again. She figured the money she liberated from Knuckles' pocket would go a long way toward gaining more information out of her.

Before he would let anyone leave, Pastor Butch Gregory insisted that they pray. Wyoming snarled his compliance as he forced himself to delay gratification with the cigar he'd already unwrapped and cut.

> Dear Lord, redeem today. We were so close, but we did not succeed. We ask that tomorrow this all be solved and Tamara be found. We ask for justice to those who are evil, and for resolution. Grant us each sweet sleep tonight that tomorrow we can continue for as long as you desire us to. We are and will remain in your service. In Jesus' name. Amen.

Butch spent the evening at home. Lucy made him a large dinner of southern fried chicken and mashed potatoes with homemade buttermilk biscuits. He needed the comfort food. He was able to spend some time with his children and play a game or two with them. Everything in life felt normal as they got bathed and prattled about the upcoming school year. Yet the plight of Tamara Rey tugged at his heart as he stood over Paul's bed after he'd said prayers and tucked him in. He tried to focus on the moment with his son; Tamara was on his mind. She had no comfortable bed and no one to hug her goodnight.

Sarah stayed up later than her little brother. Butch could tell she wanted some daddy time, so they played another two games of checkers. After Sarah went off to bed Lucy asked him all about the day. At first Butch didn't want to tell her. He felt it would be better to shield her from it.

He started to think up an alternate story that would not be as dangerous or disturbing as the truth.

Lies.

Deception had come so easily to him as he lied to Knuckles, and now here he was thinking about lying to his wife. What a dreadful slippery slope lies are? Lying to Lucy would not be good for his marriage. He decided to tell her the truth if she wanted to hear it, but first he tried to just ignore the question. When she asked about it a second time after she brushed her teeth and got ready for bed, he asked her, "Do you really want to know, because it is not pretty and it is upsetting?"

"Yes. Your burden is not yours alone. We are one flesh, Butch Gregory. Let me be someone you can talk to about it. I know you; and I know you need to process it. I also know it has been gnawing at you all through dinner and the rest of the evening. You might be able to fool a congregation or a deacon board, but you can't fool me."

Butch told his wife everything. He told her about the cages. He told her about the man named Donny. He told her about Wyoming's pistol. He even told her about his daring use of the car battery to dispatch a bad guy. Lucy Gregory was very impressed with that so he told that part of it twice.

He also shared with her his frustration. He knew time was running out and he felt so helpless. How could he enjoy a comfortable dinner and a warm bed knowing that Tamara was out there in the hands of those evil people? How could he sleep when she was locked away in a cage somewhere?

"But I thought you said the police would take it from here and that you were probably finished with what Jesus wanted from you?"

"I know what I said, but I think that is just denial. For some reason I feel like we're just getting started, not near the end." He got out of bed and paced across the room. "I want to go do something," he said, emphasizing the word "do" by raising his hands to his shoulders and flinging them outward. "I want to be searching, looking, seeking but I don't even know where to look or what to do. I feel helpless, and frustrated. We were so close Lucy, so close. We could have ended it all today but we didn't. Maybe that was our one big break and now it's all over. I failed. Now it is all in the police's hands."

Lucy pulled him close to her and said, "You forget that God is in on this too. He knows things you don't now. Have faith in him and in yourself."

Before he went to sleep, Butch turned on the local evening news. He expected to see some report or footage from A-OK because of the tip and lead the three of them had left for the Tacoma police. His previous years of experience with the police and the media led him to believe that they literally didn't miss anything. The reporters were rarely accurate, but they usually had something to say about everything that occurred in Western Washington. He'd once had three news vans in his neighborhood because a bear was spotted in a tree. He certainly thought their foray at A-OK Mekaniks would make the nightly newscast.

He was wrong. None of the four major stations had a peep about it. He checked the internet to see if there was something on the website but there was nothing. He dozed off to a deep sleep that was filled with doubt and confusion.

The next morning Butch rose early, as was his custom and got ready for work. Even though he was officially on a leave of absence he thought it wise to still use his office and study at church as the base of operations for him and his team. Even though he'd shared everything with Lucy, he wanted to keep his home life separate from the grisly nature of the work he and his team were engaged in. Butch did not want his house to become headquarters for a search and rescue detail.

As he showered and shaved Butch made a mental agenda of what he would do. First he would call that friend of his he had told Amber about, Henry, who worked in law enforcement in Everett. If that didn't produce any leads, then he would pick up where Amber had left off on the internet snooping of A-OK as well as that license plate number and the moniker "Knuckles." He doubted anything would turn up, but he didn't know what else to do. After that he would call Amber and Wyoming and they could collect their thoughts in a team huddle of sorts. We should call Nicki Jones too and find out what she knows about Donny. Why didn't we do that yesterday? We are such amateurs. Lord help us.

He arrived at his office at a little after 8 AM.

A woman dressed in very formal business attire and a man wearing a dark suit, white shirt and blue tie stood outside his office building. They both wore very dark sunglasses. Twice before Butch had dealt with people dressed like this. Neither time was it good. In the casual, laid back, informal fashion world of the Northwest there are only two groups of people that dress in suits. One was lawyers. The other was feds. A pit formed in Butch's stomach as he pulled his car into his normal parking spot, right alongside a sedan with government plates.

These are not lawyers.

As he twisted the key and pulled it out of the ignition switch his mind quickly counted the number of crimes he and his pair of accomplices had committed the day before: Assault, assault and battery, breaking and entering and leaving the scene of a crime. That was at least four. If Knuckles died from the Interstate Battery incident then it would be five.

Oh dear, this could be very bad.

"Dr. Gregory?" the sharply dressed woman said to him immediately as he got out of his Honda.

"Yes, but please call me Butch. No one calls me Dr. Gregory."

"Dr. Gregory, my name is Debra Lapp-Bench and I am a special agent with the Federal Bureau of Investigations. This is my partner, Barry Chase. Is there a place we can talk in private? We have some questions for you."

Debra Lapp-Bench was a 31 year old law enforcement professional. She served five years in the army before she joined The Bureau and spent the past three years working child abduction cases. She stood five and a half feet tall with a slender frame but an athletic build. Her shoulders were masculine. Her hair was long and blond, but pulled back into a tight and controlled bun, which gave her an extremely sleek and intimidating aura. Butch thought he detected a Northeastern accent in her staccato speech. He guessed she was from Massachusetts. There was a well-manicured scar above the glasses rim of her right eye.

"Sure, we can talk in my study, is that ok?" said the pastor, nervously.

"That'll be fine."

The three of them walked inside his office and Butch smiled at Mildred and said, "Please hold all calls. I don't know how long I will be." Then, he pivoted to his inquisitors and asked, "Would you like a cup of coffee?"

"No, we're fine."

"Do you mind if I get one?"

"No, not at all."

He poured a cup of coffee into his large daisy patterned mug. He used the precious seconds it took to pour the coffee to think about what he might say. He decided he would wait and see and not think ahead, but he did say a quick silent prayer.

> O Lord, help me not to lie, but help me to be wise. Let this meeting be for good and not bad. Protect me as I am attempting to do what you told me I should do. In Jesus' name. Amen.

With that he turned away from the office kitchen and beckoned with his hand a silent gesture for his two guests to follow him. They moved down the hallway to his study where he unlocked the door, set his satchel on the floor and offered his two guests a seat.

He sat down into his big, high back chair and asked, "What can I do for you?"

"Dr. Gregory," Agent Lapp-Bench snapped off her sunglasses and began, "it has come to our attention that you and probably two friends were at A-OK Mekaniks yesterday and called the Tacoma police about a tip regarding the whereabouts of Tamara Rey. Is that accurate?"

"How could you possibly know all of that?"

"We know everything, Dr. Gregory."

Agent Chase punctuated that bold claim with a bit of bravado by adding, "We know what you had for breakfast this morning." Agent Chase did not bother to take off his sunglasses when he spoke. The pastor shifted in his chair, frowning.

Agent Lapp-Bench continued, "We were able to trace the cell phone call that you anonymously left with the police to your iPhone. We also know you were not alone. Barry, show Dr. Gregory the photographs." She was obviously the lead on this case. On cue, Agent Barry Chase produced a piece of paper from his breast pocket and unfolded it. Butch took it from him and held it in his hands, sipped his coffee and examined it. There were three photographs on the single sheet of stark white copy paper.

One picture was of his car as it crossed the Tacoma Narrows Bridge. The time and date index on the bottom was the previous day and exactly when they crossed on their way to A-OK Mekaniks. A second picture was again of his car, but this time the blue Honda Civic sat at a red light about three blocks from A-OK Mekaniks. In this photo Butch could see a clear image of Wyoming's face in the passenger seat and Amber's shadow in the backseat. Both of those photos were grainy and pixelated. The third photograph was different. It was taken at a much higher resolution from across the street of A-OK Mekaniks and from an elevated position. It showed Butch walking into the storefront.

Butch took another sip of coffee and swallowed hard. "How did you get these?"

Special Agent Debra Lapp-Bench smiled and said, "The short answer is that we are the FBI. The long answer is that the DOT and the City of Tacoma have very good cameras set up to catch toll violators and those who run red lights."

"Looks like you use those cameras for other purposes as well. But what about this last one?" Pastor Butch pointed out with his finger. "There is no Washington State DOT or city camera across the street from an auto shop? Come on." Butch tried to sound incredulous rather than defensive. "How did you get that picture of me walking into the building?"

"That, Dr. Gregory, that is none of your business. What you need to know right now is that you stepped into a hornets' nest yesterday. I would like to know exactly what you were doing there and what you did while you were there. Confession is good for the soul, Reverend Doctor."

"I can't argue with that," he paused, sipped his coffee again, and gathered his thoughts. "Well," he started reluctantly, "we were following a lead we had on where we might find or at least get information about where a young girl named Tamara was. She was abducted out of her own apartment here in Sydney a few days ago. Some of us are trying to find her because the local police seem to be unable to act, and, quite honestly, we felt like the Lord wanted us to go find her. We care. We had no intentions or motives other than locating the lost little girl." Butch briefly recalled the Bible verses in Luke 15.

"I understand that Dr. Gregory, but you are way out of your league. There are things going on here that are beyond your pay scale and ability to understand. If you keep this up you will get hurt. You need to just stay here and pray for Tamara. Let us do the finding and rescuing."

Pastor Butch recognized a rebuke when he heard one, but this was a rebuke he was not willing to receive. "With all due respect Agent Lapp-

Bench, so far she has not been found." A bile of righteous outrage climbed up his throat and out of his mouth. "I've learned that each year over 100,000 children disappear and are never recovered. This is untenable. It is not just a travesty of justice but a societal tragedy which we feel we need to do something about. When little girls and boys are violently taken from their homes it is everyone's responsibility to do something and quite honestly it looks like the authorities often turn the other way."

"Again, I understand that Dr. Gregory. However, you made a mess yesterday." Agent Lapp-Bench was irritated. "Now, I have to ask you, who are these other two people with you in the car? I advise you, Dr. Gregory, to tell the truth; and I tell you this not only because the Good Book says to, but also as a legal matter. If you lie to us I promise you," her eyes narrowed and her nose twitched, "we will make your life miserable and ruin your career."

"I have no intention, nor have I ever had any intention of lying to you. The person in the front seat is named Wyoming Wallace. I have only known him for three days. The person in the back seat is Amber Smith. Each of us, for different reasons, I think, have been led to look for Tamara. It is the Lord who brought us together."

As he spoke the names, agent Chase was writing it all down on a small notepad.

"Very good, Dr. Gregory. We already knew that was Amber in the backseat, but we didn't have any idea who the man in the front was. Now, tell me, did you take anything from the garage or from anywhere nearby when you left. Any files, documents, boxes, flash drives, hard drives, pictures, envelopes, drugs, clothing, anything at all?"

"No Agent Lapp-Bench, we didn't take anything at all. There were rows of filing cabinets in the building behind the ally that I would have liked to have gotten into, but our visit was cut short. What we assumed, what I assumed anyway was that you, the real pros here, would find the man in the cage and the evidence and then bring it all to a speedy close."

"Are you sure, Dr. Gregory, that you left everything there and that there is not something else you want to tell us?"

"Yes I'm sure. My friend Amber looked inside the boxes and found canned and boxed food. But we left before we got to the cabinets. In hindsight, I wish we'd looked inside of them and swiped a file or two, but we just didn't have time before we knew we had to go. I wish we had."

"I wish you had too," said Agent Chase.

"What do you mean by that?" asked Butch.

"Well," he replied, "when we arrived on the scene those filing cabinets were empty. Completely emptied. There were no boxes of canned food either."

Butch stared in disbelief.

"Most of the drawers were still wide open," added Agent Chase.

"They weren't open when we left. In fact, I think they were locked. Yeah, Amber said they were locked."

Agent Chase wrote in his little notebook.

Pastor Butch wondered if he might get a little information from them, since he was so free with what he knew. "Can you tell me what you learned from the man we left you? We figured having him was more valuable than any evidence on site. What information were you able to get out of him?" He expected the agents to be hush on that topic and probably couldn't tell him anything but he figured it didn't hurt to ask, though.

"Why yes, I can tell you exactly what we learned from the man you so graciously left for us. We learned nothing." Agent Lapp-Bench pulled at her skirt bottom as she spoke.

"We didn't learn anything either," Butch said. "All he would tell us is that the children were shipped south. We asked where south but he said he didn't know. He said they didn't trust him enough to give him details yet."

"That is more than we got out of him," Agent Lapp-Bench pointed at Agent Chase's notepad, and he recorded what Butch learned from the man in the cage.

"I do apologize for his battered condition. Mr. Wallace was extremely brutal in his, well, his interrogation. He's probably just being brave. Maybe he will talk more in the future."

"No, I don't think so," said Agent Chase confidently.

"Why?"

"Because," Agent Lapp-Bench adjusted herself in her seat, "We think it was his body that we dragged out of the Puyallup River this morning. He had been shot execution style in the head. His hands were tied behind his back."

"Photo," Agent Lapp-Bench said extending her right hand toward Agent Chase and then came a snap of her long fingers. Agent Chase produced another picture, this time a 5 x 7 black and white, and handed it to Agent Lapp-Bench. She then held it in front of Butch Gregory and said, "Is this the man you saw at A-OK Mekaniks? Is this the man your friend beat? Is this the man you left in a cage?"

The man in the picture had a bullet hole in his forehead and his face was pale and soggy. There was no light in his eyes and his mouth was agape. His ugly beard and sallow face appeared even more exaggerated in the repose of death. There were cuts and bruises around his eyes and cheeks. Butch gagged.

"Yes, that's him," he said as his face turned pale and he thought about how badly Wyoming beat that man. The man who was now dead.

"Donny was alive when we left, I promise you. My friend Wyoming smacked him around pretty hard, but he was alive and talking. I promise. We certainly didn't shoot anyone."

"Donny, huh," said Agent Chase, writing.

"Yes, Donny is, was, his name. He told us that he used to date Tamara's mom and that he sold her out to cover his debts with these people."

"Did he happen to tell you his last name?"

"No. But I bet Nicki Jones could. I intend to call her today and find out what she knew about her old boyfriend." Butch adjusted in his seat and took a defensive tone. "Look, we didn't kill him. You've got to believe me."

"I believe you, Dr. Gregory. That is why you are not handcuffed in the backseat of our car on the way to an undisclosed location right now. We think we know what happened, but we're not exactly sure. That is why it is very important that you cooperate with us and share with us exactly, in detail, what you know and what you did. Tell me, was there anyone else at A-OK Mekaniks other than the man you left in the cage, this man you say is named Donny?"

"There was the other man who I talked to at the front counter. That was our plan, for me to distract the front while my friends checked around back. We were trying to avoid people."

"Knuckles," said Agent Chase. When he said that, Agent Lapp-Bench shot him a scolding look.

"Yeah," agreed Butch. "His coveralls had the name Knuckles written on it. Anyway, when my ruse was blown I had to knock him out. When we came back later to tie him up and question him, he was gone. We figured he left in fear and went to go get help. That is the reason we left so fast and called the police. Knuckles disappearance is the reason we didn't have time to check the file cabinets or the rest of the shop for that matter."

"You knocked out Knuckles?" exclaimed Agent Chase with incredulity. "I hardly believe that. Knuckles is a tough man. He is a dangerous man."

"Well, I did, and I hardly believe it myself."

"Dr. Gregory, did you give the man behind the counter your real name, or address, or any identifying information at all? If you did, you could be in serious jeopardy." Agent Lapp-Bench said this with urgency and a grim sense of worry.

"No, we thought of that ahead of time."

"Well, I hope this does not end poorly for you," she said while she rose from her seat, "or for Paul and Sarah."

Paul and Sarah? How did she know his children's names?

She stood with perfect posture and put her sunglasses back on.

The other agent followed her lead and stood by her side. Following their cue, so did Butch. Then Agent Lapp-Bench added, "I warn you, back off Dr. Gregory. I know that your motives are pure and you only want to do good. We respect that. However, you are going to get hurt if you keep it up. These people are not to be toyed with. You don't know what you're doing and you don't know who you're messing with. This situation is dangerous. Stay away."

Butch knew he should be quiet, but he couldn't help himself. He responded to her threat, "I will not. We will not. Amber, Wyoming, and I seem to all be in agreement that regardless of the risk to us personally the search for Tamara is something we must do; so we will keep at it. My only promise to you is that we did not kill that man and we do not intend to harm anyone. We only want to find the little girl."

"We're watching you, Dr. Gregory." That was the last thing she said as she pulled out a business card with her contact information and laid it on his desk. Then she and Agent Chase briskly walked out of his study, down the hallway, out the door, got into their car and drove off.

Chapter Eighteen

Things Just Got Complicated

BUTCH SAT in his study and reflected on the conversation and his false bravado while he finished his cup of coffee. Was she right and he was in over his head? Of course he was. He was way over his head. Perhaps he'd misunderstood what Shark told him the other night in his dining room. Would the law catch the bad guys and save Tamara after all and he was just in the way? Was he really okay with the idea that this might get him killed? Was he okay with the idea this might get him in prison? It could ruin his ministry? His career?

He picked up the landline from the old-fashioned wooden desk and called Amber. "Things just got complicated."

Butch then relayed to Amber the need to talk. After an early and quick lunch with Lucy at home, he picked up Amber and they drove out to Wyoming's trailer. He was afraid that the two of them would be angry because he'd shared so much with the FBI, but neither of them were. Wyoming said that he half-expected something like that and Amber could not have cared less. Her reasons and motivations had nothing to do with law. They did, however, all agree with him that they should continue in their search for Tamara.

Butch and Amber sat on the splintery wooden deck with a green aluminum roof that served as a back porch to Wyoming Wallace's trailer and watched Wyoming flip his silver Zippo lighter and ignite the blunt end of a long, thin cigar. The initials W.W. were engraved on the side of the lighter. As he smoked Wyoming pieced together the way the events probably unfolded. He suggested that Knuckles came back, cleaned out the filing cabinets, killed the man named Donny and then dumped his body in the Puyallup River. "One thing about it," Wyoming remarked, "that river stinks so bad and is so polluted it is a miracle they found his body down there. A body could be there forever before someone finds it. It is odd that it was located so quickly." He raked his hand across his curly hair, "Almost like someone knew where to look, wouldn't you say?"

As much as he hated to admit it, Wyoming had a point.

Wyoming said that he suspected the clear photograph of Butch walking into the storefront was from surveillance cameras in some kind of stakeout. He guessed the FBI or ATF or even the local police had A-OK Mekaniks under surveillance. He seemed to think they might have even had cameras or recording devices planted inside the shop. "That's how they know we didn't kill the man. They heard every word we said in there. If they thought you," Wyoming's words slowed down as he thought hard, "if they thought you and you" he pointed at Amber and Butch, "and me had done that, that we killed that man, then we would all be in jail right now instead of having this pleasant conversation."

Wyoming thought a little longer then he confidently pronounced, "I'll wager you a fifth of whiskey that the FBI is actually baiting us. They want us to keep snooping because they are hindered by laws and procedures that keep them from doing certain things. Yeah, that's it. Or," his eyes became animated and he stroked his Van Dyke to summon creative power. "Maybe they have hit some kind of roadblock and can't find any more information. But if they," again his words slowed to a snail's pace, "keep an eye on us, follow us around, then, then they just might learn some things they couldn't learn before because we don't have to file any paperwork or notify any agency or anything like that at the end of each day." As Wyoming finished the sentence his cadence increased in speed to his normal slow pace and then he flashed a wide grin to punctuate his brilliance.

Amber smiled back and shook her head in agreement. What he said made sense to her. Her experiences on the street had told her that the police often follow this type of methodology. They just sit and watch and allow all the actors to play their roles; and then they pounce. Butch, however, was less than convinced. He countered with the argument that the FBI would have never come to visit him if they had wanted him to continue.

"Why would they visit me in my office, try to scare me, try to convince me to stay away and then threaten me with arrest or harm if what they really wanted was for us to keep at it?"

"Because," Wyoming replied, "they needed some information from you. They needed to know who I was, that is important to folks like the FBI. They want to know all the pieces on the chessboard. Trust me Reverend, these government types value control above all else and the key to control is knowledge of all the players and pieces. In someone's office, today, somewhere, a crime diagram has been enlarged, and our names and pictures," he paused and thought, "have been included alongside that little girl and Mr. Knuckles and that dead Donny."

"And," Amber said, "they probably know enough of human psychology to roll the dice that we would respond like most people would to such a threat—do the exact opposite of what we're asked to do."

"I guarantee you," Wyoming slowly insisted, "that if they really wanted us to stay away, well then they would have made certain we ceased. They would have found some kind of excuse to arrest you, or me, or Amber, or suddenly your car would be smashed to pieces and your bank account hacked in order to lock up all your assets and keep you put. Why, I wouldn't even put it past them to cause an accident involving your wife or your children to keep you put, if they really wanted to. Once it gets to the federal level, they will do anything to make things happen the way they want them to happen. They thrive on manipulating others."

After they talked it out a bit more and did a little strategizing, Wyoming lit another, fatter and shorter cigar and changed the subject. He gave Amber a pistol. He tried twice to give one to Butch but the pastor refused. Amber, however, was more than willing to have a little extra protection after the events at A-OK Mekaniks and with the knowledge of what happened to Donny at the hands of Knuckles.

At first Wyoming gave her a .357 revolver but Amber couldn't emotionally handle it. She shook violently as she held the weapon. She tried to overcome the revulsion and anxiety but just couldn't get out of her head that it was a .357 caliber pistol that Steve used to kill her brother Adam. Wyoming gave her his .38 revolver and he opted to use his gigantic .45 caliber revolver.

They went around back and Wyoming set up beer bottles and Amber practiced with the pistol from 15 feet away. She learned how to load all six of the slots in the cylinder. Wyoming taught her how to hold it and then he instructed her in the proper way to carry it so that it was concealed. He showed her how to shoot and how to squeeze the trigger instead of clumsily pulling on it.

Then she learned the proper way to stand when shooting. After that, Wyoming gave her a quick lesson on the use of the firing sites. He also coached her that a pistol was not very accurate over 15 feet or so, and that if she pulled it out, she'd better be prepared to use it. "This is no toy!" he kept saying over and over again.

The daylight ebbed and a rare summertime drizzle began to fall, so Butch and Amber left. Before they left, the three agreed that the day should start out with Butch following through on his lead with his friend Henry. The other two would wait to hear from him and see how that played out.

The events of the day had been very upsetting to Pastor Butch Gregory.

He felt less like a pastor today than he ever had, but there was one more stop he needed to make before he went home. He dropped Amber off downtown then he went by the Hill house to see Nicki. There really was nothing he could say to her that would make her feel better. He told her that him an a couple other people were looking for Tamara and that they were looking into a couple of possibilities. Then he asked her about Donny.

"It's odd you ask that pastor, because two people from the FBI came by today and asked me about Donny too."

That didn't take long.

"Well, what do you remember about Donny?"

"He was very nice, really. Him and Tamara got along great, I just can't believe that he would hurt her. I mean, he was a lazy bum, but I never thought he would hurt my baby. Oh God, this is all my fault, isn't it? I let that man into my home and now he has taken my baby? Sweet Jesus no." Again the wave of uncontrollable sorrow swept throw the woman.

It was hard to ask, but he had to. "Do you know where he lives?" He didn't let her know that he was dead. He didn't think she could handle it. He wondered if Agent Lapp-Bench had told her Donny was dead?

"No, but I am glad he is dead if he hurt my baby. I hope he burns in hell?" She screamed the word hell with unguarded emotion.

So she knew.

"When you met, where was he living?"

"We met in a meth house, Pastor." She settled down and wiped her tears. "There really was nothing of his past that I knew and then the day he left, he just vanished with our piggy bank. I never thought I would see him again."

They talked a little longer, but Butch wasn't able to get any information about Donny from Nicki. He and the Hills prayed with her, and then he went home.

Chapter Nineteen

An Old Friend, A New Lead

PASTOR BUTCH called his old friend, Detective Henry Keebler at 9:00 AM the next morning from his church office. Henry had been a deacon at Sydney Community Church up until three years ago when he moved across the Sound to Snohomish County to take a considerable job promotion with the Sheriff's department there. The thrill of working in the large, mostly unincorporated area north of Seattle was too much to pass up. Everett, the largest city in the county, boasts both Boeing production plants and United States Navy docks. Outside of Everett, there are many places to hide and none too few illegal activities. Law enforcement was always in high demand in Snohomish County and this is what piqued Henry's interest.

The job change was a significant increase in pay and prestige for Henry but his transfer had been a reluctant one because he loved Sydney even though he was bored professionally. The decision had been hard for him; as well as for his family. They'd been involved in Sydney Community Church for over a decade. His wife Cynthia and their three boys were all integrated in the school and community life. But it was an offer he couldn't refuse. There just wasn't, usually, that much crime in Sydney and very little opportunity for professional growth so in the end he made the transition from the sleepy hamlet of Sydney for the urban jungle of greater Seattle.

"Henry, it's Butch Gregory, how are you doing?"

"Fine, fine," replied the seasoned law-enforcement professional. "Are you calling to tell me you scored us two more Seahawks tickets?"

"No, nothing that pleasant, I'm afraid. I actually need to talk to you about work stuff. Do you mind if I ask you some questions? I hate to talk shop with you; I've found myself in a bit of a situation and I really don't know what to do. I thought maybe you'd help or at least shed some light on what has become a very dark situation."

"Sure," replied Henry, intrigued by the role reversal. Usually it was him calling Pastor Butch for advice. "Go ahead."

At that, Butch spent five minutes telling Henry all about Tamara and his leave of absence from the church and his tugging from God to be a part of the search. He even told Henry about the FBI but he withheld most of the gritty details about A-OK Mekaniks. At the conclusion of his summary, Butch asked simply, "Do you have any suggestions?"

"I've heard about the case Butch," Henry said flatly. "All police departments and state troopers are on alert. It's a pretty tragic thing. What you might not know is that the same basic occurrence, just like it or very similar to it, has happened on Whidbey Island, over in Leavenworth, Port Angels, multiple times here in Everett, and once in Longview. Those are the ones we know about. God himself only knows how often it happens down in the bowels of Seattle or the seedier sections of Tacoma. I think we are dealing with some kind of organized crime ring here. That is why the FBI is on it so heavy. You can bet they know everything you think you know and then some."

Suddenly there was a long pause. Henry then asked, "Uh, Butch, where are you calling me from?"

"My office, why?"

There was another long pause.

"Can you come up to Everett today? I know a great little Chinese noodle restaurant."

"I will be there at 11:30. Text me the name of the restaurant and I'll find it."

After he received the text Butch called to let both Wyoming and Amber know what he was up to, then he called Lucy to tell her he'd be gone for the day and not to expect him home.

Sydney and Everett are not that far away in distance, but in terms of travel time it is extensive. Butch checked the ferry schedule and decided it would be quicker to jump on a ferry than to drive all the way around Puget Sound. During the hour boat ride he drank two cups of coffee and kept his mind off of the gloominess of the situation by finishing up the latest Tim Keller book. He liked Tim Keller, even if he was a Calvinist.

The ferry arrived right on time in downtown Seattle. Butch never grew weary of the majestic view of the Seattle skyline from the water. As the ferry slowly churned toward Coleman Dock, Butch thought about the two opposite worlds right before his eyes. The gleaming emerald city sparkled with skyscrapers. She fed her residents world class cuisine. International trade and industry kept the ports busy and the populace employed. The arts, music, and literature entertained the citizens. Technology and innovation established Seattle as a desirable place to live, a world class city by anyone's standards. All of these wonderful attributes exist parallel to every corruption known to human beings. Murder, rape and violence were perpetually in the news. Drug abuse and mental illness syphon away otherwise merry lives. Avarice and greed was weaved into the fabric of Seattle's founding as industry chopped through the land and displaced the indigenous Native Americans. Corruption was the only true glue between the past and the present. A dark void of materialism occupied the place of spiritual enlightenment. The city was a macrocosm of the individual human condition. Each soul is capable of untold beauty and majesty as well as the darkest depravity. Just like Seattle.

When the ferry landed he drove around the busy Pike's market and passed by the tourist trap called the Space Needle and found his way to the freeway and sped North up 1-5. Half an hour later he walked into the door of Noodlerama and spied his old friend at a booth in the corner with his back to the wall facing the front door. Henry stood up and greeted his old Pastor with a bear hug that enveloped Butch. Henry's girth and height swallowed Butch. The two sat and immediately picked up where they had left off on the phone.

"I'm sorry to be so cloak and dagger Butch," Henry apologized, "but based just on what you told me over the phone it is probable that the FBI is listening to everything you do now."

"I thought the government had to have a warrant to tap a phone call?"

"Technically, yes. But you're thinking about the good old days when the bad guys were easier to spot. The new Homeland Security laws, Patriot Act and such have made federal phone surveillance of United States citizens a blasé run-of-the-mill everyday occurrence. I promise you, they are listening to everything you say now as well as reading your email."

"Do you think they are following me?"

"No, not likely, at least not yet. To follow someone requires too much actual manpower. Surveillance of communications is a lot easier and can be done by fewer people than actually tailing someone. But if they suspect you any further, they most certainly will. They probably have a GPS tag on your car. So they know you are here."

"Oh joy," the pastor mumbled. "Why don't they just follow me with a drone from the sky?" Butch said, paired with an irritated chuckle. Henry shot him an icy, suspicious glare and then began to give Butch Gregory the speech he'd been working up for the past hour.

"Butch," said the cop as he pointed his chubby index finger, "go home. There is nothing you can do here but get yourself hurt, or worse. You are not just out of your league; you are out of your universe. You may even be out of your mind! I made a couple of calls this morning after talking to you and I'm telling you; this is dangerous business you've gotten yourself into. These people are not burglars smashing windows or even the meth addicts you have in Sydney. Butch, the organization you're up against plays for keeps and they don't mess around."

Butch listened to the lecture. He'd expected it from his overprotective pal but he wasn't about to acquiesce.

"Look Henry, I appreciate your concern but there is a little girl out there who is counting on me to find her. Something terrible has happened to her and we must try and make it right. It is easy for you to tell me to go home, but every night I see her face whenever I close my eyes to sleep and I'm traumatized by the thought of the awful things people are doing to such beautiful innocence.

"Now here I am, sitting across from you asking for help. I appreciate your sermon, and I know you are just trying to protect me, but are you going to help me or not?"

Henry asked, "Why are you doing this, Butch? People go missing all the time. It's a tragedy and I hate it, that is why I have the job I have, to put the bad guys away and make the world safer for all the little boys and girls, but we can't save all of them."

Pastor Butch Gregory looked across the table directly into Henry's eyes and held his gaze with pastoral intensity and then he began to talk, but his tone had changed.

"Henry, in all those sermons you heard me preach through the years, did I ever tell you the story about the boy on the beach throwing stranded starfish back into the surf?"

"Uh, no, can't say that I can remember it. But what does that have to do with anything?"

"Listen. A boy was walking on the beach one day after a violent storm had come through. He saw that many starfish were stranded on the beach, drying out in the sun with no hope of getting back into the water. The boy began picking up the starfish, one by one, and throwing them back into the water where the starfish could live. After a period of time, a wise, older man came by walking his dog along the beach and he saw the boy. The man asked him, 'What are you doing?' The boy replied, 'I'm saving these starfish.' The man replied at the boy's naiveté and said, 'There is no way you can save all of them, so why bother, why does it even matter?' At that the boy picked up a starfish and said, 'It matters to this one,' and then he cast it back into the safe waters of the ocean.

"Henry, I know there are untold tragedies everywhere. But for some reason this particular little girl has been made my specific responsibility. Plus, it matters to this one. It matters to Tamara and it matters to Tamara's mother. It matters to me and it matters to God. They all matter. I can't go looking for all of them, but I must go looking for this one."

"Okay, I get your point. I just don't think it is a good idea."

"Well, neither do I," Butch laughed, and it relieved some of the tension between the two stubborn men. "I don't think it is a good idea at all, but God told me to do it and I learned years ago never to argue with God. When you argue with God it means you are wrong."

Henry Keebler ceded that point with a smirk and a roll of the eyes.

The waitress came and took their order. Henry got a bento box and Butch ordered a General Tso chicken. Over the next hour Henry described to Butch how he'd been getting information, sporadically but reliably, on a compound located west of Monroe toward Stevens pass. It was officially outside of his job assignment, but he'd been in on a couple of briefings. The local police had been told to stay away from it because the state and feds were getting ready to move in. Henry couldn't promise that it was connected to Butch's particular case, but he indicated it felt like a situation similar to other abduction cases he'd handled in the past. Conveniently Henry provided Butch with the exact GPS location of this compound.

It was at this point that he asked Henry the obvious question that had been bothering him during the whole conversation.

"Why can't you guys, the police, just go search the place and see if Tamara is there?"

"Well, like I said, the feds have told us to stay away, plus, Butch, there really is not a legal precedence for going out there. Until we have some kind of proof of illegal activity there is nothing we can do. There is no way we could get a warrant to search anywhere like that because a pastor from the other side of the Sound thinks we might find a missing girl there. No judge would ever approve that."

Butch became angry at Henry's answer. He raised his voice slightly above the tone of polite conversation, "You mean to tell me that they can tap the private conversation of a citizen, who will never know he is being recorded and follow him with a GPS tracking device, but when a child is in danger and there is reasonable suspicion that any common sensed person would have that she might be held somewhere, we can't do anything? It sounds to me like this whole system is upside down."

There was awkward silence between them. Finally Butch looked at his friend and said, "Hey, I'm sorry. I know it is not your fault. You've been a big help and I appreciate it. It's just that this whole situation is preposterous. I don't understand why the system is built to protect criminals. I feel like we've all been thrown to the wolves."

"Well," said Henry, "I guess that is why we need pastors to be shepherds, to protect us from the wolves."

The two men spent another hour catching up on their wives, kids, and careers. Butch told Henry all about the church and how it had grown but there were also some people who had left, disgruntled over changes to the systems and strategies. It was near 2:30 PM when they finally stood in the parking lot and had prayer with each other before they parted ways. Henry went back to work, but Butch sat in his car and made a three-way-call to Wyoming and Amber. Given what he'd just learned from Henry, he was very careful about what he said.

"You two had better get up here. I think I might have found our Christmas present."

Butch was trying to speak in code hoping his two allies would pick up on his intention.

"What are you talking about?" said Amber.

"Christmas!" shouted Wyoming. "Who said anything about Christmas?"

"I'm talking about the Christmas package. I think I might have found it. If the two of you would come up here and help me pick out what color to get maybe we could get this over with." Butch was a little frustrated with their lack of comprehension.

"What the heck? Why do I care what color your Christmas presents are. Amber, what is he talking about?" Wyoming was not tracking with Butch at all.

"Can the two of you get up here to Everett this afternoon? I think we might have found something," and then he emphasized, "Im. Por. Tant."

It must have worked. Amber replied that if it was that so im-por-tant then they would be there by 5. Butch looked across the street at a Shell convenience store and told the two to meet him there. He hung up the phone wondering why it had been so hard to speak to them covertly. It always worked for James Bond in the movies.

It would take Wyoming and Amber at least two and maybe three hours to reach him. He was sitting in his car wondering what he should do while he waited. He was thinking about going out to the location by himself, but decided against it. He would not want them acting without him, so he would show the same courtesy. Then the thought occurred to him to go to a local athletic store and buy a new pair of sneakers. The escapade at A-OK Mekaniks had convinced him that he might not have the right footwear for his current activities. Then he remembered that his old friend Stanley pastored a small Pentecostal church just outside of Everett. Maybe he would stop by and say hey.

His phone's ring interrupted him. It was Pastor Philip from Sydney Community.

"What's wrong Philip?"

"Well, I sure hate to call you because I know that you are on important business, but I didn't see any other way and I thought you'd want to know."

"What is it? Did one of the deacons put pressure on you? Is the church treasurer trying to get the youth minister fired again?"

"No, no Pastor Butch, nothing like that. Actually everyone has been really wonderful to me. What I need to tell you is that last night Lester Wooley died."

"Oh no." Silence crackled on the cell phone. "Well, I guess his battle with cancer is over. I will miss him."

After another moment of silence, Pastor Butch asked, "Are you making arrangements, Philip? Mike at the funeral home will help and of course Mildred knows what to do. You helped me with the Jones funeral a couple of months ago. That will be good template for you to build on. I trust you. You can do this."

"That has all been fine, Pastor. The funeral is tomorrow. That is what I'm calling about. Butch, I've taken care of all the arrangements and worked hard to keep this from you. However, Lester's family really wants you to say some words. I tried to tell them that you were unavailable but they are very insistent. It would really smooth things out if you could just come say something. I know it is short notice, but the family wanted a quick turnaround on the service. For some reason they seem in a real hurry to get the service over with."

"What time is the funeral? Is it at the church?"

"No, it is not at the church. The funeral is a graveside service at the cemetery on the hill. It is scheduled for 10 AM. They do not expect many people, as you know most of Lester's extended family lives out of state and they are not coming for the service. Lester outlived most all of his friends. This'll be a very small gathering."

"Okay, sounds good. I'll be there, but Philip, you're preaching the funeral sermon. I'm just there to give some words. This is your work right now, not mine. Do you understand that?"

"Yes Pastor."

"I'll see you tomorrow then. If anything else comes up, call me. No, wait. Don't call me. If anything else comes up, just take care of it and I will see you in the morning at 10:00 AM."

Butch hoped he'd not sounded too distant with Philip. He had punctuated the point of not being the main officiant because he wanted Philip to know that he trusted him and believed he could do it. He also knew, from his own experiences in ministry, that the only way to learn how to do these types of things was to actually do them solo, and to even fail doing it. There were no practice funerals at seminary. On the flip side, if Butch showed up tomorrow and then took over it would undermine everything Philip had done. It would also convey the terrible theological falsehood that the minister who does the funeral is what matters. Butch Gregory believed it is not the pastor who matters, it is the church—the visible community of saints—who matter. It is the church who buries the dead. A pastor is only the spokesperson for the community; the one who gives ultimate meaning, the one who explains significance in times of crisis.

At least, that was his theology on the subject. Butch observed that most people, however, did not feel that way. That is why the phenomena of having an old favorite pastor come conduct a funeral is so prevalent. Too much emphasis is placed upon personalities and not the church. It was something that troubled him.

He hoped that he would have plenty of time to finish the investigation of the compound that Henry had told him about before he had to go back for the funeral. In his mind he planned on finding the location tonight and devising a plan and then in the morning investigating. They would need a place to sleep, though. So he decided he would use his time to find them a hotel.

The sun was still high in the sky when Amber and Wyoming arrived in Everett. Wyoming got out of his black Jeep and asked, "Where is this Christmas present you were talking about? All I ever want for Christmas is a bottle of single malt scotch and a quiet place to drink it."

Butch Gregory said, "Well, I was, I was trying . . ." but before he could get the explanation out both Amber and Wyoming roared with laughter.

"Reverend, that was the worst spy talk I ever heard, but it sure made the ride up enjoyable. Amber and I made fun of you the whole way up I-5."

After Butch got over his mild embarrassment, the three of them stood in the Shell parking lot as Butch briefed them on what he learned from Henry. He included the warning about the sophisticated and tough nature of the group they were dealing with, as well as about how the state and federal authorities were involved. He went on to share the GPS coordinates and how he'd pulled up the location on his iPhone.

After telling them all of this, Butch told them about Philip's phone call and the funeral tomorrow morning.

"We can go out tonight and look around, I think."

"No," Amber said, "Wyoming and I can do this. You go back tonight, sleep in your bed, and do the funeral. I know how important funerals can be. I remember what a great job you did at my brother's funeral. We'll go out tonight and find it, and then wait till you get here tomorrow after the funeral to do a more thorough investigation."

Butch nodded, but he didn't like it.

"What do you think about that, Wyoming?" Amber asked.

"Well, Reverend, you would probably just slow the whole thing down anyway. I think Amber and I can get in and out fairly well just the two of us—three might be too many. Maybe this is the way that god of yours has of just getting you out of the way." Wyoming smiled as he said the last line, and then added, "We'll just sleep in my Jeep."

"No, no you won't. I've already prepaid reservations at the Super 8. You even get a free breakfast." Then he looked at Wyoming with suspicion and said, "I got you separate rooms. Here are your keys."

"Thanks Preach," Amber said with a smile. "But Wyoming is so not my type." Wyoming scowled.

Butch felt extremely guilty for bringing his two accomplices up here and then abandoning them. However, he didn't know what else he could do. Somehow something just felt right about him going back for the funeral. He couldn't tell if that was from the Lord or if it was his own desire to be at his friend's memorial service or perhaps his own desire for a more familiar situation. Chasing leads and snooping around a villainous cabin in the woods was not his comfort zone, whereas funerals and church events are a part of his everyday life.

Maybe Wyoming was right; maybe Jesus wanted him out of the way on this one.

Maybe there was something he needed to learn about teamwork?

Maybe he would just slow the whole operation down?

Butch worked hard to lay these doubts aside and then do the only thing he knew to do. "Before I go, I'd like to pray with you."

"I knew you were going to say that," Wyoming lamented.

> Dear God, help us make progress tomorrow.
> We need to find Tamara and it feels frustrating
> that we can't locate her. Protect Wyoming and
> Amber and help us to find the little girl. In
> Jesus' Name, Amen.

As Butch said, "Amen," Amber added a quiet "Amen." Wyoming didn't say anything, but he did nod his head. Butch saw it and thought it was the most positive thing that had happened since he'd met the man, spiritual or otherwise.

Chapter Twenty

Pioneer Square

AFTER BUTCH left, Amber and Wyoming looked at each other with a knowing grin. "There is no way I'm spending the night at the Super 8. The best plan would be to go right now. I don't want to disrespect the Reverend and all but he's got his work to do and it looks like we've got ours." Wyoming was emphatic.

"I'm glad the two of us are likeminded. Let's ditch the hotel and go now." Amber said this while pulling out her smartphone and brought up the maps app. "It looks to be about 30 minutes from here. There will be plenty of daylight left."

"Actually," Wyoming hesitated, "I was thinking about waiting until dark anyway. It would provide more cover and you can usually see inside of buildings easier at night if the lights are on."

"You're right. But I think we should go find it now, though, while it is still daytime. It gets very dark out here at night, especially out there closer to the mountains."

"I know," Wyoming replied. Amber didn't ask, but the way he said "I know" indicated that there was a story there. Maybe someday she'd ask him about it. For now though, they had work to do.

Almost 45 minutes later the two of them turned off of highway 2 down onto a side road and then they found the glorified hiking trail that led to the compound. Wyoming drove his Jeep beyond the road then u-turned and drove off into the ditch just underneath the tree line. His black Jeep was hidden very well by the setting sun combined with the deep shadows of the Cascade Mountains.

What Wyoming and Amber didn't know, however, was that inside the compound important decisions were being made.

The compound blended into the surrounding area nicely. The Hardy Plank siding was painted green with brown trim. It was a classic rambler with an elongated garage that jutted out off the side giving the whole appearance of the building an L shape. There was a great room which included a kitchen and a wet bar. Three bedrooms were on the far end opposite from the garage. The sparse décor included two full length sofas, high back chairs, folding tables with computers, filing cabinets, and a large picnic style table in the kitchen. It was a simple design, but useful.

Knuckles was there and so was Mark. Two other tall men were also present and pacing around the perimeter of the room, as if on patrol. Mark had only seen these two once or maybe twice and never in the

United States. In the far corner of the rambler's great room a man sat in the shadows. A small river of light flooded across his feet revealing expensive tan Italian leather shoes and the bottom cuff of tailor made silk trousers.

Mark had just arrived from his trip to the holding area. Knuckles sarcastically told the sad tale of misfortune that had befallen Donny. Mark was not surprised but he was worried that Knuckles might hold him accountable for Donny's failure. Mark glanced at the man in the shadows. The man who spoke nothing yet watched everything.

"Mark, you and Donny messed up real bad," Knuckles said. "Before I shot him, Donny told me there were three of them asking questions. One was a woman. I'm pretty sure it was the woman you told me about at the gas pump. I saw the man at the counter myself," Knuckles grimaced. "It is getting too crowded here. We have to lay low for a while until I can get this taken care of. That means we need to scramble. It will be my delight to take care of our troublemakers," Knuckles said this as he rubbed his head and fingered the ugly bruise on his forehead. "Mark, you take the other two and go to California and wait until I tell you what to do. Understand?"

"Yes boss. I left that little queer Jeremy at the cabin. Right now it is only me and Carl that are up here?"

"Where is Carl?"

"He is in the city," he cursed.

"Watch your language in front of the boss," Knuckles ordered. "Go get him right now, and then pick up Jeremy on your way to California." Then he snarled one last bit of instructions, "Drive straight through. Got it? No detours."

"Yes boss."

Mark tried to mask his edgy nerves as he walked outside. He'd never seen the boss so agitated or worried. Knuckles was always serious but there was an unusually troubled look on his face. Something must be wrong. And why would he tell me not to curse? Who was this boss?

Mark thought of Donny. He tried to feel better about himself because he warned Donny. What an idiot. He told himself that Donny got what he had coming.

He grabbed his travel bag out of the green van he'd taken to the holding area and loaded it into the gray minivan. Mark worked at looking confidently nonchalant as he moved his duffle from one vehicle to another because he knew that Knuckles was watching him from the window. He also knew that if Knuckles suspected any weakness at all, he very well might find a bullet in the back of his head too.

Mark thought about Carl and where he was working. Mark really hated that part of Seattle. He drove down the long driveway and out onto the road. He dreaded this turnaround so he'd try to make it quick. He sent a text message to Carl and told him to get his stuff together and that he would be there in a couple of hours.

He needed to unwind, especially with those thoughts about dumb Donny being dumped in the Puyallup River. Mark thought about stopping off at one of his favorite clubs and unwinding a bit. He deserved it. "No detours" Mark said out aloud. The privacy of the vehicle gave him the courage to mock Knuckles.

He wondered if Candi was working tonight. He really liked the way she danced.

Forget Knuckles.

He turned off onto the feeder road for Highway 2. He never saw Wyoming Wallace's Jeep parked on the side of the road.

Amber spotted the minivan.

"That's it! That's it!" she screamed and began bouncing up and down.

"I see it and I'm on it."

Wyoming followed a bit before he turned his headlights on. When the minivan turned right onto the highway he followed it.

"I wonder where this is headed?" Amber said.

"I don't know, but knowing these guys, it could be anywhere. Should we call the Reverend?" Wyoming didn't really want to call Butch, but he knew he should at least ask.

"I don't think so, Wy. If Preach knew we were out here tonight, he'd be a little upset. Besides, right now nothing has happened. We're just following this guy to see what might happen. If it turns out to be nothing, we go sleep in the lousy bed at the Super 8 and come back in the morning."

"Okay. Just thought I would check," Wyoming said happily. Amber had told him exactly what he wanted to hear.

They followed the minivan down the two lane highway as twilight turned into darkness. Wyoming and Amber almost lost the taillights in a maze of traffic revision through the small town of Monroe. When the minivan came into Everett, they followed it to a side street and a few blocks down and finally to a seedy dive called The Tropical Punch. It was a topless bar. They pulled into the parking lot and glimpsed Mark as he got out of the minivan, watched him brush his ugly red beard, hike up his pants, and put a breath mint in his mouth as he went inside.

Wyoming checked his wristwatch. It was 11:13.

"Well, I guess we wait a while. This guy apparently has some time to kill." He reached inside the middle console of his Jeep and grabbed a cellophane wrapped stogie and began the ritual of unwrapping, cutting, and lighting it. When Wyoming Wallace smoked, he thought, and it wasn't long before he cooked up a plan.

"Hey Amber, he's never seen me before," he said slowly. "Maybe I should go in and keep an eye on him, undercover style?"

"We're just fine right here, Wy. But could you crack your window if you're going to smoke that nasty death stick."

He cranked the window down but pressed the issue about his plan. "If we put one of my ball caps on you and push your pony tail through the back, he would never recognize you and we could watch him from a lot closer."

"No, we're not going in. We can wait here for him to come out. We know what he's doing in there."

Wyoming was not giving up that easy. "I'm just saying that, a pair of sunglasses would cover your face and then we could snoop around a bit just to make sure this is not a cover operation like A-Ok Mekaniks was. What if Tamara is inside of that club?"

"You're just trying to make excuses to go in there. This is not like A-OK at all because the parking lot is full of cars and we keep seeing drunk men walk in and out of that place. You want to go in there to look at the girls, don't you? You are a perv Wyoming Wallace. A Perv!"

"Why do you say that? The women in that place are mature adults who have made the decision to be entertainers. There is really no moral difference between them, and say, an actress who goes topless in a movie. Does that make every guy who has ever seen a movie with a topless woman in it a perv?"

"Maybe, but I don't like those places and I'm beginning to not like you very much either."

Wyoming Wallace applied tactics to every situation and scenario. He considered his options in between puffs. His first option was to counter-attack and say that she had no right to push her morality onto others. The second option would be to remind her that once, not too long ago, she lived a life that many would have considered perverted. A third option he considered was to tell her the stories of some of the really nice women he'd met who worked in these kinds of places in order to support children or put themselves through college.

He could also let it drop. That was his fourth and final option. He knew Amber well enough to know he would not change her mind, so he might as well let it go. So, that is what he decided to do.

A little after midnight Mark came out of the bar and climbed into the minivan. Wyoming started the Jeep but did not turn on the headlights until they came to the first traffic light. They followed the minivan out onto the side street and then on up to I-5. From there the vehicle traveled south straight toward Seattle.

"I wonder where he is going now?"

"I don't know, but keep your eyes on him. I don't want to lose him in a glowing sea of taillights." Wyoming accelerated and added, "With any luck," Wyoming tossed his stogie butt out of the window, "he is headed home. It will be very easy to apprehend him if he is at home asleep. Especially if he is as relaxed as I think he is. Notice how he keeps swerving and his speed keeps going up and down."

The minivan exited for downtown and followed the artery toward the waterfront. Wyoming followed closely down Yesler Way not far from Safeco Field and Centurylink where the professional sports teams played. The lights were still on at Safeco following a Mariner home game but the foot traffic and congestion had all dissipated. Wyoming kept pace and followed the minivan into the fringes of Pioneer Square. Mark came to a stop beside an old five story apartment building located next to two pay-by- the-hour hotels. Mark got out and waddled inside the decaying brick building, hiking up his pants.

"If this is where he lives, then crime certainly doesn't pay. But I doubt he lives here," Wyoming mumbled as he drove past Mark's minivan and then parked in an adjacent alley.

"Me too, Wy. So what do you think he's up to?"

"My guess would be that he is either dropping something off, picking something up, or picking someone up. Do you have that pistol I gave you?"

"Yes. Why?"

"I want you to stand outside the building. I'm going inside. If he comes out, he'll probably be running. Stop him. It might get dangerous. Don't shoot him, though, unless he attacks you."

"I can take care of myself, thank you very much."

"Fine, but we'd better hurry."

Wyoming jumped out of the Jeep, which was parked a block away and briskly walked to the apartment building. Amber followed. He cautiously pushed against the graffiti covered wooden door and entered the crumbling monument to urban decay. Amber stood on the street just outside the door.

An old light fixture, so old that in another venue it might be considered vintage, glimmered as it hung from the ceiling all the way down to the main lobby. The chandelier barely lit the stairway which wound up around the outside edges of the five floors. Wyoming strained his eyes upward looking for potential enemies but all he could spy was water stained tiles on the ceiling at the top of the fifth level.

When he reached the third floor he became aware of angry voices above him in the stairwell.

His target had gone up to the fifth floor.

He slowly walked up each step. He did not pull his gun because he knew that his prey had never seen him before. He might have more of an element of surprise if he just approached. The problem for Wyoming Wallace was that he didn't know how many people were up there or what weapons they might have.

The voices got louder, and Wyoming could make out the conversation.

"I told you to be ready, man! Do you think I texted you for my health?" someone yelled. Wyoming guessed it was the driver of the minivan that was yelling.

"Don't make the same mistake Donny made. We don't fire people from this job. People get dead when they don't do right, huh? Do you want to end up like him? I didn't think so. We're supposed to be on our way south right now, but now I've got to sit heres and wait for your sorry behind."

South. Every one of these bad guys is captivated by the compass. Why didn't he say where? Keep talking—where are you going exactly?

"I know Mark," said a much weaker and younger second voice. "But I was with Tina, man, you know how it is. I just now got back from where she stays. Give me just a minute and I'll be ready."

"One minute and then we go."

Wyoming decided this was his opportunity. It sounded like there were only two of them and he already despised the loud-mouthed one who kept cursing. His best chance to get a handle on the situation was to act while they were separated. He pulled out his .45 and snuck up the stairs behind Mark. Fortunately, Mark was so preoccupied with his cell phone that he never heard Wyoming come from behind and knock him in the back of his head with the butt of his pistol. The fat man collapsed to the floor. Carl came out of the room with an overstuffed canvas bag and was stunned by the sight of Mark lying on the ground at Wyoming's feet.

Wyoming pointed his pistol at Carl and said slowly and seriously, "Get down on the ground. Put your hands behind your back and I promise not to kill you." Wyoming took care that he didn't promise not to not hurt him.

Carl raised his arms slowly and then heaved his duffle bag at Wyoming and ran back into his room. Wyoming followed right behind him and crashed into the small framed man and brought him to the ground. The two wrestled on the nasty sofa in the middle of the apartment. The room smelled of drugs and human filth.

The apartment looked as if this was not the first time people had fought here.

The two men traded blows on the ground and then both managed to find their feet. Carl lunged at Wyoming and trapped against the wall, near an open window. It was clear to Wyoming that the other man intended to push him out the window. However, Wyoming repelled the attack and pushed him away. Carl lunged at him again, but this time with a knife.

Where did the knife come from? He didn't want to hurt the kid.

Nevertheless, instinct entered into Wyoming's mind as well as years of training. When Carl lunged out of control toward the experienced soldier with his right hand, Wyoming automatically stepped around the lunge to his left, grabbed the skinny boy's arm and as a reflex forced it back toward Carl's own throat and jabbed the knife right into his jugular. The young boy collapsed. It happened so fast that Wyoming couldn't stop the flow of impulses and the firing of neurons that were programmed responses to danger.

Dangit! I didn't mean to do that.

Well, at least there is still the fat one.

But Mark was standing in the doorway when he turned to leave the apartment, and he had seen what happened. In a fit of fury Mark screamed and then charged straight toward Wyoming Wallace. Wyoming moved out of the way of the coming charge, but Mark was so large and still feeling the liquor he'd drank at the bar that he couldn't bring himself to stop in time. He tumbled right out of the opened window and fell head first to the pavement five stories below, screaming the most vulgar profanity all the way down until the cement silenced him forever.

Double dangit!

Mark's obese frame landed about 10 feet from where Amber was standing. She looked up and shook her head. A minute later Wyoming Wallace came out of the building with a freshly lit cigar in his mouth.

"Grab his cell phone and his wallet, I'll check his minivan," Wyoming said. "The other guy only had a wallet with cash in it. No I.D. and no phone."

"There was another one? My, you're efficient. Two kills in five minutes or less."

"Actually, about 5 seconds apart. Not according to plan, though."

Amber looked inside the dead man's back pocket and took his wallet then strained as she rolled him over. She recognized him. He was the one she saw at the gas pump at the Skookum Quickie Mart back in Sydney. Wyoming Wallace opened the unlocked minivan and searched for anything useful. There was a Glock in the glove box which he thought about taking, but decided not to. It was probably stolen and likely a weapon for who knows how many crimes. The vehicle was filled with trash—empty soda cups, chips, candy, and adult magazines. He spotted a large duffle bag in the back seat. Wyoming hastily grabbed it and hopped into his own Jeep.

"I'll call the police," said Amber as she whipped out her phone.

"No, don't do that! If you call the police, then Butch's friend, the Lady Suit, will pay him another visit. Besides, there is a dead body on the sidewalk. Even the Seattle Police can figure that one out. Fortunately, no one saw us so we are pretty safe but soon someone is going to find Mark over there, so we do need to go."

"Where are we going?"

He took a puff on his stogie, cranked the jeep, smiled and said, "To our luxurious Super 8, of course."

Chapter Twenty-One

Remembrance

THE COFFIN that held the body of Lester Wooley lay before Pastor Butch Gregory as he stood underneath the makeshift green awning and on top of the green carpet placed over the plywood that was covering the hole dug six feet into the ground. Pastor Philip had just welcomed the guests and begun the service with the standard funeral texts that Butch taught him when he first came on staff. Philip started by quoting Jesus from the Fourth Gospel.

> I am Resurrection and I am Life, says the Lord.
> Whoever has faith in me shall have life,
> even though he die.
> And everyone who has life,
> and has committed himself to me in faith,
> Shall not die for ever.

Then he very skillfully transitioned to the words of Job from the Hebrew Bible. Philip drew the connection between the long term pain that Job suffered and the lengthy illness Lester Wooley had suffered.

> As for me, I know that my Redeemer lives
> and that at the last he will stand upon the earth.
> After my awaking, he will raise me up;
> and in my body I shall see God.
> I myself shall see, and my eyes behold him
> who is my friend and not a stranger.

Finally Philip finished the trinity of texts with Paul's words from the book of Romans. Philip reminded the mourners that these word teach the reality of death and that even in death, every Christ-follower belongs to the Lord in a special way just as every soul in general belongs to the Lord.

> For none of us has life in himself,
> and none becomes his own master when he dies.
> For if we have life, we are alive in the Lord,
> and if we die, we die in the Lord.
> So, then, whether we live or die,
> we are the Lord's possession.

When he finished these words of comfort, Pastor Philip prayed. While Philip prayed, Butch's mind wandered to the words Shark had given him. He had studied them so much by now they were etched in his mind.

Not in the forest, but near the sea
the little girl waits in uncertainty.
You must travel through woods and sky,
and in the desert eyes should pry.
On your search there will be three;
one to die, one to cry, one to see.

He wondered if Lester was the fulfillment of Shark's prophecy. He had died, and that death had caused a hiccup in the investigation. It was possible that hiccup was God's plan all along to get the case solved. Lester died, and maybe Tamara is the one who cries and perhaps he was the one who needed to see.

See what?

He had gotten comfortable with the idea that the three in the limerick referred to Wyoming, Amber and him. One of them would die. As a theologian, though, he was keenly aware of how easy it was to misread something that was intentionally vague and not always as clear as it might seem. Butch was fond of pointing out the millions of people who, throughout history, have thought they understood prophetic oracles perfectly and had figured out exactly when the world was to end, only to be very disappointed that they were wrong. Maybe he was wrong too. Maybe no one would have to die, other than Lester, and he was already very ill. Maybe this moment was the fulfillment of what Shark had promised him.

Maybe.

He hoped so.

The prayer was over now and a hymn had begun. A woman from church struggled as she sang "In The Garden." The older folks really loved that hymn. Butch did too, but as the woman garbled it, he kept thinking about Shark. Shark died in the backyard of his childhood home, which was a type of garden. Why didn't God come to their garden then and save his baby brother? That was a question he'd been asking since he was 12 years old. He relived the moment often in his mind. Each time in his memories Butch acts quickly enough to save his kid brother. In each memory he is fast enough and strong enough and wise enough to save him.

The woman continues to sing and Butch looks to his left and there is a tree in the cemetery. The tree is eerily similar to that tree, the painful tree from his past. As Butch listens to the tones of the woman singing and sees the tree he feels himself no longer at the graveside.

Now he is in his backyard. He is a kid again and he is with Shark, who is 10 years old. The boys have climbed the tree. They have climbed far too high into the tree. Butch knows that if his father sees them, he will punish both of them, but mostly him for being the oldest and who should know better. But the tree is tall and it begs to be climbed all the way to the top. The treetop screams for the brothers to conquer it.

"Hurry up Butchy, or I'll beat you to the top." His brother always challenges him.

"Oh no you don't. Not this time Shark," says Butch as he reaches for a limb above his head.

The two boys climb and climb, higher and higher.

From the tip top of the tree's uppermost bough Butch surveys almost the whole town. He sees the school playground and the steeple for Holy Fatima Catholic Church. Just beyond that the downtown drag is before his eyes: First National Bank with the clock in the gable, the Fred Meyer grocery store, and Mr. Longmire's lumber yard. He enjoys the view and momentarily pretends he is a scout for a distant king spying out enemy territory. Shark, on the other hand, doesn't care about the view. He loves to play on the limbs. He jumps from limb to limb with the agility of a chimpanzee.

"Hey Butchy, watch this!" Shark swings upside down with his knees cupping over the tree limb. "You're upside down Butchy! The tree is upside down. The whole world is upside down."

It was just then that Butch thinks he hears a crack, but he ignores it. Now a few moments later, he hears another crack and glances over in time to see the limb splinter and then it snaps. The limb does not break completely, but jostles enough to cause Shark to lose his balance and fall. If Shark sits on the limb, like Butch does, a broken leg or broken arm with maybe a concussion is all that happens.

But Shark hangs from the limb upside down, so he falls head first all the way to the bottom. Butch reaches out, but he is unable to catch him. Just before landing, Shark looks up at his brother and makes eye contact. The gaze is only a fraction of a second, but it haunts Butch Gregory from that moment on; for the rest of his life.

When Shark hits the ground his neck breaks and he dies before Butch can shimmy clumsily down the tree.

The song ended.

Pastor Philip was now up talking again and Butch heard the introduction, "Pastor Butch has come in from a special project he is working on just to share some words with us today." With that Butch stood up, focused on what he was doing and tried to leave the backyard and Shark behind for a moment. He took a deep breath to shake it off just before he began.

"Lester Wooley was my friend and my co-laborer in Christ. He was one of the first people I learned that I could unconditionally trust when I came to Sydney. The reason I could trust him in that way was because he was honest and simple. I knew that Lester was never duplicitous and that he was never scheming or plotting, but Lester was not a perfect man. He had his faults and troubles just like everyone else. Nevertheless, he tried to always be and do better. He was simple, in a good way. He was kind, to everyone. He was filled with integrity and purity.

"Most of you already know that. But you might not know, and I would never say this publicly or even privately to anyone while he was alive, but Lester Wooley was also very generous. When Jane was still alive, she and Lester would regularly have me over for coffee at the house and ask me, 'Is there anything going on at church that might need a little extra cash?'

"I can't tell you how much carpet, paint, and audio-visual equipment those two bought over the years because it is beyond my memory. This morning, though, I did some simple math and calculated that in the past ten years alone they have given over $15,000 to send kids to camp alone. That is a lot of sunburns and t-shirts. The reason they did this was not just because they had the money or they were generous at heart. The reason they did it was because they loved the Lord and they loved his church and they loved his people. Lester and Jane valued community.

"When Jane died it was very hard on Lester. That is when he and I started getting together about once a month for pie. He loved pie, especially chocolate pie, any kind of chocolate pie. Except, one time I took him to a fancy place and made him try tiramisu. He did not like it at all. So we never tried anything else like that. Eventually our monthly meetings turned into weekly meetings, until the last month or so when he became so weak.

"The last meaningful conversation I had with him was during the most recent stint he had at the care center; we talked there in his room. He hated the care center. Not because of anything about it in particular, it's just that he loved his own home so much and being apart from it troubled him. His memories were at home. That is where he and Jane had lived for decades. I'm glad that he went home from the care center and was able to spend another week or so at home before he took this turn for the worse.

"But there at his bedside we talked about his home, his real home in heaven. Honestly, he was eager to go. His body was wretchedly sick and he was extremely miserable. I know that he is there now, in heaven, with Jane and with his own parents and with all of the believers in Christ who have gone on before us.

"He is in heaven with Christ the Lord. For now, I shall miss Lester and I shall miss his sincere handshake, his warm smile, his open heart, and his critique on pie and pie crust. In the meantime, I know for certain that I shall have him forever in eternity."

With that, Pastor Butch Gregory stepped aside and gestured with his hand to Pastor Philip. Philip stepped forward, at the head of the coffin and began to give the funeral sermon itself. Butch had taught Philip that a good funeral sermon was generic in nature. It needed to apply to anyone being buried. The funeral sermon needed to address the surety of death, the grief of people, and the doctrine of Christian hope found in the resurrection of Christ and the promise of heaven. Anything less than that, Butch believed, was just pop psychology on one hand or overzealous evangelistic enthusiasm on the other. He despised both.

As Philip talked, Butch's mind retreated back to thoughts about Shark and the tree and the riddle. He thought about the readings which had begun the graveside funeral. Paul's letter to the Romans says that whether we live or die we are the Lord's. Shark died, Butch lived, and they both belonged to the Lord. Somehow, the Lord was using both Shark and Butch to help Tamara, because they all belonged to the Lord, both the living and the dead.

There was a connection in there somewhere. The call of Jesus is to believe, and belief is a form of spiritual sight, then Job's suffering and pain is understood as tears combined with Paul's outright admission that death is in the Lord's hands—it all fits together somehow. Butch thought about it. What is the connection? Butch could feel there was something the Lord was telling him in this moment, but he just couldn't figure it out. There is a connection.

But the connection was lost. It was one of those moments Butch had from time to time when it seems like clarity is about to come and everything will somehow make sense but then it flitters away. This was one of those moments. So many huge issues about life, death, relationship, the future and the past seem to be connected in a way that is tangible and meaningful but making the connection is just beyond his grasp. It is the limits of the human mind that betray and prohibit the realization of ontological enlightenment.

Pastor Philip brought the sermon to completion and now he was praying again.

Someday he would be in a coffin too. Would that day be soon?

Then the prayer ended and a sailor from the United States Navy sounded Taps in the distance on a lonely bugle. As the somber and meaningful notes echoed, Butch Gregory began to cry. Emotion swelled within him. He did not cry for Lester. He did not cry for Shark. He did not cry for Tamara. He cried for all of them, for all of it, for how he had let them all down.

At the conclusion two other sailors, a man and a woman, both in dress uniforms, folded the flag which was draped over the coffin and presented it to Lester's oldest daughter on behalf of the President of the United States. The daughter cried tears of regret and panic. The other daughter, the younger one, the good daughter, sat to the right of the older one. The younger daughter, named Nancy, cried tears of sorrow as one tells a loved one goodbye. Her tears were not the tears of selfish panic and regret.

Butch felt shame because his tears were selfish tears.

Chapter Twenty-Two

Revelation

"YOU DID what?" Butch Gregory was listening to Wyoming's recitation of the events of the last eighteen hours. He was just now to the part where Wyoming killed the young one named Carl.

"Why did you do that?"

"Well, it wasn't exactly like I did it on purpose. He attacked me with a knife."

"What about the other one, the one Amber saw the night of the abduction, at the gas station. Where do you have him right now?"

"Uh," Amber hesitated.

"Why do I think I'm not going to like this?"

"Uh, he's in a safe place," said Amber.

"Yeah, a safe, refrigerated, dark place," Wyoming said. "It's called the Seattle City Morgue." He chuckled at his own joke and then added, "of course, hellfire and damnation is probably where he really is, if you believe in that sort of thing."

Butch shook his head at Wyoming and threw his hands up. "Look, I told the FBI agent that we would not go around killing people. Oh dear. This is bad, this is very, very bad."

Butch took another bite of his sandwich. Lucy served them a lunch of tuna salad on toast, sliced carrot sticks, potato chips, and home baked chocolate chip cookies which she piled high on a glass charger in concentric circles. The warm cookies were stacked in the middle ringed by individual bags of chips which followed into a ring of carrot sticks and then the sandwiches, which were cut into triangle halves and stacked on the outer rim all the way around the serving platter. A pitcher of fresh iced tea beaded sweat beside the serving dish alongside a small French press carafe of Starbucks Italian roast coffee.

Lester Wooley's family had invited Butch and Lucy to the reception in Lester's honor back at the church, but he'd declined. He was anxious to get back on the investigation. His plans were to change clothes quickly, grab a bite to eat and then drive to Everett and meet up with Amber and Wyoming. They, however, were waiting on him when he got home. Now he was learning why they were back so soon.

Amber and Wyoming both knew what question was coming next.

"What about the compound? Did you find anything out at the compound? Please tell me you did."

Amber started, "After we finished in Pioneer Square, we went out to the Super 8 and got some sleep. At about 7 we drove to the compound again. There were no vehicles parked out front and no one answered the door when we knocked. We had decided that our cover story would be we were from a local church trying to invite people to Sunday School. We figured this would work because no one who had seen us was still alive."

Amber fidgeted and looked down as she said this because it only capitalized the fact everyone they had tried to keep alive had come to an abrupt end.

In Amber's pause Wyoming finished the story, "Since no one answered, we just helped ourselves inside. There was no one there. There were computer monitors and keyboards, but no hard drives. The filing cabinets were cleaned out, and even the food was all gone. The place was evacuated. It is obvious they were trying to clear out because they knew things were getting tight up here.

"I've been piecing things together and from what I overheard from the two men in the stairs, the one named Mark and that other guy, I think they are all bugging out. You can bet an operation like this has multiple places to go hide. That is where they were headed. Like cockroaches they run when the light is turned on. Reverend, we may have already lost our opportunity to get Tamara back. We scared them out too soon."

The pastor objected, "No, we still have time. I know that."

"How can you know that, Reverend?" Wyoming looked him square in the eyeballs with an intensity that startled Butch. "That is twice," Wyoming's speech slowed again and he repeated the near accusation, "that is twice you've seemed to know something we don't know about this. Don't you think it's high time you put all your cards on the table?"

"I just know. Maybe I'll tell you how I know in a minute? Did you find anything else, anything at all?"

"Yes. We did get Mark's cell phone," Wyoming said.

"Great. That is the first good news you've brought."

"But it smashed when it, along with its owner, hit the ground real hard," Amber said this as she hit the table with her hand to simulate Mark's fall.

"Oh."

"We also got his duffle bag. But there was only dirty underwear and clothes, a bottle of whiskey, a pocketknife, and candy in it. I kept the whiskey, unless you want it. It was Canadian. I threw the clothes and candy away and I gave the knife to Amber to replace the blade she broke down at the A-OK. It seemed fitting, ya know.

"These guys travel light, very light. It is on purpose too. I suspect the only one who really knows all the moving pieces and how all the dots connect is the boss Donny was talking about. And the boss," Wyoming looked at Butch and grinned, "is probably that Knuckles guy you whacked in the head with the battery in Tacoma." He stroked his beard. "Had knuckles been only an underling he would not have come back and cleaned up the way he did."

Butch Gregory wiped his mouth and said, "You are probably right," and then he clasped his hands together on the table and his demeanor turned very serious. "Listen, I'm sorry I got upset earlier. It's just this is so foreign to me. I've spent my life trying to help people, not hurt people and, I don't know, this just feels odd. My world has been turned upside down all over again."

At that moment Butch's wife came into the dining room with a large ceramic bowl filled with sliced cantaloupe, watermelon, and pineapple. Lucy placed the bowl on top of the now empty charger in the middle of the table and then she sat down on the side of the table opposite her husband and looked at him.

Wyoming looked at Lucy and then at Butch and said, "I know this is hard for you Reverend. You are a man of peace, but maybe this is why God has me and Amber in this. This world is filled with terrible people who, quite honestly, need to die. That is why there are people like me. I have read the Bible, you know, and there are people like me in it too, who take care of evil people."

"Speaking of God," the pastor said, "maybe I should let you guys know why I am certain that we have more time to find Tamara and that it is not too late."

"Yeah, that would be good," Amber said and Wyoming agreed.

"Amber, the night before you came to see me in my office I sat here at this table and had a conversation with my brother, Shark."

"I didn't know you had a brother?" Amber looked confused.

"I do, I mean, I did. He died when we were boys."

"So you have a brother in heaven too?"

"Yes, and he spoke to me. I can't explain it, but he sat here and told me that the Lord wanted me to find Tamara because the police were not able to do the things we could do to find her. He told me we had ten days to find her. That was four days ago. So we still have six days."

Butch sipped his cup of coffee and took a bite of cookie as he gathered his thoughts.

"When Shark was talking to me, he also gave me a riddle, or a prophecy, or something that he said described what would happen. He said:

Not in the forest, but near the sea
the little girl waits in uncertainty.
You must travel through woods and sky,
and in the desert eyes should pry.
On your search there will be three;
one to die, one to cry, one to see.

I've been thinking about that for a while. We've tried the forest. That is what the compound was all about. For some reason I knew she wouldn't be there, but Henry seemed to think it was a good lead. Guys, from the way I understand it, one of us might die doing this. If you want out, I understand. But I have to continue on. You've both been a tremendous help. But I've got to keep looking. I have to."

"Could you repeat that again?" Amber asked. "I didn't quite get it. In fact, do you have some paper and a pencil?"

"Sure," said Butch. He took a quick sip of the coffee again then got up, walked out to his study which was on the other side of the house.

Amber looked at Wyoming and said, "Wy, that sounds pretty weird."

"I've heard weirder." Wyoming Wallace didn't volunteer anything more.

Amber didn't catch the tone, but Lucy Gregory, however, heard Wyoming's emotion and realized something else was going on inside the tough guy. She spotted a crack in Wyoming Wallace's armor. Lucy read people and their emotions like others read novels.

Butch returned with a sheet of yellow legal paper and the words were already written on it. Amber folded the paper and stuck it in one of the many pockets on her cargo style pants.

Wyoming Wallace said, "Reverend, as long as you are in this, so am I. I don't quit, and someone has got to find that girl. I would though, like to spend some time with Jennifer, get a hot shower and sleep in my own bed tonight. I also would like to think a little more about what to do next." He continued explaining, slowly, "One of the things I learned in the military is, that it is just as important to plan and think as it is to act. Mistakes happen and people get hurt when everything hasn't been thought through. I know you want to be out doing something—beating down doors and calling for Tamara, but right now we've got to regroup and figure out what is next. We've chased two leads and now we need to process what is, exactly, our next move."

Amber nodded agreement and said, "Yeah, I have an idea or two as well." She didn't say it, but she thought about talking to Janet a little more. "Plus," she chimed in, "we should probably take the evening off and see what comes up."

"That is an excellent idea," said Lucy, as she winked at Butch.

Before they left, Butch suggested they have a prayer. They bowed their heads.

> Lord, we've chased our leads and we don't know where to go next. We've tried to do what you told us to, but we're at a dead end. Please help us help Tamara. Show us what to do and we will do it. Protect us; and help us live long enough to complete the work you've laid out for us. In Jesus' name. Amen.

Wyoming and Amber both added, "Amen."

When Butch's two partners left Lucy Gregory told Butch some of the things she learned from her reading of Mr. Wyoming Wallace.

Chapter Twenty-Three

The Sydney Diner

"I FOUND something," said Amber's text message to both Butch and Wyoming. It was followed immediately by a second text.

mt in 1 hr for brkfst at sdy dnr. C U then.

Butch put down his iPhone. He'd already been awake for a couple of hours. He made coffee at about 5, then he read his Bible and prayed. He prayed for Wyoming to quit killing people off. He prayed for Tamara to have strength to persevere until she was found. He prayed for guidance. He gave thanks, again, for the life of Lester Wooley. He prayed for Amber. This must all be hard for her. He prayed for Philip and the church. Most of all he prayed for Lucy, Paul and Sarah. They were so great, putting up with him.

He had just crawled back into his bed with his wife when the text came.

"Who and what was that?" Lucy rolled over as she groggily asked the question.

"Amber. She said she found something and wants to meet in an hour. That's what, eight o'clock?"

"Oh. I was just getting comfortable," she winked. "Surely you have a few moments for your poor, neglected wife." She grinned, paused, and playfully asked, "Is the door shut?"

"Does a pastor give to missions?" he said and pulled the cover over them and then leaned in to give Lucy a soft kiss as they shared a few tender moments in the early morning.

An hour later Butch was showered and refreshed as he hopped into his Honda and made the 3 minute drive to the Sydney Diner. Over the years, beginning long before Pastor Butch arrived in Sydney, the Sydney Diner had evolved into an unofficial annex to the church building. Many church budgets had been first etched on napkins laid out onto the yellowing tables, and more than a few building improvements were diagrammed using the Diner's ketchup, mustard, and sugar bins. The food was not great but it was good and cheap while the coffee was plentiful. The IHOP and Denny's were located out on the freeway, but the old downtown mainstay is where locals ate their eggs, drowned their fries, and chomped their Monday meatloaf. At the Sydney Diner you were sure to bump into someone you knew.

Butch was hungry before he arrived, but as he walked in through the rickety front door and smelled the familiar aroma of eggs, bacon, and biscuits his hunger grew. His team was already in a booth across the room alongside a window facing the parking lot. They sat underneath a framed oversized antique print of Sydney from the 1890's. Amber ate a bowl of raisin and brown sugar oatmeal and Wyoming Wallace had a Western styled omelet with home fries, ham, peppers and onions splayed out before him, all drenched in Tabasco sauce.

The server greeted him with a familiar, "Good morning Pastor Butch."

"Good morning Joann," he replied as he walked to the booth. She followed him to his table where he sat down beside Wyoming Wallace, directly opposite of Amber Smith. The server turned his coffee mug upright and poured him a cup and then topped off the other two.

Butch looked up at the overly friendly server and said, "I'd like the special—but I want both sausage and bacon, and rye toast. I'd like my eggs over easy."

"Both bacon and sausage, why Pastor Butch you're living dangerously. Anything else?""Yeah, I'd also like a glass of orange juice too."

"Got it. You two need anything?" she asked but they waved her off.

After Joann walked away from the table Wyoming told Butch, "We've got to go to Nevada."

"Isn't Nevada your brother? Nevada Wallace?"

Amber giggled, recalling Butch's confusion when she had first introduced him to Wy, then she chirped up, "No, Preach, Nevada, as in state of. It is where we need to go next."

"What's in Nevada?"

"Sin, Reverend; lots of it. Amber thinks somewhere in Nevada might be where they hold the kids they abduct. There is a lot of wide open, unregulated, unpatrolled space there." His speech slowed down and Wyoming ran his left hand through his curly hair, which was enjoying rare exposure out from underneath the usual ball cap. "There is also a population of people who have learned over the years to not ask too many questions."

Butch felt himself sick to his stomach at the implications of what Wyoming was saying in the context of their current odyssey. He wondered if he'd be able to eat his breakfast.

Amber picked up from there and continued the briefing. "I talked to a friend of mine late last night, a girl named Lacy. She told me that she'd walked with a couple of girls who had come out of Nevada. Their story sounds a lot like Tamara—snatched right off the street and hauled off to work as slaves for pimps. To make a long story short, Lacy made a few contacts through the night with these old colleagues and got me a description of a place outside of Vegas that might be where Tamara is, was, or might be. There are no promises, but it is a good lead." Amber didn't tell him that she used some of Knuckles cash to pay two months of Lacy's rent, which in turn jogged her memory and loosened her lips.

"Good work Amber," said Butch as he sipped the hot coffee. "When do we leave?"

"Well, that's just it, Preach. I found out from a guy I used to know on the streets that there is also a place, a cabin or a hideout down in Oregon somewhere just as the Siskiyous begin that is used by a rival organization to his. He says that is where they hold girls until they can be processed or sorted out. I knew that it was bad, Preach," she said as she took another bite of her oatmeal, "but I didn't know it was this bad. From what I have been able to learn, these people are as methodical and businesslike as any computer manufacturer or retail manager. They view children as merchandise. It's the most immoral kind of capitalism imaginable. They store them in a central location until they have orders to fill, then they are sent out like cargo from the warehouse to the sales floor. What we need to do is find out which one of these places, Nevada or Oregon, is the place where Tamara has been taken."

Butch drank his coffee. Wyoming did the same.

"Here's your special, Pastor," the server broke the silent contemplation. She brought out two plates. The larger plate had three eggs, hash browns, and toast while the smaller plate held two strips of bacon and two strips of sausage. "I'll bring your OJ out in a sec."

"Thank you."

"Need anything else?"

"No, we're good."

A hasty but sincere blessing was made over Butch's breakfast and he began to butter his toast. As he peppered his eggs the pastor asked, "Well, do we go to Nevada first or do we do Oregon first?" He chewed his bacon. "Actually, if we drive we can probably cover both by cutting across southern Oregon into Nevada and drive past Reno and on down to Vegas on highway 95." Butch was familiar with most of the major highways in the west as he'd traveled to various denominational meetings and conferences over the years. Butch always thought it was ironic that Las Vegas is a popular church convention location because the rooms are so much cheaper by comparison to other meeting spots. Church leaders hated the sin aspect that subsidized such low-cost arrangements, but desire for a bargain always outweighs any righteous indignation when making block hotel reservations, booking airline tickets, and negotiating conference rebates.

"Well," Amber said, "what we're worried about is that if we show up in Oregon and its mostly empty we might just spook them again, the same we did here with A-OK Mekaniks or the compound out by Everett in Snohomish. That would ruin things in Nevada before we ever have a chance to get there. Of course, the flip side is true too; if the real deal is in Oregon but we go to Nevada first, then we might scare them away. Wyoming and I have been talking about it, and he thinks we need to find a way to hit both sites at the same time. At least that is the way I understand it, right Wy?"

"Absolutely. An ideal offensive is one that confronts the enemy on two different fronts and is timed to be synchronized." There was a glimmer of giddiness in Wyoming's eyes as he spoke. It was apparent that, even though he embodied a hard-as-nails persona, Wyoming's real passion was tactics and strategy. "We've got to find a way to be in place and spring on both locations at the same time. That is what Amber and I decided just before you arrived. What we haven't decided yet is who will go where. Since there are three of us, that means someone will be alone. I figured that the two of you should head to Oregon and I can take care of Nevada by myself."

"The problem with that," said Butch, "is that it is not a good idea for Amber and me to be on an extended road trip together. It just doesn't and wouldn't look right."

Amber smiled at the old-fashioned integrity of their partner in mischief.

Wyoming swore under his breath, "Why not?"

"Because it just wouldn't be right."

"Look, if you want to be a superhero, you're going to have to get over some of your simplistic views about the way the world works. The plan comes before any prudish church-law you're worried about. If you want to save that little girl, you're going to have to get over yourself and focus on the task at hand, not your image. Do you understand me?" Wyoming was getting hot under the collar; so his speech, in contrast to the normal slow delivery, had accelerated to a point of near incomprehension.

Butch was amazed at the irate tone in Wyoming's voice. Yesterday afternoon he had been almost sympathetic to Butch's situation.

What changed?

Maybe Jesus was working on Wyoming and changing his heart, and this was about his old temperament trying to reassert itself. Always the pastor, Butch measured his reply to accommodate whatever spiritual activity was going on in Wyoming's heart and answered him with a genuine softness. "I understand you, but Wyoming, this is not negotiable. I'd rather risk my life by going alone than risk my integrity."

"Oh for crying-out-loud this is getting us nowhere." Wyoming's face was screwing into an angry expression and his voice was getting louder. "You know what; I think I just might let you solve this whole thing on your own then. I don't care what God or some godlike spirit might or might not have told me. Maybe I imagined the whole thing anyway. But I do know that I'm not going to let the mission parameters be dictated by a Sunday School teacher."

Gotcha! Lucy was right. What did the Lord tell you Wyoming?

"Wait a minute boys," Amber spoke up. "I want to go to Oregon by myself. I've got a friend who lives in Eugene and from there it is just a couple of hours to where this cabin is supposedly located. The two of you can drive to Nevada. I say we use the rest of the morning to pack up and gas up and then meet at 2 PM. The two of you can leave, because your trip will take much longer, and I can leave in the morning. That way, we'll both be in place to pretty much spring at the same time."

"Blessed are the peacemakers," Butch said, "For they shall be called the children of God. I like your idea Amber, but since the trip to Nevada is so much longer, how about Wyoming and I fly and rent a car."

"I like the sound of that, Reverend. I hate long road trips." Butch was relieved to see that the flare up had seemed to abate.

"I'll buy us tickets later this morning and we can leave tomorrow. Amber, you should drive on down this afternoon to Oregon. Spend the night with your friend in Eugene and then tomorrow morning we'll both be in position. Once we're in place we'll contact you; then we will, uh, how do you phrase it, move-out, I guess, at the same time."

Wyoming smiled. "Move-in, not move-out. Move-out is when you're leaving a theater of operations. Move-in is when you're about to start trouble for someone else. Tomorrow we are purposefully and definitely initiating and engaging in conflict, so that is a move-in. But you're getting the hang of this operations talk. We'll make a hard nose out of you yet. Just don't talk about Christmas trees or Christmas presents anymore." Wyoming's joke signaled that the squabble was officially over by patting Butch Gregory on the back.

They spent the next few minutes planning all the details. Amber brought a map of Oregon and showed Butch and Wyoming exactly where the location of the suspected holding area was. It was located south of Medford, almost to the California border. The map showed that there was only one road in and it looked very remote.

For the Vegas trip there was far less certainty. All Amber had was a general area, not a specific address. Amber's contact only described the location as where two roads intersect. Amber didn't even have the name of the roads, just that it was 30 miles north of Las Vegas off of a highway near where two dirt roads meet. Fortunately, though, the description of the place was very detailed: A single wide trailer on a plot of land just over a ridge with an old blue cement truck parked out front.

"Well, it's not much to go on," said Wyoming, "but at least it is something. I don't think we'll have too much trouble scoping out the area. Nevada is a big and vacant desert, but you can see for a long way off." Then he somberly added with his usual deliberate tone, "And, be seen from a long, long way off."

"Yeah, I know," said Butch. "I hate Nevada. I've driven through there several times and can find no redeeming quality about it. The whole place smells like a cigarette, tastes like dirt, looks like Jezebel, and sounds like a slot machine. It is a society of sin unto itself; a place where the most disgusting and base of human behavior is tolerated as normal—no, not tolerated, celebrated." Pastor Butch tossed his hands into the air as he thought about the wasteland he was about to travel to.

Wyoming glanced sideways at the pastor. "You are looking at it the wrong way. In a place like that you'd have job security preaching against sin. I've seen Vegas up close and personal; the people there are not evil, Reverend. They are just people trying to get by. Most of them are trapped, really." Wyoming slowed, "Somehow they got stuck there, like a fly stuck in a car or a cat stuck in a tree. They're just trapped." He reflected for a moment and then added, "In many ways most of them are a lot like Tamara—stuck somewhere they don't want to be but can't really get out, don't know how to get out or too proud to ask for help to get out. Some of 'em have been lied to and promised the moon and still hold out hope that things will just turn around or that someday their luck will change. Shoot, I guess they are a lot like most people. What is it, that saying or that quote," Wyoming hesitated, "was it Thoreau, 'most people live their lives in quiet desperation.' That is Las Vegas, desperate people, and that is life."

Amber was listening to this whole conversation and she could see that Wyoming was starting to get serious. So could Butch, but the mood was quickly broken. A man whom Amber did not know came and plopped down right beside her in the booth. He looked at Butch and said, "Hi Pastor." Butch replied with a grimace, "Hi Tommy."

Butch then introduced the man to Amber and Wyoming. "This is Tommy Bothers, he is a member of our church."

"Well, I'd say more than just a member, Pastor," he swelled with pride and physically puffed out his chest as he announced, "I pass out the bulletins on Sunday morning."

Butch corrected himself saying, "That's right. Tommy is the lead bulletin passer-outer for Sunday morning worship services. The whole church would fall apart if Tommy Bothers was not there to pass out the bulletins."

Tommy had such an inflated view of himself he didn't quite perceive Butch was engaging in sarcasm. Tommy was in his early 40's, well dressed, and spoke in such a way that his nose tilted up ever-so-slightly when he finished a sentence. It was with this certain demeanor of superiority that Tommy began to speak.

"I heard about what you're doing, Pastor Butch. Me and my daddy were talking about it and we think you are a fool. You and these two misfits, no insult intended, do not have any chance of finding that little girl. She could be anywhere, or nowhere by now. She's probably been cut into a hundred little pieces and thrown somewhere into the bowels of Puget Sound. You are just wasting precious time—God's time, that is. Your job is to take care of the church and take care of us, not to go gallivanting around beating bushes and tramping hedges and chasing windmills. This is ridiculous. Besides, I've heard you will not even be at the Annual Missionary Tea next week. What kind of a pastor doesn't go to the Missionary Tea? That has upset my dear sweet precious mother quite a bit, knowing that her pastor is skipping the Missionary Tea. She is just heartbroken over your lack of priorities. She told me yesterday that it will be the first time in 47 years that the pastor of Sydney Community has not been there to give the invocation for the Missionary Tea. I tell you, Butch Gregory, you've got a lot to learn about how church works and what really matters in this world. My daddy is thinking about bringing it up at the next meeting and having you disciplined for dereliction of duty. Mother has already written a strongly worded letter to the district supervisor. You will be called on the carpet for this rash, childish behavior. There will be a day of reckoning. Mark my words—you'll regret this."

If this had happened a week earlier, Tommy's cliché avalanche of mean words and hateful attitude would have worried Butch more than he would have ever admitted to anyone. He would have felt a defensive posture sweep over him as well as words of conciliation rise up within his throat. The truth was he had faced these types of accusations before. Every pastor does, and every pastor who is able to stay anywhere for more than two or three years has learned to deal with it politically.

But this morning was different because Butch was different.

He ignored Tommy, took out his cell phone and dialed Mildred at the church office. "Mildred—yeah, hi—this is Butch. Yeah, can you get me two tickets for flights out tomorrow morning from SeaTac direct to Las Vegas? Yeah, the earlier the better. I prefer Alaska Airlines if possible, even if it costs more. One ticket is for me, and the other is for my friend Wyoming Wallace—yeah, hold on a minute."

Butch asked Wyoming, "Wyoming, what is your birthday and how does your name read on your driver's license?" Wyoming told Butch and Butch relayed the information to Mildred. Then he finished the conversation, glaring at Tommy the whole time. "Oh, Mildred, two more things. I'd prefer to be on the aisle and please make sure and put this on the church credit card, okay. No, I will not need the airport shuttle, I think my friend Wyoming and I will drive to the airport and park in the terminal parking lot. I'll get you a receipt for that when I return. I will also need some spending money for the trip, so would you please pull $300 out of the petty cash and put that in an envelope on my desk for me to pick up. Just have the reservations emailed to me—Thank you—you are wonderful, but you already knew that."

When the conversation was over, Pastor Butch Gregory simply stood up, grabbed the ticket which the server had left on the table and said, "Wyoming, I'll let you know when our plane leaves and Amber, I'll call you later this morning." Then he looked right at Tommy Bothers and said, "Good morning, Tommy. Have a blessed day." He walked to the counter, plopped down $40 and walked out of the front door. The events of the last few days had placed petty church politics into their proper perspective. Tommy was the least of his concerns. There was a girl to be found.

Amber followed Butch's lead, "Excuse me, Tommy," she said as she indicated she wanted out. He stood up and she scooted out of the booth. "Bye Wy, have a good trip with Preach in Vegas. Don't corrupt him down there," she said and walked out of the Sydney Diner. Tommy Bothers watched her leave, the way some men watch a woman walk, and then sat back down.

Wyoming finished his coffee and said, "Can I talk to you outside for a moment."

"Sure," replied Tommy. Tommy was anxious to learn if Wyoming might have some inside dirt he was willing to share about Butch Gregory that he wanted to relate in private. He greedily stood up and walked outside. Wyoming grabbed his hat from the coat and hat rack at the front door and walked outside. Tommy followed.

Once they were outside the diner's doors Tommy stopped, but Wyoming kept walking. He walked down the sidewalk and around to the side of the restaurant where the delivery alley led to the loading dock behind the building. Tommy followed. When they reached the back, Wyoming stopped, looked around to his left and to then to his right and finally behind him. He lifted his ball cap off his head and re-adjusted it.

Then, with a sudden explosion of pent up energy he punched Tommy Bothers in the side of his face with his left hand. It was a hard punch that surprised Tommy, knocking him to the ground. Blood began to spurt from a cut on his cheek.

Wyoming then bent down to him, grabbed him by his perfectly styled hair. "Look here, boy. I'm not a religious man like the Reverend is. I don't have to be nice, but the way you just talked to him is wrong, and it's not the way a man talks to another man. If I ever catch you talking to him like that again, I will put a scar on your other cheek."

Wyoming stood up and walked away in the direction he had come.

"You can't do that," Tommy whined. "I'm going to call the police and have you arrested for assault."

Turning around, Wyoming pulled a dark cigar out of his shirt pocket. Then he slowly pulled a stainless steel guillotine cutter from his back pocket. He snapped it closed over the rounded end of the stogie, decapitating it in one violent motion. He lit the cigar with his silver Zippo. After taking a couple of puffs, he spit on the ground. Only then did Wyoming Wallace reply to the weak threat.

"Go ahead, sissy. Call the police. That is about what I'd expect from a wimp like you."

Wyoming turned his back and walked away in the confident knowledge that a man like Tommy Bothers would not call the police and file any charges because his ego would never allow him to admit to anyone what had just happened. Before he got to the corner to turn away, he glanced back and added salt to the wound by saying, "Make sure your mamma puts some ice on that."

Chapter Twenty-Four

A Thousand Wails

"I HATE this city!" Butch Gregory exclaimed with a large amount of disgust and remorse. How did he ever let himself get talked into being the one to come to Las Vegas? Why couldn't he and Wyoming take care of Oregon and let Amber investigate this God-forsaken land.

"I love it, it's my kind of town," Wyoming said as the two men drove away from the airport car rental office. "Why do you hate it so much Reverend?"

"There is very little about this place that is redeeming. I feel like Lot in Sodom and Gomorrah, and I keep looking up to check for sulfur falling from the sky."

"Well, I feel like a soldier on leave, so I guess we're even."

"Well, soldier, should we check in with our northern flank?" Again, Butch had hoped he'd used the right terminology. He and Wyoming were from such different worlds. Apparently he'd communicated enough because Wyoming plugged the cell phone into the car's speaker system and dialed Amber.

"We are just outside of Vegas and headed toward our lead. We should know something before tonight on whether or not this has been a wild goose chase. The pastor here is a little edgy though. I don't think the desert agrees with him."

"Be nice Wy," Amber's voice crackled over the speaker. "I've learned that where I need to get to is even more isolated and rugged than I thought. It will probably take me half of the day to get up there. I'm glad it's summer and not snowing. I probably will not have much in the way of cell phone reception up there though, so, don't worry if you can't get in contact with me. Tonight I'll give you a call."

"Okay. How about we pray a bit?" Butch asked.

"Now? You're driving?"

"He prays all the time Wyoming."

"Even when he's driving?"

"Yes, I do. So let's do it now." With his eyes wide open and attentive to the road, Pastor Butch Gregory offered a prayer.

> Dear Lord, we've split up to take two
> different paths chasing two different leads.
> My prayer is that you keep us safe—that no
> harm comes to Wyoming, Amber, or myself.
> Please help us to find Tamara, alive and well
> and unharmed and to bring justice. At least
> we ask that you intervene in a way to let us

> discover some clues that would help us locate her. We are doing all that we know to do; and have left nothing undone. But we can't do anything without you. Please guide us and open our eyes to see and our ears to hear. In the name of Christ Jesus our Lord, Amen."

Butch drove the car out of town along I-15 and then turned onto Highway 93 as they traveled north toward the mountainous desert. He drove for another 15 minutes when Wyoming said, "Slow down, I think this is it."

What they were looking for had only been vaguely described to them: Two dirt roads which crossed the highway about 30 miles outside of Las Vegas—Take a right and follow the dirt road until it comes to a single wide trailer with a blue cement truck parked out front.

Butch would have preferred precision such as mile markers, road numbers, or even better yet a physical address or GPS coordinates. As a pastor, precision was something he appreciated—chapter and verse, declension, definition, and paradigm were the type of words that fueled his daily work on a normal day. Now he was made to embrace guesswork on this murky mess that Shark had sent him on. His plausibility structure was changing every day.

The guesswork had started as soon as they left town. There were only two highways which left north from Las Vegas that might intersect a dirt road. One was US 95 and the other was US 93. Judging from the topography and assuming a certain desire for anonymity he guessed US 93; as it was far from the beaten path. The only people who really traveled this highway were those UFO enthusiasts headed up to Rachel to try and sneak a peek at Area 51. Butch had a few of those types in his congregation. He once heard there was good pie in Rachel. He thought of Lester.

Butch obediently slowed the car to a crawl at Wyoming's hunch and turned right onto the chalky dirt road. It was a road in name only. A few cattle stood out in the open field to the left; they ignored the invading car as Butch drove it turtle-like down the road in the Lexus. Mildred reserved them the full size option.

"Speed up," Wyoming ordered.

"But the road is bumpy and uncertain."

"It's a rental. Speed up."

Again, Butch obeyed. He gassed it and the car zipped forward. A giant plume of dust trailed from behind their red car. No trailer was in sight. Neither men would say it but they were both beginning to assume nothing was here and maybe they should turn around and try the other highway out of town, or that the trip down was indeed a wild goose chase. Butch even wondered if they might be on government land. He knew the military owned most of the parts of Nevada that weren't casinos. They had not seen a posted sign, and Butch had been diligently searching for one.

Did he miss it? Did it say trespassers will be shot? He hoped not.

The road took them up the side of a slight ridge. As they crested the bluff Wyoming shouted, "Got it!" as he pointed to the valley below. Far off on the opposite side of the arid valley was a blue speckle. "Stop here. Let's take a look."

Butch didn't bother to pull the car over to the side but stopped the vehicle right in the middle of the road. He jumped out of the car and was greeted by a trail of dust that blew by him. It was the dust he had made by driving through the dirt. Wyoming laughed at the pastor as he waited inside the car for the dust to roll by. When it did, he opened the door and pulled out his binoculars. He was looking to see if anyone was at the trailer.

"I see no cars and I see no people. In fact, it looks like it is abandoned."

"I guess it is a dead end then." Butch was disappointed. He'd hoped to find Tamara here.

"Not necessarily. Let's go."

They got back into the comfortable air conditioned cabin of the luxury vehicle and drove towards the bottom of the shallow valley. As they progressed deeper the blue speckle grew. Eventually the shimmer of flashing glass in the desert sun caught their eyes as the mirage turned into reality. The road ended right in front of a single wide trailer with the blue cement truck parked in front.

The windows were closed and venetian blinds were shut. Other than the cement truck, no other automobiles were parked there. There were no wires going to the home from poles—no electricity, no satellite dishes, no phone cables, nothing. Just the trailer. It certainly appeared that no one was there.

Butch shouted, "Hello!"

"This place is empty. There is no one here but you and me." Wyoming said those words with confidence, but deep inside of him there was an uneasiness. The landscape felt like Iraq. The dryness in the air smelled like danger to him. It was a danger he was ready to confront and conquer. It felt dangerous.

To help him stay focused, he pulled out a cigar and lit it.

"Do you have to do that now?" the pastor asked.

"Have to do it now, no. Want to do it now, yes. Care what you think about it, no. Going to do it now, yes. Besides, I've already lit it. This is an eighteen dollar stogie."

"Those things are deadly and nasty. They will kill you."

"Everybody dies."

Wyoming walked around to the back of the trailer. Butch thought of following him, but decided not to. He'd learned it was just one of those things Wyoming did. In two minutes he returned, accompanied by a cloud of smoke, and reported that there was absolutely nothing in the back, which was odd. There was no sign of water, septic, or trash. There were, however, tire tracks. After making the perimeter sweep report he said, "Now let's go have a look inside."

Wyoming crossed the sandy, rocky terrain that served as a front yard for the trailer house and climbed up the three wooden steps and turned the door knob. It was unlocked and opened easily. There was a pause before he entered. The pause was not out of fear, but caution. Wyoming reached to his waist for his pistol holster, only to remember it wasn't there because he couldn't fly with it as a carry on.

Pastor Butch Gregory approached, far more slowly than his partner, and stood at the foot of the front steps.

"What do you see?" asked Butch.

Wyoming didn't answer as he walked into the trailer. The floor sagged beneath his weight. His brown work boots forced the floor into a groan as he entered the metallic shack. It was dark inside and there was no electricity. The only light was from the bright sunlight exploding through the front door. Wyoming opened two of the blinds to illuminate the room. All of the interior walls had been removed, leaving no bedrooms, bathrooms or closets. There was a stove, a wall mounted oven, and a sink in the kitchen which had faded yellow linoleum flooring that pealed up around the walls and edges. There was a place for a refrigerator and a dishwasher, but the appliances were absent. The floor was bare and exposed the subfloor where a serving bar had once been. The rest of the house's floor was covered in threadbare faded brown carpet. The bathroom fixtures had all been removed. Folded neatly along the back wall was a card table and a metal folding chair. That was it. Nothing else was in the trailer.

Butch finally stepped behind Wyoming and took in the whole scene. "What do you think this is used for?"

"Well, I don't really know. My guess is that this trailer is some kind of transfer point. Perhaps the kids are brought here, forced into this room and made to wait until the different transports arrive to take them in different directions. That would explain the different sets of tire tracks. From this one spot the children can be tagged, counted, and then shipped to wherever there is a buyer. They might even end up in Miami or Los Angeles. It's like a clearing house; or maybe an inventory warehouse for people." Wyoming cursed.

"One thing is certain, our target is sloppy. Look at this," Wyoming picked up a curly piece of white paper and handed it to Butch.

"It's a receipt. It's a receipt from a Burger King," Butch said.

"What is the date? Most receipts have a date."

"My soul, this is dated yesterday. Someone bought a coffee and a sausage biscuit."

"Breakfast means they were here yesterday morning," Wyoming deduced as he took a big draw on his smoke.

Butch too, was analyzing, but in a different way. "It's a slave auction block," he mumbled as he thought aloud. The longer he stood there the worse he felt. Part of his ill-feeling was the thought of countless numbers of people, children, being inhumanely handled and abused in this one spot, for only God knows how many years. A deeper psychic sickness, though, spewed from the well of his own soul. He thought of Tamara. Had that sweet little girl been here? What happened to her here? Before he knew it tears were streaming down the caked dust on his face.

Butch Gregory hears a thousand wails and feels the shriek of endless pain. He now is a little child in the room. In his mind's eye he sees, as through a haze, children standing in the room. They are mostly girls but some are boys. There are no chains or shackles, no manacles to hold them in place. These little ones have no place to run. Three men are here, guarding. One man is older, in his sixties with short gray hair. He sits at the card table. On the card table is a laptop and a bottle of cheap bourbon. Butch sees the computer screen, for he seems to now suddenly float above the table such that he can see everything. The old man is typing physical descriptions of each child including approximate age, coloring, eyes, teeth, and size. He is matching those descriptions with pictures and creating folders for each one and then storing them onto flash drives. The other two are much younger, in their twenties. One man is Caucasian and the other is Hispanic, with a moustache above his hair lipped mouth and he keeps talking to the older man sitting at the table. Butch strains to hear what they are saying, but all he hears is San Diego, over and over again, at least four times he hears the old man say San Diego. The white man looks familiar; Butch shudders; it is Knuckles. A sound comes from beside Butch in the room; and he glances and sees a little girl—Tamara. Butch attempts to grab her, but he cannot move. Tamara is crying and she pleads, "I want my mommy. Please take me to my mommy." Knuckles hears her and grins like a devil as he tells her, "You will never see your mommy again. Your mommy is dead. I killed her," and then he slaps her across the face. The room erupts in loud wailing as all the children, Butch estimates about twenty-five of them, begin to cry and lament. The man with the moustache shouts, "Shut up!" and then whips out a pistol and fires two quick shots into the ceiling. The sound is deafening. Butch covers his ears. The shots have the intended effect. The children are quiet.

Butch hazily became aware of Wyoming, the room, cigar smoke, and who he was. He did not know what had just happened, but he felt a cold chill down his spine. His sobbing had stopped, but he felt great spiritual and emotional pain. Trembling, he stepped to the back wall of the trailer where he had been standing in the vision and looked around to the position of the gray haired man drinking whiskey and making computer files. He could see where Knuckles had assaulted Tamara, and where the man with the moustache had stood when he fired. Butch walked to where the shots were discharged and looked up. He gasped. There were two small bullet holes in the ceiling.

"Tamara was here," said Butch. "She was here with about twenty or thirty other children, right here in this place. You are right, they use this trailer to sort and to organize. There were three men guarding them and one of those men was our friend Knuckles."

"How do you know all of that?"

"I saw her," Butch mumbled.

"What?"

"Don't ask me to explain, but just now I saw her. I saw them. All of them. Somehow the Lord gave me insight. I don't know why or what it means, but for some reason the Lord wanted me to know that we are on the right trail and that not too long ago there were people here, in this very room, who are responsible for Tamara's abduction. I also think they are in California."

"What makes you say that?"

"San Diego, California. A hunch from the vision I just had, I guess." Pastor Butch was still shaking and a cold sweat soaked through his shirt and covered his dusty brow. "I believe our next step will be to go to San Diego, California."

"Well, when do we leave?"

"Let's wait and see what Amber comes up with," Butch said, panting. "But we can fly out tomorrow." Butch noticed that Wyoming did not argue about his experience. Wyoming just accepted the supernatural experience he'd just had. Butch wanted to follow-up, but decided not to.

"Good, I'll at least get one night in this spectacular city you've brought me to. But first, I want to sit out here on this makeshift porch and finish my smoke."

Wyoming changed the subject, and Butch noticed.

Butch felt better immediately after he walked out of the trailer. The spiritual darkness and oppression of that evil building was a tangible reality he was glad to be rid of. The desert sun blazed down upon them, but it was not too hot. It was a far different world from Western Washington, yet not unpleasant.

"What do you make of that cement truck, Reverend?" Wyoming pointed with his cigar.

"I don't know. It does seem oddly out of place. Maybe it was derelict before the slavers ever started using the trailer. It seems evident to me that this is just an abandoned piece of property they have somehow found and now use as a stop-over, probably because it's central to the Midwest and the coast. Maybe the truck is just a part of the scenery and has nothing to do with any of it."

"Maybe, but that doesn't seem right to me. Something," Wyoming said, "is not right. Let's have a look."

Wyoming Wallace took a big puff and walked the forty yards to the cement truck and the pastor followed. The truck was mostly blue, except for a little red trim. Butch noticed that it matched the color scheme of Knuckles uniform coveralls back at A-OK Mekaniks. The side door said, "All American Cement Company, Las Vegas, Nevada." Butch noticed that "Las Vegas, Nevada" was new paint. He picked at the sign with his hand and discovered it was not paint at all, but a magnetic sign made to match the paint of the truck. Underneath the "Las Vegas, Nevada" peel-off was the words "San Diego, California." Butch peeled off San Diego and revealed "Tacoma, Washington" was painted directly onto the truck beneath it.

As Butch was making that discovery, Wyoming climbed into the cab. He found the keys to the truck in the sun visor. He put them into the ignition and turned the engine over. It started. Wyoming let it run for a moment and then killed the engine and shouted to Butch, "Not so abandoned after-all. There is three quarters of a tank of gas in there." Wyoming put the keys to the truck in his pocket.

"Yeah, I see what you mean," said Butch as he held up the peel-off sign so Wyoming could see it. "But why, why would they have a concrete mixer."

"Things are not always as they seem." Wyoming jumped out of the cab and surveyed the vehicle. He pulled off his hat and ran his hand through his hair and then stroked his beard. Then he crawled underneath the distinctively large oval drum mounted behind the cab of the construction truck.

"This shouldn't be here," he mumbled.

"What shouldn't be here?" asked Butch. There was no reply. Thirty seconds later Wyoming disappeared.

Wyoming opened a secret latch underneath the mixer and climbed up inside the drum. Needing a flashlight and not having one, Wyoming used the LED from his cell phone to illuminate the small cavern. He discovered that concrete had never been mixed inside the concrete mixing truck. Instead there were blankets, some articles of clothing, a five gallon bucket and a couple of trash bags. The smell was awful. Having his suspicions confirmed, Wyoming quickly left the way he had come in.

"Where did you go?"

"They use this cement truck to carry the kids in. There is even a bucket for them to use the bathroom inside. God—who knows how long they make those kids stay inside there as they move them from one spot to another. Can you imagine the torture? When I find these people I will break every bone in their bodies. Then I am going to castrate them and finally I will kill them. Slowly." He spit.

Butch wanted to calm his colleague down. He knew he should say something about revenge being of the Lord, and forgiveness, and of justice and such pastoral counsel, but he couldn't. He mostly agreed with Wyoming's sentiments. The scope of his emotions had moved from being about one little girl who was abducted to thoughts and feelings about the injustice done to all these children and their families. One way or another, he would see this through to completion.

Chapter Twenty-Five

The Fire of Hades

AMBER PUSHED end call on her cell phone after Butch's amen ended the prayer he offered from the rental call just after they landed. Unlike Wyoming, Amber really did believe in the Lord. She had been raised by good parents and her brother was a Christian minister for years before he was murdered. But her first instinct was never to pray, it was to act. When threatened, Amber would either throw a punch or run away. Fight or flight was hardwired into the way she lived. Life on the streets did not teach her that; it only reinforced her natural *modus operandi*. Butch Gregory lived differently and Amber could tell that whenever something important was taking place Butch had learned that prayer was the first order of business. It was one of the things she liked about the middle-aged preacher.

She also liked that he was just about the only man she knew that did not have getting her in bed in the back of his mind. She could tell from his expression that he simply cared for her as a human being and that he was driven by a decency and innocence absent in most men she knew. Even Wyoming, as great a guy as he was, would not hesitate to take the opportunity to sleep with her. She was well aware that his words and actions were usually calculated to impress her or any other woman who might be nearby. Amber was pretty, and she knew that in a matter-of-fact way, but she also knew that beauty really didn't play into most men's sexual appetites. Experience taught her that most men would sleep with anyone, and they often would pay for it with money or gifts. But Pastor Butch Gregory was different.

Before leaving the college town of Eugene to head south Amber had her car filled up. She liked that in Oregon gas stations had attendants to pump gas. She also bought provisions for the trip up the mountains: Chips, soda, sweet-n-sour candy, and chewing gum. Butch had given her $200 for the road trip.

She sped south out of town in the 7 year old, light green Toyota Corolla her father bought her last year. Eugene was roughly halfway through the state while her destination was further south close to Medford. There she would find highway 238 and head toward the Rogue River. That highway road would lead her out of the Rogue River Valley and into the part of the mountain range that formed along the border with California.

The Siskiyou Mountains provide both the geographical and psychological barrier between the Pacific Northwest and northern California. The range begins to form along the freeway near the town of Roseburg, Oregon and rolls south past Mt. Shasta and then levels out at Redding, California. It is the most treacherous part of the I-5 Corridor, except for the city of Los Angeles. Los Angeles is dangerous for entirely different reasons than topography.

Amber would not be going further south through the Siskiyous, though. Her location was on the northern side of the range. The scenery for her journey was absolutely beautiful. Amber had spent most of her life in Washington. Her only forays into Oregon were trips to Portland or long journeys through the state on their way down to Southern California with her family when she was a child. Her only adult experience in the state was the better part of a winter she lived on the streets of Eugene. That is where she met her friend, who was now a college student at the University of Oregon. Amber believed that Eugene was the most unique place in the world.

The mountains in Oregon were different than the cascades in Washington. The Oregon mountains seemed steeper and more angular; and the roads were not as developed. Amber used several of the pullouts to stop and look. The clean air, birds, and breathtaking beauty of mountains in summertime brought joy to her soul. It was a joy she didn't know really existed within her. She even snapped a few pictures with her phone.

Why have I never been here before?

How was it she had lived so much of her life in hard concrete jungles and surrounded by urban grey and industrial brown?

She wondered how her life might have been different if she'd been brought here as a child and allowed to dream. Maybe she would have become an ecological worker or forestry officer. Even though she was on her way to engage in grimy work, she was falling in love with this beautiful and pristine landscape. Had she been on a sightseeing adventure this would have been one of the most enjoyable times of her life. But this was not a sightseeing tour. It was a mission. The grim reality of what brought her to this utopian countryside kept reeling her imagination back in. She had work to do, and time was running out.

Amber drove a few more miles until she reached the remote area where the cabin was located. She turned off of several gravel roads and made many of the familiar switchbacks found on mountain roads until she discovered the exact mile marker she was looking for. It was another four or five miles until she came to a large highway department sign in the middle of the road that said, "ROAD CLOSED".

Amber stopped and checked her map and information. She knew this was the right place. The bad guys den was only three or four miles beyond where she was. She tried to check her location with her phone GPS, but there was no signal. She was a very long way from any signal. She had to make a decision—go around the safety barrier into risky terrain or turn around.

It was an easy decision. Amber had spent her whole life going around society's barriers. This one was no different. She would just be careful this time because more was riding on it than her own life. Tamara was counting on her. She pulled her car out and revved the engine to accelerate around the obstacle and trudged on. The road was fine. She decided that the bad guys had probably put that barrier up to keep access limited to the road. It even occurred to her they might have even had someone in the highway department on the payroll.

There might be people at all levels on their payroll.

After a few more minutes of very slow driving due to hairpin switchbacks Amber arrived at her destination. The road was marked exactly the way it had been described to her: A private drive with red reflectors, a sign on a pole that said, "PRIVATE: NO TRESPASSING," and it was across from a yellow traffic warning sign indicating a curve ahead.

Deciding to leave her car on the side of the road, she prepared to walk in. Her only fear was that some safety patrol would come by, see her car, assume it was abandoned, and then tow it away. She thought about leaving a note on the car, but then she thought better of it. If things went right, then she would be back soon with Tamara and maybe others. If things didn't go well, it probably wouldn't matter.

It was cold outside. It had taken her most of the day to get here, and the sun was setting. Amber anticipated some cooler temperatures in the high elevations and pulled a coat from the back seat and wrapped it around her. She pushed her blonde hair up inside a blue knit cap. The walk wasn't far. She found the driveway about a quarter of a mile and then saw the cabin. There were no cars out front, but she saw a light on through a window. Her pulse raced as she thought that perhaps Tamara might be inside.

She fought her instinct to run straight toward it. Instead Amber squatted down behind a tree and looked around. It was eerily quiet, the way it always is in a dense canopied forest. Birds were singing and the breeze was rustling in the treetops. The cabin seemed idyllic against such a backdrop; like a painting of a frontier way-of-life that no longer existed.

This cabin, though, was entirely modern. There was a satellite television dish mounted on the roof along with what appeared to

Amber to be electric cables coming in from the main grid along the road. Amber took a deep breath, stood up, and slowly approached the front door.

Should she knock? She hadn't thought about that until right this instant. What would she say if someone came to the door? *Hello, are you a child abductor?* No, that wouldn't work at all, now would it, Amber?

She darted quickly away from the front door and eased along the side of the cabin toward the back. There was a back door with firewood stacked along the exterior wall. A trail of sorts led away from the cabin toward the forest. She could hear a stream running in the distance. It sounded refreshing.

Amber peeked inside the small vertical window in the door and could see no one inside. Part of her was relieved, but the other part had wanted to see Tamara.

She turned the knob and entered. The cabin had one large room with a kitchen, a cot, and a small closet-like half bathroom. There was a large but dormant wood burning stove in the middle of the room. A flat screen television was mounted on the wall. Between the television and the kitchen area was a table. On the table was an overflowing ash tray, a cheap yellow Bic cigarette lighter, a pack of Camels, and a laptop computer.

Amber could smell the cigarette smoke.

Greedily she flipped open the PC and powered it up. As Windows was resuming she glanced around and noticed that along the back wall, opposite the television and behind the stove there were large metal rings bolted to the floor. Chains and handcuffs were hanging on the wall above the rings. She didn't have to guess too hard to imagine what those were for.

Finally the PC was ready and she noticed that it was linked into the internet, apparently through the satellite dish. She opened the browser and accessed the history. The majority of the sites were either sports or pornography but one URL stood out. She clicked on it and found it to be a portal to an online business of some sort. The site asked for a login password, and Amber did not have the slightest clue as to how to hack through it.

She checked the documents folder and discovered photographs. There were hundreds of photographs of little girls and boys. The pictures were not taken at the cabin, but somewhere else.

The shop.

The back wall framing the pictures was the wall near those cages in the auto-shop. She scanned through the pictures. Most of the children were somewhere between the ages of eight and fifteen. She scrolled quickly through the digital images until she found the one she was looking for.

Tamara Rey was crying in the picture. Her thick black hair was a mess and her dark eyes were blood shot and held a frightened look.

She's still alive.

Another thought entered Amber's mind and she quickly raced to the email application and launched the Microsoft program. Nothing was password protected. She moved through the inbox and discovered the email address recipient was a Gmail account with the username Cabinman. Fortunately, he had not deleted his sent mail and she was able to see that most of the outgoing email went to one single address stoner@hotmail.com. She read the most recent sent message.

> *got back last night from the drop in vegas. knuckles is still there. he wants me to wait here till you bring the next batch from spokane. supposed to lay low for a while. things getting tight in seattle. donny, mark and carl are all dead. its not the feds. boss says its some cowboy and his friends. keep your gun loaded and watch out.*

Knuckles! She checked the email's log and gasped. That email had been sent 30 minutes earlier. Where was Cabinman? She looked around and saw no one. Tamara clearly wasn't here either. Amber guessed that Tamara may have been the "drop" in Las Vegas.

Preach and Wy!

Amber thought about taking the whole laptop, but decided against it. Perhaps stealth would be best. Fortuitously she found a memory stick lying on the table behind the laptop. She stuck the flash drive into the USB port and saved the email, copy-n-pasted the history and saved it, then she saved all the pictures and all the documents—she didn't have enough time to sort through them, so she just saved them all. It took a while to download all that information onto the flash drive. While she waited for that to finish, she checked if there were any contacts which might have been uploaded from a cell phone.

The silence of the cabin was pierced by a gunshot. On the wall in front of Amber a pock mark flashed into existence. Amber jumped and swiveled around and saw a small framed man with a tiny head and protruding eyes standing in the doorway with a pistol aimed at her.

"I missed," the weasel shouted in disbelief. "I can't believe I missed."

He pulled the trigger again. Nothing happened.

"What the –?" exclaimed the man as he looked at his pistol.

Amber suddenly regretted that the gun Wyoming Wallace had given to her was in the car. Why hadn't she brought it with her?

Nevertheless, she took advantage of his hesitation and ran hard toward Cabinman and kicked him in the groin. He doubled over and fell to the ground. Reaching for the first thing that came to her mind, Amber grabbed the laptop computer and raised it high above her and smashed it down on top of his head.

His crumpled body lay on the floor with the pieces of the laptop beside him. It was open when she swung it and the monitor ripped off the base. Amber smirked at the destruction of the computer. She'd hoped to get more information out of it. She was able to recover the memory stick that was jutting out the side of what was left of the Toshiba frame. After putting it in a pants pocket for safe keeping she contemplated what to do with the sicko on the floor.

The sun was now on the west side of the mountain peaks and it was getting dark. She could stay the night in the cabin; but the prospects of that did not seem savory to her. She looked at the man again and surveyed her surroundings and that gave her inspiration. She dragged him to the floor mounted shackles and chained him. Underneath the sink she found a roll of duct tape. She could only imagine what it had been used for, but now she would turn the tables. She taped Cabinman's mouth—all the way around his head. Then she taped his feet and legs together so he could not wiggle. She then cleaned out his pockets and found over $1,000 in cash as well as a prepaid VISA card.

No sense going to waste. Janet or Lacey might be able to use this.

She grabbed his pistol, a 9mm Glock, which she stuck in her coat pocket.

Wy will like this.

She checked the kitchen to see about something to eat. Her years on the street had told her to never take the next meal for granted. The kitchen was well stocked, but with mostly canned food, the same stuff that was in those boxes at A-OK Mekaniks. Inside the small refrigerator there was a plate of sliced cheese and lunchmeat. Amber munched that while drinking the can of Coke that was stuck in the refrigerator door.

She stared at him while she ate his food. A thousand questions about him ran through her mind: Why had he turned out like this? What makes a person do these things to children? What kind of power trip is it? An overpowering sense of anger and revulsion slowly took command of her emotions. Fear gave way to loathing and loathing turned into hatred. Her original mission into the cabin was to find Tamara or to find information to help locate her, but as she sat and looked at him she wanted to hurt him. It only seemed fair. Amber did not like the feeling and she recognized these were negative and unhelpful emotions. She imagined Preach telling her, "Calm down Amber. Leave him chained up and call the police. Let them deal with it." Amber, though, suppressed Pastor Butch Gregory's voice. She fed her inner vigilante. She knew it was wrong, but it felt good to turn the tables on evil.

He will get what he deserves.

When the man woke up, Amber Smith began her cruel interrogation. She kicked him in the side.

"So, they just leave you up here, without a car, only a computer, and let you hold onto the girls until a buyer can be arranged," she put a slice of cheddar onto a piece of ham and popped it in her mouth. "Then when the time is right, you drive down with them—I suspect a delivery truck of some sort comes and gets you, and takes them to Las Vegas? Is that right?"

Cabinman, groggily nodded. Then a slow realization of his situation was betrayed by an emerging panic in his eyes.

"Where do you take them, exactly?"

Cabinman just stared at her.

She pulled his pistol from her pocket and pointed it at his eyebrow. "I said, where do you take them?"

No answer from Cabinman.

She moved the gun lower and pointed it between his legs.

He tried to move his mouth to speak, so she ripped the duct tape off, pulling the better part of two days beard growth with it. He screamed in pain.

"That hurt!" he yelled.

"Where do you take them, or I will pull the trigger and hurt you even worse."

Cabinman looked at her to see if she was bluffing. He decided that she was not bluffing.

"First they go to Nevada, then on to San Diego. It is easier to get through from Vegas than up here. There is a pier just outside of town. That is the final holding location until they are sent overseas."

"Why do you go to Nevada?"

"We meet up with the other ones and take them all at once to San Diego."

"Anything else? Where is Tamara Rey? I saw her picture on your computer. She is the one I know, and she is the one I'm looking for."

"We don't go by names, but by numbers. If we gave them names, then it would make it harder to sell them off. You know, like naming cattle you intend to slaughter."

Amber pointed the pistol at Cabinman's face and said, "Say something stupid like that again and I will kill you. Her picture was on your computer. The picture was taken at the auto-shop in Tacoma. She would have been here within the last two or three days. Was she here?"

Cabinman sat silent, getting braver as time ticked by.

"Was she here or not?" Amber asked again, this time pointing the weapon directly at his face.

"Yeah, she was here. She was with, let's see, there were four other girls and a little boy. They all came from Tacoma."

"Did you drive down from Tacoma with them, or were you waiting here when they arrived."

"I drove down with two other guys."

"Were their names Carl and Mark?" Amber asked.

"Yeah, how did you know?"

Amber reached inside her jeans pocket and pulled out the pocketknife Wyoming had given her from Mark's duffle bag. "I think this used to belong to Mark before we killed him. He was the fat one, right?"

She had his attention now, and she knew it. A sense of justice swelled inside of her. She wanted to make this man pay for all that he had done, and for all the others like him who hurt kids. Compassion and mercy were draining away from her like water out of a bathtub drain. Her heart was becoming a basin filled with the dry heat of revenge and retribution. She anticipated the purifying lather of justice.

"Why did they leave you here?" Amber asked the question out of sheer curiosity.

Cabinman did not answer.

"Tell me!"

He still did not answer. His refusal to cooperate unleashed a burning fire inside of her she'd never felt before. While holding the gun in her right hand she used her left thumb to open the pocket knife's pointed middle blade. She waved it in front of him.

"Tell me why they left you here."

Still, he was quiet.

Amber plunged the knife into his right thigh.

He screamed so loud Amber was certain if anyone were anywhere nearby they would have heard it. She did not care. She pulled the knife out of his leg and blood spurted out like a volcano, then pulsated rhythmically down his thigh and dripped onto the wooden floor.

"Tell me why they left you behind."

"I asked to be left behind."

"Now that wasn't so hard, was it? Why did you ask to be left behind?"

He was silent.

Again, she waved the now bloody knife in front of his face. "Tell me."

"Okay, just don't stab me again."

"I will not promise, but if you don't tell me, I promise I will stab you again."

"I wanted to stay behind because, I liked the boy."

It took Amber a second to figure out what he meant. When she did, down came the knife blade into Cabinman's left thigh.

He screamed and cursed. He cursed her and he cursed God.

When he stopped screaming, Amber asked him, "How long have you been doing this?"

"About two years."

"How old are you?"

"I'm 21."

"Where are you from? How did you get wrapped up in all of this," she waved the gun around, "were you born into it? Is this a family business?"

"I am from Tukwila." He was breathing heavy and his face grew pale.

"I never meant to hurt anyone. But ya know, I ended up owing someone a favor and the next thing you know they called that favor in and it involved snatching little kids off the street. Most of the kids don't have no home and no kind of life, so, it seemed like it didn't really matter. After a while, I kind of got to where I liked it, ya know."

"No, I don't know."

"Hey, don't judge me. No one is perfect," he seemed more indignant at the thought of Amber judging his perversion than he was at her stabbing him.

Cabinman was getting lightheaded and pale. The blood was pooling thickly on the floor, dripping through his denim pants. After a moment of silence he continued in a hushed, almost whispered voice. "The boys are so sweet and innocent and scared when they come to us. It gives me a chance to play the nice guy, ya know. I leave the girls all locked up, but I give the boys a soda and some candy and let them watch television. They kind of bond with me, ya know. Then I'm able to tell them, that if they let me have a little fun, well, then I might be able to let them go."

Amber interrupted, "But you never let them go. You lie to them and build false hope."

"Yeah, but false hope is better than no hope at all."

"What was his name?"

"I told you, we never ask their name. We go by numbers."

"No, what was the name of the man who abused you when you were a kid?"

Cabinman was quiet. Amber couldn't tell if it was from blood loss or he was unwilling to say. Amber waved the knife in front of him and said, "I lived on the streets too, buddy; and I know that for every person who hurts, there is usually a story of being hurt. What was his name?" She waved the knife in front of him.

"Michaels. John Michaels. He was my mother's boyfriend. When she was gone shopping or something he used to touch me. At first it scared me. After a while, though, I adjusted and kind of got used to it. I guess, it just became a way of life for me."

Amber sat in silence and drank the rest of her soda.

"If I let you out, or at least let you live, do you promise to get help and to stop doing this?"

Cabinman answered quickly, "Sure, anything. I'll do anything. Just stop stabbing me and let me go."

"You're lying. You will never change, will you? You and your kind never do."

His eyes shifted left and right, frantic of what to say next. He took a chance and decided to agree with her and tell the truth. "No, you're right. I probably will not. I like it too much. If you let me out, I will turn right around and keep at it as soon as possible."

"I admire your honesty," Amber replied. It gave Cabinman a glimmer of hope.

"Of course, I'll probably just call the police and they will pick you up. If that happens, then you'll never get the chance to hurt anyone again."

"I've already been in jail once. It's no big deal. I'll get out again."

Of course. What use is jail?

"There is one more question I have for you, and I want to ask it before you pass out from blood loss. Tell me where, exactly where, I can find this warehouse in San Diego. If you do, I might let you live."

He was silent.

She waved the knife in front of him again.

"I'm tired of you, you witch."

Amber shoved the knife into his left foot.

"Go to hell!" was his angry scream.

"That's your job," she said as she stood up. She stashed the Glock back into her coat pocket, then looked at him and growled. She had enough of this lousy human being.

Amber snatched the cigarette lighter that was still lying on the ground from their earlier altercation and flicked it to life. Lifting one of the sofa's cushions, she set it ablaze and held it until half of it was inflamed. Then she dropped the cushion back onto the sofa. Quickly and intensely the sofa erupted. Amber kicked the sofa across the room toward the table and the kitchen area and looked at Cabinman for the last time. He desperately and futilely wiggled in his bonds.

"What are you doing? You can't do this."

Amber ignored him and walked out of the front door into the darkness that had settled around the cabin. About thirty yards up the road she heard the screams of the bound captive. Amber turned around and saw the cabin inflamed, totally consumed by heat. It startled her how quickly and completely smoke and fire engulfed it. She thought about going back and rescuing the evil man. His screaming and agony beckoned to her sense of humanity. It would be the right thing to do, the moral thing to do, the Christian thing to do. It is what Butch Gregory would want her to do. But, she decided, it was not what she wanted to do. Instead she declared to her conscience that this was justice.

Welcome to hell, Cabinman. You will never harm another child in that place again. Ever.

Part Four: **One To Cry, One To Die, One To See**

Chapter Twenty-Six

Out of the Desert

AMBER WAITED until she was clear of the mountains and back on the freeway headed north before she called Pastor Butch Gregory and Wyoming Wallace. The three intrepid amateur sleuths compared information. Both had learned, in different ways, the same basic thing—that there was a main location in San Diego that likely held Tamara and many other children. Wyoming and Butch both wanted to fly directly to San Diego from Vegas. Butch had already looked up tickets and they could leave mid-morning the next day.

They talked through the logistics and travel needs and decided that the two men ought to go ahead and fly to Southern California but book a hotel near the airport in San Diego for all three of them. Amber would turn around on the freeway and drive down I-5. In the time it would take her to get back to Sydney she could be halfway through California.

"Are you okay driving like that, through the night?" Butch asked her. It was a very parental question.

"Of course I'll be okay. I'll stop and get a large coffee and I'll be great. I've done a lot harder things in my life. What I really need to know, Preach, is did you bring your laptop computer with you?"

"Yes, why?"

"I downloaded lots of information onto a memory stick and I think it could help us pinpoint exactly where we are going in San Diego and what we might be up against."

Wyoming Wallace was ecstatic, "That's outstanding. Good work soldier."

Neither Wyoming nor Butch told Amber about the vision inside the trailer. They had only talked about the next step. The men agreed to book the hotel for three separate rooms, near the airport. They would expect Amber sometime around three in the afternoon. Butch was very worried about her driving that far, alone, through the night.

Butch insisted upon praying before they hung up.

> Dear Lord, thank you for protecting all three of us in today's work. We are disappointed that we have not yet found Tamara, but we trust soon we will have her. Please grant Amber travel mercies on the road tonight, and help us all to arrive safely in San Diego. Most of all, Lord, please watch over Tamara, and if there is any way possible, let her know that people are looking for her, and that people care about her. In Jesus' name. Amen.

As soon as they were finished with prayer and Amber had disconnected, Butch looked at Wyoming Wallace and said, "Let's buy those tickets, and then I want to hit the hay."

"Sounds good to me, Reverend," agreed Wyoming.

It took Pastor Butch a while to make the reservations. It had been a long time since he'd done that himself. Mildred or Lucy made most of his travel arrangements. He was certain that he probably paid more money on the flight than he should have, but it would be money well spent if they found Tamara. Their flight departure time was 10:15, and the Vegas airport was easy to navigate so they didn't have to leave the hotel until around 8:30.

"I'll knock on your door when it is time to go," said Butch.

"Great," Wyoming said as he picked up his hat and walked out. "See you in the morning."

Wyoming's room was right next to his. When they arrived he had considered sharing a room with Wyoming in one suite, but Wyoming was insistent that he have a separate room. Right now, Butch was glad of it. He wanted some privacy as he talked to his wife and he wanted to be alone.

He spoke to Lucy for well over an hour. He told her about the trailer, the vision, and the cement truck. He also told her that Amber had found the same conclusions in Oregon and that they were going to

San Diego tomorrow. Lucy shared with him that Sarah had gone skating with a boy she met at summer camp. Paul just lost a tooth.

Lucy instructed him quite sternly that he should be careful in Vegas and she teased him about all those pretty girls everywhere. "None of them are half as pretty as you, my dear," Butch told her. He meant it too. It was not his spirituality, or his vocation, that led him to a somewhat prudish view of the world. Instead it was simply his temperament. He found more beauty in integrity, hard work, and kindness than in evening gowns, make-up and phony baloney glitz. It was the integrity of his wife that had attracted him to her twenty years ago and it still did; nothing could sway him away from that.

Nothing.

After he finished his phone call with Lucy, Butch drank several glasses of ice cold water. The desert dried him out, and he felt like Charlton Heston as Moses crossing the Sinai. He drank the water standing in the middle of his room. For most of the day he'd been sitting—either in a car or on an airplane. It felt good to stand and stretch. While he was on his third glass of water Butch became self-conscious of the large number of mirrors in the hotel room. There was a mirror hanging on the door. There was a mirror above the dresser. There was a mirror behind the bed and there was a mirror above the sink, which was just outside of the bathroom. The hotel room was like a dressing room in a department store. All that was missing was canned Christmas music. Butch thought of Christmas music because the only time he ever bought clothes was at Christmas.

Butch Gregory gazed at himself in the mirror. His 49 year old stomach was catching up with him. In college he'd actually played tennis and was athletically thin. Butch sucked his gut in and then let it out as far as it could go.

Where did the spare tire come from?

He didn't remember that before. Something about this trip was making him feel old. He was old enough to be Amber and Wyoming's father. He didn't know their ages, but he guessed Wyoming was 29 or 30 and that Amber was around 25. He had a hard time keeping up with their energy level. He also felt old, in a worldly kind of sense. The world was changing on him. He wondered how the bad guys had gotten this powerful.

When did we lose innocence? He felt irrelevant, a relic of a different time.

Reaching up, he ran his left hand through his hair. His once dark, full and thick head of hair was now thinning noticeably. He hadn't reached the classic male pattern baldness oval at the top of his crown just yet, but it was only a matter of time. There was a little gray at the temples and above the ears. Butch had noticed that on some men gray looked distinguished and noble. On those people gray added a sense of wisdom or the perception of experience. But on him it just looked tired. He felt tired.

His face was bloated and the lines under his eyes and the wrinkles on his chin stood out. He used to have an angular, hard lined jaw.

When did those turn puffy?

Too many macaroons.

Maybe he would grow a beard? He'd never had a beard before, but it might hide some of this oldness.

Oh, why bother, It'd just come in gray. He drank more water, perhaps in the futile hope that it would help him feel better.

The desert didn't agree with him.

He'd be glad to get back to the soft rain and cool temperatures of home. He missed it. As he thought about how much he missed his family, Tamara came to his mind. If he was homesick, how much more did Tamara Rey feel it too? That thought led him to pull out of his notebook the dingy parchment paper Shark had left in his filing cabinet. He plopped down onto the soft bed and repeatedly read over the familiar lines.

Not in the forest, but near the sea
the little girl waits in uncertainty.
You must travel through woods and sky,
and in the desert eyes should pry.
On your search there will be three;
one to die, one to cry, one to see.

That odd conversation with his long dead brother happened only a week earlier, but it felt like a lifetime. When he first heard the riddle; it made no sense to him. But now there was clarity. Snohomish had been the forest, Amber had been in the woods, and they were in the desert; now they were flying in the sky to San Diego, which is by the sea.

If he read the oracle correctly; one of his team would die. As much as he wished it to be, Lester Wooley's death was not the fulfillment of the prophetic warning. Someone from his team was going to die and he knew it. Would it be tomorrow? Would it be him? Wyoming? Maybe Amber? Oh, he hoped not. Pastor Butch Gregory tried to force his mind to work on these ultimate reality questions, but physical, spiritual, and mental exhaustion took hold of him and he fell asleep fully clothed on top of the bedspread.

He woke, without an alarm, at 6:00 A.M. After winning a death match with the in-room coffee pot he opened his Bible and said his daily prayers. The Old Testament reading was from Genesis 19—the destruction of Sodom and Gomorrah.

How ironic.

The New Testament reading was from the Gospel of Matthew.

> At that time the disciples came to Jesus, saying, "Who is the greatest in the kingdom of heaven?" And calling to him a child, he put him in the midst of them and said, "Truly, I say to you, unless you turn and become like children, you will never enter the kingdom of heaven. Whoever humbles himself like this child is the greatest in the kingdom of heaven. Whoever receives one such child in my name receives me, but whoever causes one of these little ones who believe in me to sin, it would be better for him to have a great millstone fastened around his neck and to be drowned in the depth of the sea.

As he knelt beside the hotel chair he asked the Lord to show him unconfessed sin. Butch couldn't always remember his sins; he depended upon the Lord to show him. The first thing the Lord showed him was that he had given into his own anger with these evil people. He was on God's mission, not his own. He must resist every urge to get revenge. Then the Lord told him that he had acted mean to Tommy Bothers and had abused his privileged position as pastor by showing off in front of him with the way he bought the airline tickets. Finally, he got the definite impression that he needed to talk to Wyoming about faith. It had been a sin to avoid the issue.

After prayers Butch showered, put on a pair of tan trousers and a nicely pressed blue oxford shirt, his brown wingtips and a matching belt. Then he packed his little bit of luggage, left his hotel room, walked across the hallway and knocked on the door to Wyoming Wallace's room. There was no answer. Butch's heart raced. Had Wyoming skipped out on him?

Butch banged on the door again. This time Wyoming answered, fully dressed and ready to go with his bag packed.

"Shhhh," said Wyoming with his left index finger pressed against his lips.

"Are you leaving?" a pouty female voice asked from inside the room.

Wyoming looked at Butch crossways and whispered, "Why did you wake her up?"

Butch shrugged his shoulders to demonstrate his confusion.

Wyoming left Butch standing in the doorway and walked back toward the bed and said, "Yeah, I have to leave, but last night was wonderful. If I'm ever here again, I'll definitely look you up." The red headed woman in the bed looked at him and smiled. "You do that," then, as if she was suddenly aware of someone else in the room, she looked at Butch, flashed a radiant smile and said, "Hi there." Butch just smiled back and said, "Hi."

When Wyoming and Butch got into the hallway Butch asked, "Who was that?"

"I don't really know what her name is, but she is a great blackjack dealer and a pretty good dancer."

"I'm confused. I thought you had a girlfriend."

"I do. But what happens in Vegas, stays in Vegas."

Butch rolled his eyes in disgust. What happens in Gomorrah stays in Gomorrah, until the brimstone starts to fall! He wanted to confront Wyoming about it head on, but thought better of it. This was not the time or the place. Being a pastor for two decades had taught him that "right now" was not always the best time for action. A large part of being guided by the Holy Spirit was waiting for the moment.

Now was not that moment.

But the moment did come during the flight to San Diego. The trip was a short one, only an hour and a half. The Boeing 737 had just reached 33,000 feet when Wyoming started the conversation.

"Reverend—what made you decide to spend your whole life going to church?"

Butch was a little taken aback by the question. It startled him because even though Butch prayed earlier that morning for an opening to talk about faith with Wyoming he didn't expect Wyoming would be the one to start it. Wyoming's question revealed that he was thinking about Butch as a person, not as a title or position.

"Okay," Butch replied. "Well, after I decided to become a Christ-follower in college I discovered that my desires had changed. Before, all I had wanted to do was get a good job in the financial industry—I was a business major—and make lots of money and live the good life. I always imagined myself with a boat, a million dollar home, a luxury car, and a Rolex."

"That's not a bad plan Reverend," Wyoming interrupted.

"True, and there is nothing inherently wrong with any of that, but after Jesus came into my heart, I changed. Possessions, boats, cars and such didn't appeal to me that much anymore. What I really wanted to do was study the Bible. The more I studied the Bible the more I realized that following Christ meant caring about people and sharing life with them. I also discovered that one of the things I wanted to do more than anything else was to help people grow in their own connection to God. That sounded to me a lot like the job description of a pastor and when I graduated from college I felt led to go to seminary and, since then this has been my life. It has its ups and downs, but I can honestly say that it is a privilege and joy to be a pastor. I can't imagine doing anything else with my life."

"What about that Tommy fella from breakfast the other day, is he a 'privilege and a joy' in your life?" Wyoming didn't ask the question sarcastically, but with a deadpan look.

"Well, Wyoming, no one is perfect. No, Tommy is not one of the highlights of my work. However, if I could just spend a few moments introducing you to some of the wonderful people who are kind, generous, and completely dedicated to Jesus that I get to spend time with on a daily basis, then I think you would understand that it is worth putting up with a few rotten apples. Church is actually a great place to work.

"Anyway, people like Tommy help us to remember that grace and tolerance are important Christian virtues. The church, being in church, forces us to learn how to live together in community. That is one of the great purposes God has for us; to teach us how to love one another, even annoying and mean people. To be honest, I failed rather badly with Tommy yesterday morning in the diner. I could have done better."

Wyoming looked intently at Butch as he spoke, but did not reply with another follow-up question. Butch knew it was his turn.

"What about you, Wyoming? I know you were in Iraq, but before that what did you want to be or do?"

"Heck, I just wanted something stable. My parents loved me, but they were always all over the place growing up, gypsies really. When I finally graduated high school all I wanted was something permanent and stable. The recruiter painted me a picture of the Army that I wanted to hear and so I enlisted. That was the summer before September 11. I was 18, couldn't find work out of high school, so to me it was a blessing. I didn't know we'd be facing the kind of combat that would come so soon after I joined."

"Did you like the Army?"

"Yeah; I really did. It was a good life and in many ways I miss the structure, the camaraderie, and being honest, the action of it."

"When you were in the Army and risking so much every day in Iraq, did you ever think about dying, or faith or heaven? I mean, the closest thing I've ever come to battle, before the last week that is, was a heated church board meeting. So, I've never been in battle and I just wonder what a man thinks about when other people are trying very hard to kill him?"

"That's a fair question Reverend," Wyoming stroked his whiskers and then ran his hand through his hair. Butch could tell he was thinking deeply about the subject because his typical slow speech pattern emerged.

"When I was first deployed to Iraq I thought about dying every day. I talked to a chaplain about God and heaven and he told me that if I am a good person, and follow orders and do the right kinds of things then I will go to heaven when I die. He said I've got to try my hardest to be a good person."

Butch bit his lip. In his ministry he'd known several military chaplains and had discovered that chaplaincy was a dice toss. Sometimes, a chaplain can be really great—regardless of denominational affiliation. Other times, though, chaplains could be lousy and offer the worst theological and spiritual care imaginable.

It appeared that Wyoming Wallace, at a very fragile moment in his spiritual awareness, had found the latter, a lousy chaplain who peddled good works and a Christ-less heaven.

Wyoming continued to tell his story, "I took that as a good way to understand things and it made sense. So, I tried very hard to be good. But then I messed the whole thing up and something bad happened." Wyoming Wallace's voice cracked. It was the first emotion besides anger Butch had seen in the man since they met.

"What happened?"

"I don't want to talk about it. But suffice it enough I was a part of something that forever put my balance sheet on the negative side. So, Reverend, I've given up on God and heaven. I know that there is nothing I can do, accomplish or achieve that will undo what I've done so I'm doomed. What I do from now on is irrelevant. So I figure to just squeeze what little joys I can get each day out of life as it comes. That is the best I can hope for."

Butch insisted, "That's not true. It is never too late. Look, I don't know what happened and I don't need to know but I know the Lord I serve is gracious and forgiving. Wyoming, Jesus has a purpose for your life and that purpose is not to carry around this pai—"

"That's enough!" Wyoming said in a firm but agitated voice, raising his left hand and making a cutting motion, chopping off the dialogue.

"I understand." Butch backed off.

Wyoming pushed the call button over his head and ordered a Jack and Coke from the flight attendant and silence fell between the two men. In the silence Wyoming Wallace thought about the little girl named Leyla in Iraq whose blood was on his hands. He thought about her future; and how it was robbed from her. She would never know joy. She would never go to school or read a great book. She would never learn to play a musical instrument. She would never drive a car. She would never fall in love or get married. She would never have children or grandchildren. Most of the good things in life he'd help take from her. He thought about his future and how he was doomed to forever be guilty. He deserved whatever punishment he got.

In the silence Pastor Butch Gregory prayed for his new friend, and for some reason, the memory of Shark came to his mind again.

Eventually Butch glanced at his watch and checked his itinerary. The plane would be on the ground in thirty minutes. In ten minutes the obnoxious FASTEN SEAT BELTS sign would ding and all the passengers would be condemned to airplane purgatory; sitting until the plane had rolled to a complete stop at the terminal gate. Butch was doing this calculation in his mind because his bladder was telling him he would not make it to the terminal bathroom. One of the realities of aging was knowing that he'd better go now or the next half-hour would be very uncomfortable.

He stood up and stepped over Wyoming and made his way to the aisle. Three minutes later, he was back.

Wyoming turned to Butch and said, "I reckon I'd better do the same." It was the first thing he'd said since he'd closed the book on their spiritual conversation. He then finished off the rest of his Jack and Coke in one gulp and stood up.

"Excuse me, Reverend," he said as he stood, stretched, and then stepped into the aisle. Ten minutes later he returned.

"Was the line long?"

"No, I was busy getting this." He handed Butch Gregory a slip of paper with a phone number on it. Above it was written, "Marsha."

"Unbelievable. You are unbelievable."

"It gets even better. She's based out of Seattle," he smiled widely and then added, "and she's a redhead."

Chapter Twenty-Seven

I Am Not A Murderer

DURING THEIR conference call Amber did not tell Wyoming and Butch that she killed Cabinman. She didn't even mention him. This made her feel a little guilty because she knew they were in this together and that they needed to know. But they might not understand. Well, Preach would not understand. Wyoming would have wanted to know all the gory details and then he would have made strategy notes for her next interrogation.

Amber had never intentionally hurt anyone before; she'd always been the victim. At the cabin she heaped upon one depraved man all the pain that had been done to her and to so many others whom she knew and cared about. Then she cleansed the evil with hot fire. It was a purifying, cathartic fire which she did not regret. Not even a little. Wyoming was right, some people needed to be dead, and Cabinman was one of them.

She did, however, regret not letting the other two know about it. The truth was she didn't know how to tell them. How exactly does someone admit to murder? Was it even murder? Did her actions constitute murder or justice?

She was not a murderer.

She thought about her brother. Adam had been murdered at church, while preaching, by a crazy man with a pistol. Did her actions match her brother's assassin? No, she decided. She wasn't entirely sure of that definition legally, but she didn't feel like a murderer. Even if she was, she didn't care.

After a few more miles Amber talked to God about it. She wasn't as eloquent with God as Preach was, but Amber knew the Lord. She decided that was why it was gnawing at her so much. The Lord was convicting her. Maybe it was murder. She talked to God, and it seemed God was answering. She knew she would have to tell Butch and Wyoming eventually. Not now, though. For now, she pondered the curious limerick that Butch said his dead kid brother gave him. She had it committed to memory.

Not in the forest, but near the sea
the little girl waits in uncertainty.
You must travel through woods and sky,
and in the desert eyes should pry.
On your search there will be three;
one to die, one to cry, one to see.

Up until the cabin, Amber had assumed she would be the one to die. But she might be wrong. Maybe the one who was to die was Cabinman? She thought that it might be a play on words, though. Wy had accidentally killed Mark and Carl in Seattle and she had killed Cabinman. Maybe that was the three? Maybe three are going to die, and three are going to cry? Could the three who cry be the two FBI agents and Butch's friend Henry, because they couldn't do anything to help? Then the three to see would be her, Wy, and Preach because they see what to do and how to help?

A sobering thought crossed her mind. What if the one to die was Tamara? Oh no. No. No. No. No. It can't be. God would not do that. Would he? Would God drag all of them all over four states and through many dangers just to let the little girl die anyway? Sadness filled her thoughts: Tamara looked so frightened in the photograph on Cabinman's laptop. What kind of torment had she lived through? And then Amber thought of all the other kids; every picture was a torture victim. Tamara was the one they were after, but there were so many victims of these awful people.

She rehearsed the prophecy and thought about her own mystical experiences.

Amber drove down the freeway weeping and praying.

> Dear Jesus, I'm not as good at this as
> Preach. But I want to tell you something.
> I'll do whatever it takes to save those kids,
> to save Tamara and all of them. Please
> rescue them, even if I am the one to die.
> You've already saved me once in my
> lifetime, so I'm sort of living on bonus time
> anyway. I'm okay with whatever you do
> through me or to me. Just help us to save
> the kids. Amen.

She continued to weep all the way until sunrise, at which time she was so emotionally drained that she had to exit and get a Pepsi and some Skittles at a convenience store. All of her life Amber had been strong. It was unlike her to cry yet it felt good and right. With each passing mile through central California clarity and perception had swept over her and for the first time Amber Smith knew what it all meant. She also knew that there would be a price to pay for killing Cabinman.

She sat at the little plastic table in the convenience store, under the familiar glare of florescent tubes and ate her early morning snack while she wrote a letter.

Chapter Twenty-Eight

Theodicy and Steak

"THIS FEELS like a final meal before battle," Wyoming Wallace said as he chewed his porterhouse steak. After Amber arrived they let her take a nap, but when she awoke, Butch suggested they have a decent meal together and so he splurged and took them to the Outback Steakhouse. Wyoming ordered the biggest steak on the menu, Amber was only nibbling a New York strip but she had devoured most of the Blooming Onion appetizer. Pastor Butch went big time and was enjoying his lamb.

"Well, I felt like we needed it after the past couple of days." The meal was indeed refreshing to him.

"But I feel guilty," Amber said. "We probably should be working on finding Tamara right now. I mean, every second counts."

"That is true," Wyoming said chewing. "But we are of no use if our bodies don't work. We need to eat and we need to recover. You've been on the road for the past 36 hours and Reverend was traumatized at the trailer. We are no use to anyone else if we are not optimum when we act."

"I can't believe this, but I agree with Wyoming, Amber. Yes, I feel the frustration too, but even Jesus stopped and ate and went to sleep in the midst of a storm. Now, let me share with you what I've pieced together."

Butch spent the next few minutes describing what he had learned from the memory stick Amber had brought back. While Amber slept and Wyoming did whatever it was that Wyoming did, he had used his laptop to retrieve as much information as possible. Most of the data on the flash drive was files filled with pictures of boys and girls. Butch described how the pictures were apparently catalogued in some intentional order that he was unable to decipher. Some of the photographs were of children wearing clothing, and some were of them stripped naked. The way the data was arranged, it matched the usage he saw during the vision in the wasteland.

When Wyoming heard Pastor Butch's description of the digital information he cursed so loudly people looked at him from all of the surrounding tables.

After he calmed down, Butch continued his report by telling them the emails on the flash drive were interesting, but most were mindless chatter between the Cabinman and another person named Miles, who, Butch suspected, lived in Spokane. Judging from the emails he guessed that Spokane was a holding area for children who were snatched from the upper Midwest.

The last thing Butch shared was the good news and this was that in one of the emails there was an exact address of the location the children were at in San Diego. It was a pier warehouse outside of town along an old highway. Butch had a picture from Googlemaps and showed it to them. The bad news, though, was that he learned by deducing together three of the emails that the children were scheduled to be delivered day after tomorrow. Shark had been exact in his estimation of how much time they had before it would be too late.

From what he gathered, the plan or procedure they used was to bring a boat in the early morning darkness, load the children in pitch black, and then ferry them off, out to international waters and then they met another boat that would take them down the coastline into Mexico. From there the children were sent all around the globe.

"It would have been nice to have had the actual laptop, because I think we could have gotten more information. It is too bad Amber forgot to put it in her backpack when she left." Butch gave Amber a glance, a glance she took to indicate he gave little if any credence to her cover story.

"From what I've been told," Wyoming said after the briefing was over, "many of them end up back in the United States working the streets as prostitutes. They are brainwashed or have some kind of Stockholm syndrome effect where they identify with their captors so much they think they are doing the right thing for themselves by doing what their told."

"I've heard the same thing," said Amber.

Wyoming asked aloud, "What I don't understand is why this happens? How can any human being do that to another one, especially a child? It makes me sick."

"Well," said Pastor Butch, "part of the problem is that people are just rotten. But further than that, the more a person feeds their own depravity, the more debased they become and the more gruesome is the need for stimulation. Certainly there have always been sicko people in the world, but I blame the escalation of the problem in our culture today to the rise of pornography, the pornographic industry, and the mass technology that broadcasts it into people's homes in ways never dreamed even thirty years ago."

"That's crazy Reverend. Dirty pictures have been around since the Romans. We haven't invented anything new."

"True, pornography is old and we all know what the oldest profession is but, think about when you were growing up Wyoming, and you too Amber, for a person to consume pornography and sexually explicit images he, and it was almost always a he, would have to go into a shop, in public where he might be seen or his car spotted, and purchase it or view it. In big cities that was no problem, but in small towns, like Sydney for example, the stigma of being spotted engaging in that behavior was enough alone to keep most people from going down that path. And that is not including the public pressure aspect that made it nearly impossible for sexually oriented businesses to operate in town because of zoning restrictions. Pornography used to be bad policy.

"The result was that it took a lot less—Marilyn Monroe's skirt flying up or Cheryl Tiegs in a bikini—to arouse most men. But now, people can view pornography anonymously and without limit in their home from their computer or television. They can even take it with them on the go on their mobile phone or tablet. More and more graphic images are bombarding people and desensitizing them to the point where it takes even more quantity and more shocking images to generate arousal. For some people that means more and greater explicit content. For others, with a dangerous streak, it means real world contact, abuse, and destruction of someone else in order for them to live out their fantasies. Once a human being, whether it is a male or female, adult or child, is objectified in a digital media format it is a very small step to do the same thing to a flesh and blood person right in front of him or her."

Amber was hanging on every word Butch was saying.

"So you're saying that the internet is to blame?"

"No, Wyoming, the internet is neutral. Good things are on the net as well as bad things. But if you want a villain, a true villain who caused all of this, I suggest you look no further than Hugh Hefner. It was he, and primarily he alone, who convinced the civilized world that it should indulge their every sexual whim. Those of us who oppose that way of life argue that it objectifies women and debases the gift of God into something frivolous. But we were called prudish and puritanical and marginalized to the extremes. We attempt to try and protect our children and safeguard them, but the world is increasingly dangerous, frightening, and scary for children."

"Okay, I've had enough Reverend. I can see why you are a preacher. You are very convincing. Not sure I'm buying all of what you say," Wyoming ran his hand through his curly hair. "I mean, I do enjoy a good centerfold. But I can see the logic. How about another question, though, while we're talking about things all philosophical like. Why us? I mean, all of us have felt, in some way," he slowed down and ran his left hand through his short curls again, betraying uncertainty, "coerced, yeah, coerced into doing this. If I had my druthers I would be having dinner with Jennifer right now instead of you. Amber, you'd be working your job and saving money and doing the things you love and Reverend here would be saving souls at church.

"But why us? It doesn't feel very safe. God doesn't seem to be acting in a safe kind of way. I mean, you'll have to excuse me if it offends you, but it seems rather foolish. Why would God use such a foolish plan to save a little girl?"

"The Bible teaches us," said Pastor Butch, "that God uses the foolish things of this world to confound the wise. Sometimes God just doesn't make sense. Dying on a Roman cross in an embittered part of a dusty ancient world seems a foolish way to save the world—and then trust the message to fishermen, slaves, and a curmudgeonly Jewish Pharisee as the main way of evangelizing is equally as foolish."

Amber spoke up, "I've been thinking the same thing, Wy," she pointed at Wyoming. "I know you would rather be doing other things and so would Preach. But me, I've got, really, nothing else going on. My life is all extra time anyway. About three years ago I nearly committed suicide because I couldn't see any way out of the mess around me; so really, I'm just grateful to be in the game, so to speak. So I'm not complaining, but it feels very unsafe and haphazard."

She continued to explain, "Wy, you have the most experience, but really, none of us knows what we're doing and we're just making it up as we go. If it hadn't of been for a bit of luck here and there, we'd be nowhere in our investigation. It just seems so, inefficient and odd."

"What you call luck might be understood as the hand of God."

"Okay," Amber answered Butch, "Maybe so. Maybe the luck was God's doing but I really agree with Wy, The Lord doesn't seem to be acting very safe now, does he?"

"God is not safe!" Pastor Butch Gregory said that as an exclamation point. He was thinking about the quote from the C. S. Lewis classic about the lion Aslan where Lewis informs the reader that Aslan is not safe, but he is good. Butch repeated the line, "God is not safe, but he is good. His desire is to change the world with those who are willing. Perhaps as he searched our heart, he knew we were all willing. I also can't get away from this idea that, even if it is unsafe, it is not only good for Tamara that someone looks for her, but also good for us. We need this for our own personal growth as individuals."

"How do you mean?" asked Amber.

"I told you a little bit about Shark at my home. What I didn't tell you is that he died while we were playing together. I have carried the guilt my whole life that I couldn't save him. I would have gladly exchanged my life for his and have prayed that prayer often—that if there were any way for me to go back in time and make the exchange, I would. That is why it was so curious to me that when the Lord called me to this, he did it through my dead brother. Shark was the one person that could talk to me about my inner pain. A better way to put it, he is the one person who could talk me through my inner pain. This mission might be more about my healing than I even know right now. I don't know for sure, but my suspicion is that the two of you, in your own way, have something similar. There is some kind of history, a part of our individual pasts, which God is letting us atone for," he paused and then corrected slightly "or maybe helping us work through."

Wyoming sat stone faced. Part of him wanted to share about Leyla. He wanted to tell about Fallujah. He wanted to open up and expose all his inner darkness and pain to the light that was being shared at this table but he couldn't. He just sat there and took another swig of beer and ate another bite of steak. Perhaps after tomorrow he would. Not right now.

Amber, however, was an open book.

"I know exactly what you mean, Preach. Ever since this started happening, I've thought more about my brother Adam than I have the last year combined. I also think about Steve and I think about the voices that I used to hear. Looking for Tamara, and facing the bad guys, feels, in many ways, like I am undoing some of the wasted time, the wasted moments of my life. What is the word you used?"

"Atonement," said the pastor.

"Yeah, atonement. Or healing."

Amber's thoughts were about Cabinman. Part of her wanted to share that story right now, but she just couldn't. There would be a time for that to be known, but that time was not now. Not right now.

"Alright, one more question." Wyoming said to Butch. "Maybe I buy the issue about us growing as people or about healing and such, but that still doesn't answer the biggest question of them all. Why," his words crept out of his mouth in a syllable by syllable crawl, "Why does God allow all this evil and badness in the world to start with? If you could answer me that, I'd appreciate it very much."

"That is a universal question Wyoming, one that people have been asking for a long, long, long time. Some people believe that it is logically inconsistent, and therefore, God does not exist. Others have adopted a view that God would like to end suffering and evil, but he is not strong enough to do so. I find both of those unsatisfying. From my own experiences I know that God exists and I believe he is all-powerful. So what we are left with is something else. That something else is the paradox of love."

"Wait a minute," Amber interrupted. "Evil's in the world because of love?"

"Yeah, I don't get it either." Wyoming took another drink of beer.

"Exactly," Butch said. "It is a paradox. Here is the way I see it. God loves us so much that he gives us freedom. Freedom is something great—I have it, you have it, all people have it. But with that freedom comes the capacity to do evil things. Some people abuse the freedom to do evil. The only way to remove all evil is to remove freedom. He loves us too much to take away our freedom, our right to choose. Therefore, God allows evil so that freedom may thrive. Only a truly free person can love. Therefore, love and evil must both exist in order for love to be legitimate."

Wyoming snorted, "Humph."

"There is one more aspect to it, though. God's answer to the problem of suffering and evil cannot be taken into consideration without the work of Christ Jesus. Christ suffered under Pontius Pilate, says the old creed, he was tortured and killed. God's answer was to suffer with us. Because of that, he knows how we hurt. That is why Jesus is so great. Our hope is that just as he reversed his crucifixion and turned it into resurrection, somehow he will reverse all the evil in the world in heaven. Somehow. I don't know how, but somehow."

Amber said, "I guess that is why it is called faith, and I have faith that tomorrow we will rescue Tamara Rey." Her confidence came as a result of her early morning experiences driving down the California highway.

The trio sat in the restaurant and talked a lot longer. Butch and Amber ordered a dessert and Wyoming ordered a cocktail. Finally, they all got up and Pastor Butch drove them back out to the airport where their hotel was and they all three went to bed. Even Wyoming forewent his usual philandering and went to sleep.

They each prayed, in their own way; that tomorrow would bring their odyssey to an end.

Chapter Twenty-Nine

The Angel In My Dream

THE DRIVE out of town to the isolated pier took longer than they had planned because of the winding seaside road. It was a little after nine that morning when the three arrived. They drove past the pier about a half mile and turned down a country road. After parking Amber's Corolla on the side of the road they walked back through the brush to the edge of the pier. The pier was long and jutted out into the deeper water. An old fishing vessel was moored to the pier on the opposite side of the warehouse. Wyoming surmised that was the boat they used to transport the children off and out into international waters.

As they lay in the prone position beside the highway opposite the pier Wyoming formulated a plan to gain access to the warehouse. He pointed at the front door, "It'll be guarded, you can bet on that."

"How do we get out there?" Butch realized the weakness of the question as he said it.

"We've got the element of surprise on our side," Wyoming replied and then asked Amber for the binoculars out of her bag. He studied the situation for several minutes; then he began to speak, slow and methodically.

"I'll walk out there straight on and get their attention on me. The two of you slip down into the water and move from pylon to pylon until you get to the boat. I can see that there is a little rigging out where the boat is docked. You can use it to pull yourself up. While I'm keeping the guards busy the two of you can go down the pier to the back door; which is probably where Tamara and any other children they have are being held."

"I don't like it," said Amber. "It separates us. Plus, you probably will not get very far by yourself with those guards."

"Do you have another idea?"

Silence.

"I didn't think so. I never said it was perfect, but we don't have a lot of options. Besides, don't worry about me. I've been in tight situations before. If something happens to me, no matter. After all, that prophecy Butch is always talking about says one of us dies. Haven't the two of you figured out yet that the one who will do the dying will probably be me?"

It was the first time Wyoming had spoken about his internal contemplation, and apparently, his acceptance of, the prophetic utterance. Butch noticed it, and so did Amber. What Butch didn't understand is why Wyoming had assumed it would be him who would be the one to die.

Each one of the three people fully expected to be the one to die and each one of them, in a supernatural way, was completely at peace with that idea.

Wyoming had settled it all in his mind. Now what mattered was the plan, and so he spoke up. "What I am really worried about though, is the two of you. Can you swim?"

They both glared at him with incredulity.

"Well, I had to ask. If you can slide down the rock facing on this side of the pier, away from the warehouse, you should be undetected. The pylons on this pier are not as thick as the ones downtown, so you should be able to grab them, and then move from pylon to pylon until you get to the rigging."

"Okay, we'll try your plan. But before we do anything, we must pray. This is crunch time."

"Again?" protested Wyoming. "We prayed at the hotel before we left. We prayed in the car on the way here. I know good and well you prayed this morning in your room. I mean, come on. Do you really need to pray again?"

"Yes. Again."

"Fine, fine. Just make it snappy. I'm certain the Good Lord wants us to get on with it."

Pastor Butch ignored his partner's agitation and simply began to pray.

> Dear Lord, we've come this far. We believe you asked us to do this and we feel that now is the time. Help us to make it safely and for our plan to work. Let us find Tamara and any others who are being hurt and get them out of here. In Jesus' name, Amen.

Both Amber and Wyoming added their, "Amen" to Butch's prayer.

"Butch, you'd better take this," Wyoming said as he pulled out a small .22 pistol from his pants' pocket. "I brought this just in case we needed extra help. I think you should take it."

"No, I can't take it. I am a man of peace. I am not a warrior. I'm not against the use of force, but, I," and he hesitated, "I just can't see myself shooting at another human being."

"Well, suit yourself. I hope you, and I hope we, don't regret it."

"Wait a minute, how did you get your pistols down here? You didn't have them in Las Vegas because of the airplane?" Butch was trying to piece it together.

"As soon as I knew we were coming here and you made the hotel reservation, I had Jennifer overnight these. They were waiting on me at the lobby when we arrived. Sometimes I really think I love that girl."

"You can mail a handgun?" Amber was amazed.

"Yes, if you know what you're doing. Trust me, Jennifer knows what she's doing. Amber, do you have the pistol I gave you?"

"Sure do."

"Good. If you have to use it; remember what I taught you." Amber nodded.

Immediately after the next car passed by the pier, Amber and Butch hurried across the two-lane highway and crawled down the jagged rock wall to the beach below. It wasn't as much as a beach as it was the place where the large rocks ended and the smaller rocks began. The pier's bottom was about head high on Butch as he stood at the base of it on the water's edge. The warehouse was about thirty or forty yards away at the end of the pier. It would not be a long swim, but it would be tedious. Just as he was about to step out into the water, Amber tapped him on the shoulder.

"Look," she said and pointed above. Mounted on the side of the pier were two—not one but two—white, circular life preservers.

Butch whispered, "Nice work," to Amber and then he looked up toward heaven and said, "Thank you."

Amber pulled out her pocket knife, reached up and cut the rescue line for both of the floats then she reached down to her waist and took out the pistol and put it inside her shirt and tucked it into her bra. "I think it will still shoot if it gets wet, but just in case, I want to keep it dry."

Butch didn't argue, but he did add, "Oh, I hope it doesn't come to shooting. I've had my fill of violence. But," he paused and his face blushed as he said, "isn't there a better place to put it than there? I mean, really?"

She ignored him.

The two of them eased into the water directly underneath the pier. The morning shadows made it ideal to hide all the way down to the end. Butch was pleasantly surprised at how nice the water in Southern California felt compared to his experiences in the frigid hypothermia inducing waters of Puget Sound.

The two swimmers couldn't afford the luxury of kicking full tilt on their floats for fear of being heard. Stealth was more important than speed. Nevertheless they made good time moving from pylon to pylon until they reached the boat. The boat was named El Diablo, written in red letters outlined in yellow.

Wyoming had been watching their progress through the binocular lens. As they neared the boat he pulled out his .45 and checked the rounds—six bullets, one in each hole of the revolver. Then he felt in his pocket for extra bullets. He had plenty. When he saw that Butch and Amber were climbing up the rigging, he put the weapon back in his shoulder harness underneath his teal colored light windbreaker and stood up. He walked out onto the highway, adjusted his ball cap and then marched out onto the pier. He strolled with certainty and confidence right up to the warehouse door.

Act like one who belongs here.

Just as he suspected, two thugs immediately came out from the side door and approached him.

"Ya not supposed to be here," said the first thug in a New York accent.

"Yes, actually, I am supposed to be here you knucklehead."

"Why?" said the other one. He had a gold tooth and a pony tail and said "Why" with a distinct southern drawl. Wyoming picked up on that and replied in kind.

"Becuz the boss sed I culd come pick me out one of them there pretty little things."

Wyoming had spent a lot of time in the South and with Southerners; so he knew how to throw the accent. Even though some of the smartest people he'd ever met are from south of the Mason-Dixon Line, there was something about a southern dialect which made the speaker sound stupid or naïve; innocent. It tended to help with gaining the 'benefit-of-the-doubt' when bluffing. Wyoming needed the benefit-of-the-doubt.

Butch and Amber watched the conversation play out with their heads just over the side of the pier. They dare not climb up all the way yet. Wyoming was still working his subterfuge. However, neither one of them knew how long they could hold themselves in that position. With each passing second their fingers, hands, and arms grew weaker. Butch was certain he would make quite a large splash in the water beneath him. The climb up the rigging had been far harder on him and his middle-aged gut than on Amber. Hanging there he thought about how all those years on the street had made her very strong and powerful, while all those years at fellowships and potlucks had made him slow and weak. If he made it out of this alive, he promised the Lord to take better care of himself and join the gym.

If he made it out.

Wyoming was waiting for the reply from the two guards. If New York called his bluff; then he would have to act fast. He was already imagining himself taking a swing at Southern Boy and then shooting New York quickly. Or should he go the other way around. He supposed that New York would be quicker on the draw; so maybe he should swing at the Yankee first and then take Dixie out. Maybe his best move would be to run right between them quickly and then dart inside the first door office. That was, of course, if the office was unlocked. It might be electronically coded to lock automatically when shut. If that were the case, then he might be better just turning around and running. That would force the other two to chase him which would draw them away and open the front for Amber and Butch.

New York paused for a moment, and then said. "Let's go inside and take a look at da book."

"Okie dokie bubba," Wyoming said. This was going to work.

The three of them walked around to the side of the warehouse and entered the door. It was tinted glass with no lettering on it at all. Once they entered, Wyoming stood right in front of the door to block the view while the two men took positions directly in front of him.

Amber nodded to Butch and the two quickly crawled onto the wooden planks and, on all fours, crawled past the door. They had no way of knowing for sure that the two bad guys inside couldn't see them, but they had learned to trust Wyoming. Once they were clear of the door they stood and eased down the boardwalk to the end of the warehouse where the back door was. They knew it was there because Wyoming had seen it with the binoculars; what they didn't know is if it would be unlocked.

It wasn't.

Butch groaned, but Amber went to work. "Give me your credit card." Obediently Butch dug through his soaked wallet and surrendered the church Visa card. Within seconds Amber had worked her way past the simple doorknob and into the warehouse. What other dangerous but helpful things did she know about? He thought her to be like the runaway slave in the Bible whose name was Onesimus, which meant "useful." Amber's time as a runaway on the streets had surely proven useful now, and that was the most useful way that church credit card had ever been used.

Amber and Butch entered cautiously and walked down the corridor and around a corner. What they didn't see was the security camera mounted on the wall, but it saw them.

"Where do you think they are at?" asked Butch in a whisper.

Amber shook her head, "I don't know for sure, Preach. I was kind of hoping we would hear them by now."

"Me too. It is not that big of a facility. Maybe they aren't here."

"They are here. I know they are."

"Amber, how do you know?"

"You're not the only one who has visions and dreams."

"What? What have you seen?"

"Later, Preach. I'll tell you later."

The two took a few steps down the half-light of the hallway. Their heavy breathing and squeaky wet shoes were the only sounds in the corridor.

A door behind them, which they had not seen before, burst open. A large, red faced man rushed out and yelled profanities as he lurched toward them. Butch and Amber ran down the hallway. Two shots were fired in their direction. Amber could feel the air of the first bullet when it breezed by her ear, just nearly missing her head. The second shot found a target, hitting Butch in the shoulder. He screamed in pain but kept running. They both darted left in unison through a door.

Butch collapsed into the far corner of the room yelling in agony.

Amber's agile mind and quick wits took over. She slammed the door closed and then crouched in the corner behind where the door would open. She sucked in her breath and yanked out the .38 pistol from her shirt and cocked the hammer back. Her urge was to shoot blindly through the door but knew that wouldn't work. She had to wait.

She winked at Butch. He didn't really know what that meant, but, as with Wyoming, he'd learned to trust her. His shoulder hurt, but not as much as he thought it would, given that he'd never been shot before. He winked back at her.

They both heard the feet outside run to the doorway and stop. The handle turned and Amber caught her breath. The door flung open and the goon pounced. He saw the pitiful sight of Butch lying on the floor. Amber could not see him yet, as she was behind the open door. She counted to herself. One. Two. Then she kicked the door with her left foot and lifted the pistol. Amber squeezed off a shot at near point blank range. The sound echoed in the metal room and hurt Butch's ears more than his own gunshot wound. The evil man fell onto the floor and clutched his gut as blood spurted out. The bullet had gone through his back near the spine and came out just above the navel.

Amber stood over him.

"Where are they?"

The man was silent.

"One more time," she demanded as she put the gun's barrel in his face. "Where are they?"

Again, silence.

Amber squeezed off another shot.

"Oh, no," Butch said, shaking. "Was that necessary?"

"Justice," replied Amber.

She grabbed the pistol from the corpse and stuck it into her pants. She found a smaller semi-automatic in his breast pocket and she took it too.

"Are you okay?" she asked Butch.

"Yes. It hurts, but the bullet went clean through."

She ripped at the shirt on the body and stuffed it into the entry and exit holes of Butch's shoulder. With another piece of shirt she tied a makeshift bandage and said. "We've got to keep moving. Everyone around heard those shots. Where should we go?"

"Probably through the door he came out of. I would wager he was guarding something. Or someone. So we need to go back the way we came to the other end of this hallway."

"You're right. Let's go."

Butch stood up and Amber gave him the small semi-automatic and ordered, "Be ready to use this. All our lives might depend on it." Butch did not argue but he felt a little odd holding the destructive weapon. Amber could see the hesitation in his face. "Look, Preach we are at a place where it is us or them. I pray you don't have to use it, but please take it." He took the gun and held it. Then he threw it down onto the dead body. "No."

"I didn't think you would, but it was worth a try. Let's go."

He felt a little dizzy and the first couple of steps were difficult. But once they left the room adrenaline kicked in and he moved swiftly. All pretense of being quiet was now gone. They trotted down the hall and quickly ran through the still opened doorway.

This doorway led to another hallway that ran to their left and they walked steadily down it, passing what looked like storage rooms. Large boxes and crates were stacked high. As the hallway neared an end it opened up into a larger warehouse. Butch and Amber ran to the other end where there was one small door. They looked at each other and

Amber pulled out her two pistols and stood ready. Butch turned the knob and then with a quick thrust he pushed open the door.

It opened to the warehouse room which was rowed with cages, just like A-OK Mekaniks in Tacoma, but many more. It looked like a zoo holding area; except inside these cages were little children. Slivers of natural light glimmered through small slats in the top of the walls. Ceiling fans circulated the fowl septic air. Butch and Amber ran up and down the rows between the cages shouting.

"Tamara," called Butch.

"Tamara," echoed Amber.

Finally a weak yet hopeful voice sounded back, "Pastor Butch? Is that you?"

"Yes, yes it is. We're here to get you."

"I knew you would come. I knew it would be you."

"We're going to get all of you out of here," Amber screamed this so every child could hear it.

"That's right," Butch said. "We're all getting out of here right now. Tamara, do you know where the keys are kept?"

"Yeah, in the desk."

Neither Butch nor Amber had seen the small green metal desk pushed against the back wall. Amber tucked the .38 pistol into her pants, walked to the desk, and opened the center pencil drawer. A key chain with one large key was all that was in the drawer.

"Got it!" she shouted.

Amber ran to Tamara's cage and tested the key. Seconds later the prison door swung open and Tamara ran out and hugged Butch. Both of them were crying uncontrollably. Butch held Tamara's face in his hands and temporarily forgot all about the pain in his shoulder. He winced, though, when he saw the deep bruise on her face where Knuckles had hit her in his vision of the trailer. A shiver ran down his spine.

"Thank you Pastor Butch," said Tamara. "I knew you would come." Then she looked directly at Amber and said, "You're the angel in my dream."

"I dreamed about you too, Tamara," she replied and quickly went to work releasing the other captives. Most of them did not immediately leave their dungeon when the lock clicked. They sat there stunned, unsure of how to respond. Their hopes had been crushed long ago and there was very little left of independent will.

Amber yelled back to the sobbing Butch and Tamara, "Help me get these kids out. We probably don't have all day. This isn't over yet."

Butch and Tamara began gathering the children and coaxing them out of their cages while Amber moved through the room unlocking all the cages. Butch made a headcount and tallied 27 children, mostly girls but a few boys. He said a silent prayer over each one of them as he passed by them.

> Dear Lord, heal this child
> from the evil encountered.

Once all the children had been gathered, Butch shouted, "Let's go!" Butch led the group out walking briskly while Amber took the rear position. Butch was carrying Tamara. She had latched onto his non injured shoulder and was not letting go. Likewise, Amber had a sweet little blonde girl with big blue eyes attached to her neck. They walked by the rooms filled with boxes, through the door where the goons had attacked them and back into the main hallway. The group then moved to their left and opened the door to the outside. The light was bright and the sun was glaring. Butch's eyes took a moment to adjust but there was a collective shriek from the children who all winced with pain as they came out of the darkness of captivity and into the sunshine of hope.

Neither Butch nor Amber said anything about him, but as they had made their way out of the warehouse they were both thinking about Wyoming. Their wondering soon found an answer. Wyoming was at the wheel of the El Diablo, with the engine running, and a big fat black cigar in his mouth. "What took you so long?"

"We ran into a couple of problems."

"Looks like you ran into a bullet too," said Wyoming as he pointed to Butch's shoulder. "Get those kids on this boat and we can scoot on into San Diego Harbor and find the police there."

"What happened to the two men?" Amber asked.

"You mean Tweedle Dum and Tweedle Dee? I took care of them. I didn't even break a sweat."

"You didn't kill them did you?" Butch looked worried.

"No, Reverend, I didn't kill them. They are tied up with their own belts and shoe laces inside that building over there. I didn't gag them, though, because I want them to have to listen to each other."

"Why didn't you come help us then?" asked Butch. "We could have used an expert?"

"Well, I did, sorta. That office has security cameras all over the place. I could see your progress and I saw Amber plug that guy. Nice work by the way. After I saw that all the bad guys were cleared out and that you had made it to the kids, I went ahead and planned our getaway. Now hurry up, get us untied and get into the boat."

Amber and Butch scurried all the children aboard.

When Wyoming saw Tamara clutching onto Butch he saw Leyla. Her features, coloration, and even countenance looked to him to be identical to the Iraqi five year old from a decade earlier. A wave of healing swept over the young and bitter man. The best word to describe what he felt in that moment was hope. Wyoming Wallace experienced hope for the first time since Fallujah.

It was an unexpected emotion.

Butch put Tamara down and told her, "I've got to untie this thing, go on into the boat. I'll be there in a second. You're safe now." Amber did the same thing, putting Britney down and the two soaking wet rescuers fumbled with the rope.

The serene marine air of the Pacific Ocean was shattered by the roaring boom of a gun as a bullet hit the hull of the boat. Butch looked down the walkway and saw five men jumping out of a van. Either someone called for backup, or they accidentally interrupted a fresh delivery.

Maybe the security cameras are tied into another remote computer and they saw everything. Butch hoped their rescue would not be short lived. He looked up into the boat, all of the children were down below, out of immediate danger.

The five men bore down on the boat and opened fire. Wyoming Wallace shouted, "Oh no you don't, not this time," and then he returned fire with his .45. It sounded like a cannon. His second shot found a target as the head of one of the attackers exploded. So did his fourth, destroying the kneecap of one of the assailants, knocking him into the water.

Amber likewise returned fire with both of her pistols, keeping the attackers, who lacked any cover at all, at bay.

Butch was still wrestling with ropes. "Get on the boat!" Wyoming shouted to them while he reloaded, taking cover behind the sturdy wooden helm of the boat. When he finished and jumped onboard he ushered the children to the relative safety below deck.

"Stay down," Butch shouted toward Tamara and the others.

Two more shots were heard from the approaching men, and one of them struck the cigar in Wyoming's mouth and it exploded.

"That was a Cuban!" Wyoming shouted and returned two more volleys with anger. The boat had been freed from the pier, but it floated out on the water aimlessly as Wyoming tried to steer and reload at the same time. Amber and Butch both came topside to help Wyoming get the boat safely away. Amber fired both of her weapons in the general direction of the pier. Wyoming emptied his pistol, but none of his bullets were successful. He reloaded again and Butch tried to steer. The boat began to get some distance from the pier, but the outlaws kept firing at it.

They were all too preoccupied to notice the sleek white boat with blue trim that appeared and flashed its sirens, but they all heard the voice over the speakers of the boat. The voice demanded, "Put down your weapons and place your hands over your head or we will shoot. Put down your weapons and put your hands over your head or we will shoot." The three heroes on the boat looked at each other inquisitively and each wondered the same thing, but only Wyoming said it, "Is he talking to us, or to them?"

Butch spotted Agent Debra Lapp-Bench with her pistol drawn on the bow of the incoming boat as it nudged itself between the *El Diablo* and the pier. He breathed a sigh of relief. The cavalry was here, right on time.

Butch lifted his hands and when he did his shoulder roared with pain. In the rush of the moment, he had forgotten all about being shot. Slowly, very slowly he stepped out into the open from behind the wall he and Amber and Wyoming had been hiding behind. Amber switched the lever on the engines and the boat came to a stop. It seemed like the fire fight was over and Agent Lapp-Bench was in firm control. Now Wyoming, Amber and Butch were all on the bow of the *El Diablo*, but the pastor turned backward and told the children to stay down below. "Tamara, keep all the other kids down there for now. We don't know what might happen next."

"Yes Pastor Butch."

The three rescuers took protective positions directly over the open hatch to where the children were.

Butch looked over to the pier and saw the remaining sex traffickers. Standing head and shoulders above the other two was the blonde headed baddie Knuckles. The El Diablo had drifted back against the pier and the two men were only about twenty feet away from one another. The boat kept drifting. Butch hadn't been this close to Knuckles since he bonked him on the head with the battery. The police boat was just reaching the pier and Agents Barry Chase and Lapp-Bench along with what looked like an entire swat team were spilling over onto the pier to surround the evil ones who had dropped their guns.

Knuckles growled at Butch. Butch just glared back.

Butch saw motion from Knuckles and at first didn't understand, but then realized he was going for another gun tucked in his pants. Butch shouted, "No!" and when he did everyone looked at him. Knuckles pulled his weapon and fired in Butch's direction. But he missed. Instead, the fated bullet sailed through the air and struck Amber Smith in the chest. She collapsed sideways and fell onto the pastor.

Agent Lapp-Bench then sent Knuckles straight to eternal death with a bullet right between his eyes. She put two more into his chest before he finally collapsed onto the wood decking of the pier.

Shock filled the pastor and he collapsed over Amber's body and pulled it to himself.

Wyoming Wallace stood helpless. All he could do was watch.

Amber tried to talk, but words were having a hard time forming. The breath of life was leaving her. Finally, with one last exhale she said, "I see my brother Adam with Jesus, and Shark. And," she gasped, "Leyla." She died seconds later as the pastor held her hand and told her how brave she was, and how Jesus was waiting for her, and that she had done well. The children were saved.

Butch Gregory held the young woman in his arms, like a father would hold a child. It was a reverse pieta of sorrow. He looked up at the heavens and screamed, "Why not me? Why her? Why not me?" Butch kept shouting it over and over and over again. Then the tears came. Butch cried for the rest of the day as he was taken into custody, handcuffed, and led away. He cried as they took him to a local hospital and his shoulder was cleaned, sutured, and his arm put in a sling. He cried all night as he rode in the back of a windowless armored vehicle. He cried the next day as he sat alone in a room.

Chapter Thirty

Nothing But Abiding Contempt

TWO DAYS after the rescue and Amber Smith's death, Butch Gregory was allowed to shower and given a clean change of clothes. They were his clothes; his favorite tan trousers, a white button down and a navy blue sweater vest. He assumed Lucy had brought them from home. Or was he back in Washington? He did not know where he was. He longed to hold his wife and hug his son and daughter. He wanted to talk to Tamara and her mother Nikki. He wanted to tell Wyoming thank you. He wanted to tell everyone about Amber.

The only company he'd had that morning was a medic who came and changed the bandage on his wound.

He was served a ham and cheese sandwich and a Coke for lunch. He was not hungry. He did drink the soda. Not long after his lunch, a tall man dressed in a black suit came and escorted him out. "Follow me, Dr. Gregory."

Without saying a word Butch got up and walked out of the room and across two corridors and finally he was brought into a small room with one light hanging overhead, a wooden table and three chairs.

"Have a seat Dr. Gregory."

"Do I have a choice?"

"No."

"Then I'll have a seat."

He sat down and the tall man left the room.

Five minutes later Agent Lapp-Bench came in, alone. Agent Chase was not with her. Butch assumed he was behind a two-way glass or watching on a monitor somewhere.

"Dr. Gregory, we've reviewed all the evidence we've found. You friend Mr. Wallace has told us all about his part in the scuffle at the A-OK Mekaniks in Tacoma, the compound in Snohomish, the two men he killed in Seattle, the trips to Nevada and Oregon and finally how the three of you planned everything in San Diego. Do you have anything you'd like to add?"

"Are the children safe? Have they all been put back with their parents?"

"I can't answer that. This interview is about you and your activity. Do you have anything else you'd like to add voluntarily?"

"No, not really, except that, if you'd asked me two weeks ago to do what I have done, I would have refused. However, having lived this week and experienced what we've experienced, I can tell you I have no regrets and, regardless of what you do to me, I would do it all over again."

"But, Dr. Gregory, what you did was to get your friend Amber killed. You have no regrets about that? You have no regrets that your actions directly contributed to the death of someone you cared about? Do you not realize you have to answer for your actions?"

"With all due respect, Agent Lapp-Bench, I answer to a higher authority than you. I know that I will be accountable for my actions; it was he, him alone, who sent me on this mission and I have acted accordingly. As to Amber, we all knew that one of us was going to die. It was in the prophecy. We just didn't know which one of us it would be. But we all settled in our mind that reality and went forward.

"Tell me, Agent Lapp-Bench, if you knew that doing the right thing to help someone else, to do what you've been called to do could result in your death, would you do it? Would you play it safe and let others perish and live awful lives of slavery and at the whim of a sicko's perversion? Or would you accept that the Lord was the Lord of both life and death and decide to make the best difference you could for others?" Then he added, with a bit of spite and disdain, "There are worse thing than dying, Agent Lapp-Bench."

"What is worse than dying?"

"Disobedience."

The Agent looked down at her lap and then she looked up at the ceiling randomly and took a deep breath.

"Dr. Gregory, the bureau has decided not to file charges against you or your friend Mr. Wallace. In addition, we are providing immunity for any crimes, and there are many, which you committed in these ten days. An agent is waiting outside the door and she will take you home."

"Not so fast. I have a question for you, since I have you here and may never get the chance to ask it again. You guys knew all along what was going on with that nasty group of people, didn't you? You knew what Knuckles and his vile gang were up to. You knew about the children, you knew about the holding areas, you knew about the websites, you knew about the sick disgusting demons who buy human beings to be used as sex toys and you didn't do anything about it." As he spoke, Pastor Butch did not raise his voice, but his intensity level steadily increased.

"Don't tell me you don't have a file thick enough to have put them all away forever, and you've had that file long before Tamara was ever abducted and long before we ever got involved in it. Isn't that right Agent? Why didn't you intervene sooner? If you had acted when you could have, none of this—not the deaths, not the hurt, not the trauma, not Amber, none of this would have ever happened. If you people had done your job I would not be here right now and I wouldn't have to sleep at night thinking about the boys and girls we didn't save and the little ones who were shipped out last week or last month or last year. Tell me, I demand an answer from you and from my government as to why you let this injustice go on day after day after day?"

"I don't have to answer any of that, Dr. Gregory."

"I know you don't, but as one human being to another, not as professionals, but as humans, please tell me, give me a reason."

"Dr. Gregory, you should be glad that you are not in prison right now. You are the one being questioned here. I suggest you take your opportunity to go before we decide to change our minds about your long-term future."

"You win, Agent Lapp-Bench, and I am ready to go home. But you, and all of you," he stood up and waved his hand around the outer darkness of the room, gesturing at the assumed eyes and cameras pointed at him, "have lost your sense of direction. You've forgotten who the good guys are and who the bad guys are, and you have neglected those you've sworn to protect—the innocent and the vulnerable. You have forgotten that you are accountable to us—the people, and to God Almighty. I have nothing but abiding contempt for all of you, you pathetic and worthless pen pushers."

He walked toward the door and was escorted out by the agent who was waiting for him.

Chapter Thirty-One

Home

THE RIDE home was not what Butch expected. He assumed the overnight journey in the windowless armored vehicle was to Washington. He was wrong. He was not in Washington at all. He was, as best he could tell, at some installation located in northern Nevada or maybe Southeastern Oregon. It had been dark when he arrived and it was daylight as he left. Maybe he cried so much during the journey that he couldn't remember. Or maybe they gave him some pain medication for his wound that kept him sedated and he was unconscious for part of the trip. Everything had been a numb blur since the pier.

The agent drove him to a helipad where he was put on a white and blue helicopter and flown to an airstrip. At the airstrip they put him on a small jet piloted by two FBI agents. The jet landed at the small regional airport just outside of Sydney, where another car met them and whisked him off to his home.

When he got out of the car, the agent left. For the first time in three days, Butch Gregory was, apparently, a free man. Lucy threw open the door so hard that it crashed against the stair rails as she ran out to meet him. She gave him a big kiss, and Paul and Sarah came running. He swung his arms around all three of them and gave them the longest, biggest and best hugs of his life.

"I have a surprise for you," his wife whispered in his ear.

She walked him up the sidewalk and into the front door. His surprise was sitting on the couch. It was Nikki Jones. She exploded out of the seat and ran to him and hugged him. Tears were streaming down her face. "Thank you, thank you, thank you for saving my baby. Oh, Pastor Butch, I don't know how you did it, but thank you."

"Is Tamara here?" Butch asked.

"No, the really nice FBI woman said that they were holding her, and the rest of the children for a few days of evaluation and counseling. She said that Tamara will probably need counseling for a long time, and that they would help her get what she needed."

"Have you been able to see Tamara?"

"Yes, yes, I spent yesterday with her. She is not far away."

"When she gets home, Nikki, I'd like to see her. I didn't really have a chance to talk to her at all at the pier."

"Sure thing, right after I get all my hugs and kisses out of her then we will come see you."

"Deal."

"Where are your friends, honey? Aren't they with you?" When Lucy asked him that question he realized they didn't know anything about what had happened. Butch walked into the dining room and sat at the oak table. He sat in the chair Shark had sat in when he had visited him, and this was the chair he had sat in when he shared the prophecy with Butch and Amber. He cried.

"I have not seen Wyoming since they arrested us at the pier." He gulped. "Amber Smith was shot in the chest and died in my arms. She was shot saving them. Mrs. Jones, we would have never saved Tamara had it not been for Amber. She saved my life, and she saved all of theirs. It is to her and Wyoming Wallace to which you owe your gratitude. Those two are the bravest people I have ever met."

Three days later, Butch finally was able to see Tamara. He and Nikki decided it would be best to meet at the church building. Nikki had not brought Tamara back to the apartment where she was abducted yet. The FBI counselor had suggested moving, and never letting Tamara go back because she would never feel safe there. Butch understood the logic. Meeting at the church, a place which had safe, happy memories for Tamara seemed like a good idea. Butch was waiting for her in the library. When she arrived, she broke loose from her mother and ran toward Butch and jumped up into his arms. He winced at the pain in his shoulder, but didn't say anything.

The hug lasted a long while.

"You are so brave Tamara," Butch told her after they sat down into the chairs around a small coffee table. "And I am proud of you."

"Do you like my new dress?" Tamara stood up and pirouetted for him.

"Yes, did your mom get that for you?"

"Yeah. I'm not afraid any more."

"You must have been very afraid?"

"I was at first. But then, then I started having dreams, especially after they took us to the water by the ocean. Inside the cage I could hear the water beating against the wood and against the shore. I could hear boats and their horns out on the water. I kept thinking about that story in the Bible of Jesus walking on the water and I prayed for Jesus to walk out and save us. Then I dreamed about you. In my dream you walked on the water and came and saved me. That is why when you showed up, I wasn't surprised. I expected you. God told me you were coming."

Tears formed in the eyes of Pastor Butch Gregory.

"I also dreamed about that pretty woman. Mommy says her name was Amber."

"Yes, her name is Amber. Amber Smith." Butch emphasized the "is" instead of the "was" that Tamara had used. It is a subtle difference, but meaningful.

"Pastor Butch, was she a police woman?"

"No honey, she was a janitor. A janitor who listened to God."

"While I was still in the cage, she came and talked to me in my dreams. She told me that she was taking my place and that was okay, it was what she wanted and it was what God wanted. She was so beautiful in a white dress and radiant blonde hair in my dreams, like an angel. But when I saw her in real life she was so strong and powerful with you there. I felt like she could do anything. When I grow up I want to be strong and powerful and help protect and save people like her."

At that point Butch could not hold back the tears any longer. He swept Tamara up in his arms and held her tight. "You do that; you grow up to be strong and powerful. But the important thing right now is that you will grow up."

Chapter Thirty-Two

Confession

TWO WEEKS after he met with Tamara, Butch tried to return to work on a Monday morning. It was the middle part of September and some basic things needed to get figured out. Soon there would be fall preaching schedules to arrange, Advent was not too far away and then there was Christmas. He preached the day before, and it felt good to be back. He did not preach the sermon on prayer he'd pulled from file a month earlier. He instead preached about Jesus walking on the water.

He truly loved preaching and it acted as a healing balm. It was pastoring that was hard.

Mildred greeted him with a smile as he came in around 9 AM, which was later than normal, but he was trying to ease into it. She talked to him about all the happenings at the church and how Pastor Philip had done a great job in his absence, but it was nice to have him back. She had a thousand questions about the Tamara case and about Amber. She said she'd heard everything on the news and in the papers.

Butch had seen those reports too, and he assured Mildred that she had not seen everything and that only about half of what was reported was accurate. This was the second time Butch Gregory had been involved somewhat in a major news story, and it amazed him at how inaccurate reporters were in details and storyline. If he did his work that sloppily he would be fired.

Mildred handed Butch his mail, which was considerable. He filled his favorite coffee mug, the daisy one, and carried the correspondences to his study. He told Mildred to hold any calls until the afternoon. He was still trying to find his way, he said.

Butch sat in his big comfortable high back chair. He pulled his laptop out of his satchel and powered it up and then began flipping through the mail. Most of it was junk—promotions for conferences and advice on how to grow your church. There were a couple of books in there he'd ordered the week before Tamara was abducted. Four denominational letters were in the pile. He assumed those were in response to people like Tommy Bothers who were trying to get him fired.

One letter stood out. The address on the front was hand written, and there was no return address. Odd. It was a plain white envelope. It was postmarked almost three weeks earlier from someplace in California. Butch ripped it open. It was written in beautiful penmanship.

Dear Preach,
I pulled over just after sunrise and bought some candy and a soda somewhere here in the middle of California. There are some things I need to tell you, and I don't know if I will get the chance in person or not. The first one is, I know that I am the one who is going to die. Remember that day I first came to your office and told you about the dream. Well, I held something back. I didn't tell you that in the dream I died. When you told us about your brother's prophecy, I knew it was all coming together. At first I was afraid. But the longer I've been around you, the more I know this is right. If it is the right thing to do, then regardless of the consequence, it must be done. In the last few hours I think I understand how it all fits. Jesus is teaching me this.

Thank you for letting me in on this. I respect you so much, and wish I'd spent more time in your congregation and getting to know you. I lived most of my life running from people like you when I should have been running toward them. Keep on making a difference and helping people and being you. And don't be so hard on Wy. He is a good man, he's just tough. I think you can help him.

The second thing I need to tell you is something else I hid from you on the phone when we talked. I did recover the information on the laptop with the memory stick I found and I did burn the cabin, just like I told you. But what I didn't tell you is that I chained a man I found working for the kidnappers and I left him inside, on purpose, to die a horrible death. I could hear his screams as I walked back to my car.

I needed to confess that to you. I still do not know if it was wrong or not. But I do not think justice would have ever come to that man any other way. He needed to die. But it was wrong that I didn't tell you and Wyoming about it immediately. We've developed too great a trust to not be completely forthcoming. Please forgive me.

Okay, I gotta get back on the road again to meet up with you and Wy. Hopefully by the time you get this, it will all be over. Tamara will be with her mother, you will be back at the church, and I will be in heaven with my brother.

Amber.

P.S. I almost forgot. I also took a wad of money, close to $700 off of Knuckles when you and I hid him at A-Ok. I didn't keep it, but I used it to get information from my contacts. You should know that just in case it ever comes up.

Chapter Thirty-Three

I'm A Pastor, Not A Detective

THREE MONTHS later Butch Gregory walked the neighborhood around his church building. It was something he had been doing for years. In the past as he walked he prayed for the homes, and for people he saw in their yards, walking on the sidewalk or in the park. There was a little park not far from his study that was nestled in between some of the homes. It was not big, but it had large trees, a swing, a picnic table and a little stream that ran alongside of it. In the summer Butch had been known to bring his Bible, a writer's notebook, and a thermos of coffee and prepare sermons here.

Butch wasn't praying today or preparing sermons as he walked in autumn's drizzle. He walked the sidewalk with an empty mind. He was just walking. He'd been attempting to get back into a normal rhythm of life, and had been taking this walk daily at about this same time. It helped him center.

When he neared the park he noticed a sedan parked on the street opposite the park and a woman standing by the alder which guarded the entrance. He frowned, for he recognized the woman.

"Good morning, Dr. Gregory," said Agent Lapp-Bench.

"Is it good?"

"Fair enough, but I think you will find it, at least, satisfying. Can we talk for a moment?"

Butch hadn't noticed it before, but Agent Lapp-Bench's voice was deep and pleasant. "Sure, let's go inside the park. There is a picnic table over here under this giant evergreen. We can talk in privacy there."

"Good, privacy is what I need. How is your shoulder?"

"Almost completely healed now. It still hurts in the morning, though, when I wake up."

"It will do that for the rest of your life. I took a bullet in the thigh about seven years ago. It is healed, but it still hurts in the morning."

They walked across the park and sat down opposite each other at the picnic table. Gigantic brown leaves had fallen onto the table and covered it. Butch brushed the soggy foliage off the table and onto the ground. The two sat in silence for a moment, and the pastor inside Butch Gregory knew that meant the other person needed him to start. It was something he'd learned from years of ministry. People want to talk, but they don't know how to start the conversation. So he began with the simplest question, "What is on your mind?"

"The day we let you go, you asked me some tough questions about why we didn't act sooner. I told you I didn't have to answer and then you left. Do you remember?"

"How could I forget?"

"Well, as you probably know that whole situation is under deep surveillance. There were cameras and microphones all over the place, so, I couldn't really answer your questions fully without professional and legal repercussions. Enough time has elapsed; I think we're clear so I wanted to give you the answers you have a right to.

"First, we did have plenty of information on the gang, but legally we had nothing absolutely airtight to prove our case. Many of us, me included, wanted to go ahead and act about a year ago, but the more cautious side of our leadership kept us from moving in. They were worried about coming up short and spooking the whole operation into hiding. That is always a concern and it is legitimate. You should know, Dr. Gregory, that is very nearly what you did with your escapades up here in Seattle. Once you stirred the pot at A-OK Mekaniks they were going into shut down mode."

He nodded agreement. He knew she was right and Wyoming and Amber came to the same conclusion after the incident in Snohomish and Seattle.

"In fact, we're still not quite sure how you turned it around and figured out so much so fast. In five days you learned more than we had accumulated in our thick file in eighteen months. Some of us think you had an inside man."

"We did," Butch said. "His name is Jesus. He is the ultimate inside man."

"The Bureau does not accept God as an informant."

"It should. Maybe you guys would get more accomplished if you trusted the Lord as much as you trusted forensics and lawyers."

"Message, or rebuke, received. However, there is more I need to share with you. Let me ask you a question, who do you think the boss, the string puller of that group was?"

"That would be Knuckles."

"Dr. Gregory, Knuckles was mid-management. He was funded, directed, and supplied by someone else from somewhere else. We still do not know who, and given the way everything in The Bureau kept gumming up, we think we have a bigger problem."

"Gumming up? Please explain."

"I told you that we kept having problems getting hard evidence and the green light to act, right?"

"Yes, you said that it's a legitimate concern."

"That's right, it is." Agent Lapp-Bench looked around, almost nervously as she spoke. "But what I didn't tell you is that each time we were nearing the hard evidence—a wire-tap conversation, a squealer from inside, or captured client ready to testify—something would happen to erase or lose the recording or we'd have a new corpse on our hands. Dr. Gregory, I believe the sex traffickers were helped by someone inside The Bureau. We have a mole that kept us from doing our job. Part of my reasoning for believing this is the incredible rarity of the organization. There are thousands upon thousands of people or gangs that swipe children and force them into the sex trade. This group was different. It was very ambitious in its reach and scope. They were global. Those children you rescued were headed overseas. Usually child abductions stay domestic—small town kids shuffled off to the big city. But not this group, it was greedy, and we believe, it was highly profitable."

"Unbelievable."

"You'd think. The truth is, we would have never, ever been able to shut down that organization as fast and save as many victims without you and your friends. To be truthful, many of us think of you guys as heroes. On behalf of all of those who are trying to do their jobs, and who know whom they are accountable to, I thank you."

"You are welcome, but we are not heroes. I was petrified the whole time. Amber was the true hero. She gave her life so others might live. I have never seen a more Christ-like act. Ever. And Wyoming. Wyoming was exactly what we needed."

"Are you still in contact with Mr. Wallace?"

"Yes, he and I have breakfast at the Sydney Diner every Tuesday morning. He has also started coming to church. We are working through some of his history together."

"We know about his history. Our file on Mr. Wallace is quite extensive. He was highly decorated and respected, even after the ugly incident in Fallujah."

"Stop—don't tell me anything more," he raised his hands in protest. "Wyoming has slowly started opening up, and I want to hear it from him and not from the raw data of a file with clips and pieces of paper."

"Suit yourself. But be warned, Mr. Wallace can be a very dangerous man."

"I know. But he is, I think, finally beginning," and he paused and thought of Shark's prophecy, "he is finally beginning to see."

Agent Lapp-Bench stood up and shook his hand and walked off, leaving him sitting there at the table. When she reached the alder tree guarding the gate to the park, she turned back and said, "Oh, Dr. Gregory, there is one more thing. Do not be surprised if, at sometime in the future we don't solicit your services again."

He raised his hands to his waist with palms turned upward, shrugged his shoulders and said happily, "I'm a pastor, not a detective."

EPILOGUE

This book has been a very difficult book to write, but not the way you might think.

I began working on it in the summer of 2009 right after my first book, *The Haunting of Pastor Butch Gregory and Other Short Stories* was released. In many ways I planned a follow-up book from the beginning as I made it clear to my publisher the only thing I was concerned about was keeping the rights to the characters in THOPBG. The first new character I developed was Wyoming Wallace. In fact, his name came to mind as my family and I drove through the state of Wyoming on our way across country toward our ancestral home in Texas. I worked on him for the rest of our vacation.

Over the next few months I began to see more and more material come across my desk regarding the plague of child sex trafficking. This is a problem of national and international proportions. For me, it was also a problem of regional scope. Western Washington on down through Olympia and into Portland is one of the most worked areas for these demons of society that prey upon children. Part of the reason for this is the easy access to international borders as well as large ethnic populations. Immigrants and their children are especially vulnerable to the problem.

With that thought process, I began to plot the story arc of a tragic child abduction and how my intrepid yet hapless Pastor Butch Gregory might be involved. I was nearly half-way through the novel when the unthinkable happened. A scandal emerged in the midst of my own congregation that caused most of my emotional energy to simply slide away. It was not the same issue as is faced in the story, but a close colleague and trusted friend was arrested and found guilty of harming a precious little girl in a monstrous way. Suffice it to say, that was close enough to the subject that Pastor Butch deals with in this novel that it hurt enormously.

I closed the file on the book in the spring of 2011 and intended to never reopen it again. I did write, however, spending most of my energy with my friend David Caddell on a biblical studies work on the book of Romans in the New Testament. But most of my energy was focused on helping our church heal and overcome what was the worst time of my ministry and our church's history.

The story, however, would not go away. Writers will understand, but a story demands to be told. The writer is helpless under its pull. I kept seeing more information on the issue, particularly at a Catalyst West Conference where I heard a great speaker challenge me and the other people attending about what we could do to solve the problem of child sex trafficking. What could I do? I could write! Then I spoke to some friends who work closely on the issue. They grew up in our church but have since moved off to make a life for themselves in Oregon. They informed me about some of the issues and put some great resources in my hands for inspiration and for knowledge. Thanks Joan and Griff.

By Christmas 2011 I was beginning to dream again about what the book might look like. Thanks to my wife, Kim, who encouraged me to finish the book. And that is what I did throughout 2012.

None of the characters in this novel are intended to be portrayals of real people. It should be stated again that this is a work of fiction. In fact, it is near fantasy at some points. At other points it is gritty and contains a realism that is necessary to tell a good story. However, there is also a darker side to this tale; and that probably reflects my spiritual and emotional pain as I wrote. My first book was much more playful. This book is not as playful.

I want to thank you for reading the novel. I appreciate anyone and everyone who picks up something I worked on and reads it. It always surprises me that anyone would want to, so I am thankful for you, my reader. My greatest desire in writing this is not just to entertain you, but also to move you. The issue of child sex trafficking is a terrible problem. Get involved in some way in solving the problem. Find more information, research, study, and talk to law enforcement professionals. Would it be too scandalous to ask that you pray about it? I would suggest praying for the boys and girls in your life and take steps necessary to protect and educate them about the dangers they might face.

I also write for pastors. For nearly twenty years I was a full-time vocational pastor of Baptist churches. A pastor is a shepherd, spiritual leader, and a protector.

Most of all, a pastor is a physical presence echoing and reflecting the passion God has for people. Every human pastor works under the tutelage of the Good Shepherd who laid down his life. True pastors do not shine only for the T.V. cameras or sparkle for the magazine covers. Celebrity is not the same thing as the pastorate. (However, some of the great pastors are, indeed celebrities--thank you Rick Warren and Bill Hybels for making the world better.) But the greatest pastors are anonymous servants known only by the Triune God who called them. The best pastors in the world are people you've never heard of.

In their work of shepherding there is often risk and challenge. Sheep don't want to be led. Church is hard work. Shepherds are human, and often too frail for the task laid out. But the greatest risk is the ever stalking wolf who seeks to destroy the shepherd's work and undo all he or she has labored for.

Pastoring is hard labor. Anyone who wants the call, who wants to be a pastor, should be immediately viewed as insane and unstable. Only a lunatic would want such thankless, painful, and risky work. There is a reason why the attrition rate amongst pastors is so high. The pay is low. The benefits are lousy. The stress is high. There are no true vacations. The spiritual responsibility is sometimes more than any one person could ever carry. The ones who make the best pastors are those who would gladly walk away from it if they could. But the calling holds them steady.

If you have read this book and felt any affection at all for Butch Gregory, then give your pastor a hug the next time you see him or her.

Jamie Greening
Good Friday, 2014.

www.ingramcontent.com/pod-product-compliance
Lightning Source LLC
Chambersburg PA
CBHW020558250626
47154CB00004B/1264
* 9 7 8 1 9 3 6 8 3 0 6 5 7 *